# Doll House

# Doll House

Amour

*www.urbanbooks.net*

Urban Books, LLC
97 N18th Street
Wyandanch, NY 11798

ISBN 13: 978-1-60162-560-1
ISBN 10: 1-60162-560-X

First Printing September 2013
Printed in the United States of America

10 9 8 7 6 5 4 3 2 1

Distributed by Kensington Publishing Corp.
Submit Wholesale Orders to:
Kensington Publishing Corp.
C/O Penguin Group (USA) Inc.
Attention: Order Processing
405 Murray Hill Parkway
East Rutherford, NJ 07073-2316
Phone: 1-800-526-0275
Fax: 1-800-227-9604

# Dedication

This book is dedicated to my heartbeat. Without him I don't know where I would be in life. You gave Mommy a reason to try, strive, and succeed. Love you, Sexyman!

# Acknowledgments

First and foremost, I have to thank the man upstairs, who works wonders for me. For without Him, I definitely wouldn't have the gift to write. So . . . thank you, Jesus! For so long I wondered what my gift was, and the whole time I was practicing it and never knew. You showed me it just in time.

My mommy and daddy, thanks for taking the time out of your night to conceive me. You guys are great. Mother dearest, you made the impossible possible. You made nothing everything. You've been so good to me and my sibling. Love you so much.

My ace boon, my sidder, and my best friend, Sanny, what would life consist of without you? You definitely are my backbone and are there when needed. Not to mention you're my assistant, publisher, promoter, body guard, manager, and whatever else I need. To my favorite little sister, Carlina, love you more than words could describe. You can have whatever job Sanny didn't take (LOL).

To my reason for living, you don't know how much you mean to me. You make my life complete. From your waking up smiling to your going to sleep dancing, I know you are more than the son that I imagined you to be. All I do is dedicated to you. To my granny, the backbone of the whole family, we would be all over the place if it wasn't for you. You were so strict and tidy while we were growing up, but that made us the people we are. We couldn't ask for a better granny, because I don't think there's one better. You and Jerry are awesome!

To my niece, Miss McKenzie, love you like you were my daughter. You remind me of myself, from your sassy mouth to your intelligent conversations. I know you're going to be a genius. To my cousins: To my editor, Nikki, my book was good, but you made my book *good*. I appreciate you and your advice. Dora, now you know you'll always be my favorite cousin. I called you for your opinion on anything and everything, and I will continue to. Love you, ladies!

To my better half, me plus you equals better math! Thanks for helping me become the woman I am today. We may not be perfect, but it's worth it. Over all the years, we have got a lot accomplished. Thanks for our bundle of joy, xoxo.

To my ladies, I absolutely adore you chicas. Tia Marie, my promoter, love you like we share the same parents. We may have had one disagreement, but no matter what, I have always felt our friendship was true. BG, my bestie, we done been through it all, from laughing to crying with each other. I value our friendship and love you like a sister too. Chrissy C, we may not talk every day, but when we do, it's like we just got off the phone an hour ago. Love you, doll, and I can't wait for your baby. Hope it's a boy! My other ladies, Ariana, Shaniqua, Mariah, D-Money, and my OVG Girls, love you all. My Burn Family—well, some not all—love you guys too.

To my guy friends: LL Cool LA (LOL), you're the brother I never had. I can tell you anything and know that I'll receive your honest opinion and that you won't judge me. You and I definitely stay laughing when we communicate, so love you for your silliness. Geo, you already know our friendship holds so much value. Ever since gym class at Rogers, we been cool and been tight.

Deborah, God sent you to me. It went from me asking you about a review to you offering to distribute my book for me. I am thankful for you. You truly are a mentor to me. I appreciate you showing me the steps in the game that I was so clueless about. You have been a blessing, helping me to make my dreams come true.

To the reviewers who loved my story and made other people love it too: To my very first reviewers, Toledo, the first day I put my sneak peek on my Facebook page, you guys showed me so much love. I knew you guys would like it, but you guys actually loved it, so thank you all. Toledo, Ohio, has talent, and I'm destined to show the world.

To anyone who has purchased this book or read this book and told a friend about it, thank you. You make me get closer and closer to reaching the world. To anyone I may have forgotten, thank you all.

*They say love ain't always complicated, but I'm convinced life is. . . .*

# Chapter 1

"So Unc is in jail?" Kola asked. She was obviously worried, almost to death.

"Yeah, I just walked in to Auny, crying, and she told me they just picked him up," I said, barely mustering a response.

Life had really kicked my ass the past couple of years. My mom was back on drugs, and my provider was incarcerated. What was a girl to do?

My name is Sommer Jones, but everyone calls me Doll. I'm fifteen years grown. . . . I say "grown" because I've been through more than the average person can imagine. My uncle Jim, whom everyone calls Unc, and his wife, Leslie, whom everyone calls Auny, took me in when I was almost ten years of age.

I have a younger sister named Autumn. Her nickname is Fall, and she is two years my junior. It's odd, because I was born in the fall and she was born in the summer. That's just how backward my mother, April Jones, was. She was on drugs very hard, so it was either foster care or a family member taking us in, and I thank God that we had family. My aunt Sasha took custody of Autumn when we were younger, and moved her to Atlanta to be with her and her daughter, Jasmine.

My mother got hooked on drugs a long time ago. It was way before my sister and I were even born. Sad to say, my father had gotten her hooked on the shit. My dad was abusive, and he was a crackhead—what a

combination. My mom was on and off of drugs; whenever she quit, something made her crawl right back. I
figured she loved coke more than she loved Fall and
me. My dad's family blamed her for everything, but
how can you blame a young, naive girl trying to keep up
with her older boyfriend?

Hell, them bastards didn't even try to gain custody of
us. When the judge asked who would step up, his whole
family sat silent in the courtroom. Fuck them, though.
We didn't need them. Unc assured me that I didn't, and
he spoiled me to remind me of it.

I remembered it like it was yesterday. I was nine,
and Fall was seven. My mother was in the kitchen with
her junkie boyfriend, sniffing lines. Her black hair was
matted, her eyes were big, and sweat was dripping
from her forehead. My sister and I were hiding in the
corner of our front room. We knew them being high
meant a fight was sure to follow.

About thirty minutes after she and her sickly-looking
boyfriend got done snorting, they began to argue. I
guess he felt she had had more of the coke than he did.
That wasn't going to fly with him. He grabbed her by
the neck and pushed her up against the wall, leaving a
hole. She slid down the wall, holding her neck and crying for him to stop. My sister and I began to cry also.
He turned to us and yelled, "You little bitches better
shut the fuck up!"

I put my hand over Fall's mouth, but I couldn't stop
her from screaming. He grew angry. He began walking
over to us with hate in his eyes. He grabbed us both
by our ponytails. He held them so tight, I could feel
my hair being pulled by the roots. We both began to
scream loudly. My mother just sat there watching, with
tears falling from her eyes. She never told him to stop.
She never got up to try to make him stop. She didn't
give a fuck.

Her boyfriend, whom she called Babe, threw us on the floor. We grabbed each other, trying to get closer to one another. He began unbuckling his dirty pants.

Our eyes got big as we both sat and wondered what was on his mind. My mom stood up, finally.

"Babe, no! Them my babies," she cried.

"Shut up," he yelled. He made us all jump.

My mother sat back down. I wondered if she felt as if there was nothing she could do, but she could have done something.

He let his pants drop, and his little penis was hard.

I covered my eyes. *Ugh!*

He motioned for us to come closer.

Babe was all we knew him as, because that was all my mother called him. We never called him anything, though. We never needed to. He was in his twenties, but coke made him look fifty. He was missing one of his front teeth, and the rest were rotten. He had the nappiest hair I had ever seen, and he always smelled like beer. When he saw we didn't move a muscle, he got angrier.

"Bitch, get over here now and suck my dick," he yelled.

I didn't know who he was talking to, but I knew that neither one of us was going to do it.

He snatched my little sister up by the arm. "Are you deaf?" he asked.

She shook her head no.

He told her to suck his dick again, and she shook her head no again.

"So you think you can disobey me?" He asked as he let go of her arm. He took his brown leather belt off and started hitting our bodies anywhere and everywhere.

We screamed and tried to take cover, but it hurt like hell. He whupped us for what seemed like forever.

When he was done with us, we had welts all over our bodies. He ran some steaming hot water in the bathtub for us and forced us to get in. We cried, as the water made the welts sting badly. He just kept yelling at us, calling us bitches, and laughing. My mom never came in the bathroom to save us.

When we got out of the tub, there my mother was again, snorting. She acted as if the situation had never happened. I didn't understand her. I went to lie on the floor with my sister, and I held her close. I prayed we'd see a brighter day.

The next day in school, I tried my hardest to hide my welts, but they were everywhere. The fact that I was wearing a short-sleeved shirt didn't make it any better. My fourth-grade teacher, Mrs. Dressel, called me up to her desk. She had been looking at me crazily the entire day.

When I approached her desk, she asked me if there was anything I wanted to tell her. I told her no, and then she sent me to the office. I grabbed my things and made my way to the office. I walked kind of funny because it hurt when my jeans rubbed against my legs. When I made it to the office, there was a blonde Caucasian lady sitting in a chair with a notepad.

Moments later Fall arrived. The lady took us to a secluded room and began questioning us. I told her that nothing was wrong, that our life was normal. Fall told her we had just got our asses beat for not sucking my mother's boyfriend's dick.

They took us straight to CSB, and the rest was history.

When I first moved in with Unc and Auny, my mother went to rehab. After she completed rehab, which took damn near three years, they thought it was a great idea for us to visit her on the weekends. My aunt Sasha wasn't having that, and besides, she was all the way in Atlanta. To me it sounded cool, and my mother did seem as if she was doing a lot better.

People always ask me if I love my mother. I can honestly say no. Why should I? There's no reason to. She made my life a living hell, and for that reason she doesn't even deserve a piece of my love. I was just too kindhearted, though. It didn't matter if someone did me wrong; I always found some way to give them another chance. Even if they fucked me over a million times, I always forgave them, and that was the only reason I went to visit her. I didn't want to hurt her feelings by not going.

My mother lived in Brand Whitlock, a very gritty and rugged place on the south side of Toledo, Ohio. It didn't bother me much, because I had lived there the majority of my life. When I returned, it was more like a hood reunion with my old friends.

When we pulled into the complex, everyone eyeballed Unc's money-green BMW 745. I swear, a couple of niggas were even drooling.

Once we got in front of my mother's building, I spotted some eye candy. He was mixed in with four other people. I had been going over to visit my mother every weekend for almost two months now, and I had never seen him before.

He was about five foot six, probably a buck fifty, and had a low-cut fade, hazel eyes, and a tasty caramel complexion. He rocked a Bulls jersey and the latest Jordans on his feet. I knew they were the latest because I happened to have the same ones on my feet.

I'd always grabbed the attention of the niggas in these projects. Practically everywhere I went, niggas just flocked to me! I was a five-foot-four, 115-pound, light-skinned beauty with sandy brown hair that hung past my shoulders. I had a nice shape too. Not too much, not too little . . . and, boy, could I dress! This gave anybody in their right *or* wrong mind just enough reason to want me!

Seeing that my future fling was right there in my presence, I made a mental note to make sure I threw an extra swish into my strut.

I said my good-byes to Unc and Auny and stepped out of the car. I must admit, all eyes were on me, and I was loving it! Mr. Eye Candy gave me the head-to-toe look as he licked his lips. I knew that after Unc pulled off and I got rid of my bags, I was coming for him.

When I walked into my mother's place, it smelled like rose petals. Surprisingly, it was clean! She came from the back with a big smile on her face. It kind of felt good to see her smiling. It was a warming feeling.

"Hey, baby," she said with her arms extended toward me.

"Hey, Mom. How are you?" I asked. I acted as if I cared.

We embraced each other, sharing a dry hug, and then I hurried to sit down. I gave her place the routine inspection. You know, checking for creepy crawlers, like I did every weekend. She passed the test: no roaches, mice, spiders, or anything else that would make me want to go home immediately.

We sat and watched *Judge Judy,* and eventually I fell into a deep sleep.

I was shaken and awakened by my ex–best friend, Imani. She was a very pretty black and white mixed cutie with light caramel skin. She had long curly black hair, which she kept in a ponytail at all times. She was boy crazy and kept a new boyfriend. I didn't see how they liked her, because her house was always junky. I didn't understand how it was humanly possible for anybody to live there, but they managed. We had been friends for four years, but when I moved in with Unc, we drifted apart.

"Wake up, funky bitch! I missed you," were the first words out of her mouth.

"Didn't yo' mama ever tell you it's rude to wake up someone? Damn, I do need my beauty sleep, Mani," I said while rubbing my eyes.

"When you become so proper?" She asked and chuckled.

"I don't have to be ghetto all the time," I told her.

According to Imani, my mom had left with one of her sugar daddies, so she decided to keep me company for a while. She enlightened me, telling me everything I had missed out on since my departure from the projects last week, like who was still a virgin and who wasn't, and who fought whom, and so on and so forth. She got up to go in the kitchen to get something to drink and came back running her mouth again.

"So, Doll, you still ain't got you no dick?"

"Imani, how many times do I have to tell you I ain't thinking about doing it. It seem like you tryin'a pressure me into fucking." I rolled my eyes. This had become the weekly question.

"I ain't tryin'a force you. I'm just saying you missing out." She chuckled. I sat there imagining how the boys' faces screwed up when they walked into her nasty-ass house. If they did it to her in there, then they clearly had no respect for her. I decided to change the subject.

"So who's that caramel nigga with the hazel eyes?" I didn't waste any time asking, knowing she would know. I regretted leaving my mission unaccomplished and putting sleep before it.

"Who? Zae?" She seemed puzzled. She knew who the hell I was talking about.

"How do I know when I'm asking you?" I asked, rolling my eyes.

"Had on a Bulls jersey?" She asked, making sure we were talking about the same guy.

"Yeah, that's him," I replied.

"Mmm-hmm, that's Zae. He sexy, ain't he?" The expression on her face didn't match her words.

"Is he? Girl, he is fine!"

Then she went on to tell me that she was really good friends with Zae and that she was messing around with his cousin, Malcolm.

We decided to go outside to see if he was still out there. I guess we were a little too late, because homeboy was pulling off in a two-door, red candy–colored old-school Monte Carlo that sat on some dubbs.

"That's his car?" I was astonished. My mouth hit the ground.

"Yes, he's paid, girl! Plus, I heard he got that magic stick too!"

Owing to the fact that I was a virgin, I knew damn well that the magic stick wasn't going to be doing any types of tricks on me. I was only thirteen, and in my mind I was too young to even think of having sex.

We decided to walk to a corner store. It seemed like a much farther walk than it had been three years ago, since I hadn't walked there since then. You would think there would be a closer store in the neighborhood, but I guess since we were in the hood, they didn't give a damn. The store was on the 1100 block of Belmont, too damn far for me. I complained the entire time.

"Girl, it ain't even that far. We almost there," Imani said.

"You've been saying that for what seems like forever, and we still ain't there yet," I told her.

Somebody honked a horn that sounded like a whistle. Impressive. We turned around, and there he was. Rims sitting high, seat back, music blasting, with a gorgeous smile on his face. It was Zae.

There was a guy on the passenger side, and they pulled over to the side of us. We stopped.

"Imani, why the hell y'all walking by y'all selves?" asked the guy in the passenger seat as he stepped out of the car.

"Malcolm, whose daddy are you?" Imani answered as she headed over to him. I stood there watching and felt Zae's eyes all over my body.

"Man, get in the car! If something happens to my baby, I'm going to shoot up this whole block," Malcolm said, referring to Imani.

I figured that was his way of running game on her.

She smiled. "Come on, Doll."

Malcolm pulled his seat up so we could get in the backseat.

"Hey, Ma, you can get in the front," he told me.

That definitely wasn't a problem for me. While they climbed their asses in the back, I jumped my happy ass in the front.

As we passed the store, I grew nervous. Yeah, homeboy was fine as hell, but I didn't know much about him. I played it cool, though.

We pulled up to this nice house on Tecumseh. I assumed the house had been built recently, because it looked new and it sat a nice distance from the other homes.

The car stopped, and Zae looked back at Malcolm.

"So what up?"

"Shit, I'm trying to chill with Mani," he said, looking at her for an answer. "If that's possible. . . ."

"Yeah, that's cool, but I got my homegirl with me," she told him while patting my arm.

"Well, I can take her home since I see you got my cousin all sprung and he dying to chill with you," Zae offered.

"Doll, you cool with that?" Imani smiled, knowing that I was cool with it without a doubt.

I sarcastically paused for a second and looked back at her. "It's cool. Have fun, sweetie," I replied.

They got out of the car and disappeared behind the door. I watched, wishing we could have kicked it a little while longer. Now I had to revisit boredom. When I got out of my trance, I found Zae staring at me.

"Can I assist you, sir?" I asked.

"Yeah. Actually, you can. How old are you?" he asked as if he had been dying to ask me that the entire trip.

"I'm thirteen, but I'll be fourteen in two weeks," I replied, wondering if I should have lied about my age. "And you?"

"I'm sixteen. I'll be seventeen next month. The fifteenth of October, to be exact."

He was even sexier up close. In my thirteen years of living, never had I ever wanted to have sex with someone just by looking at them. Zae definitely had me wet, and I fell in lust.

"So you going to that same apartment you went into earlier?" he asked. I knew he was trying to make sure that was where I lived.

I played dumb.

"Earlier? When did you see me?" I asked, trying to pretend that I hadn't noticed him then.

"Shit, you hopped out a Beemer and went into apartment two-forty-five. I couldn't help but watch you, young buck," he replied.

"Young buck? What an insult." I was offended and knew that I really should have lied about my age.

"Sorry, baby. You are young, though." He chuckled.

"Age wise, yes, but mentally, I'm grown," I said, pointing to my head. My eyebrows went up.

"Well, Miss Grown Ass, is that where I'm taking you?" He pulled off of Tecumseh.

"Yes, it is." I wanted to go with him, but my number one life rule was "Always hungry, never thirsty."

He pulled up to the apartment, and I hesitantly opened my car door.

"Thanks," I said with my head down.

"No problem," he replied.

As I was getting out, he grabbed my arm.

"Write my number down," he suggested.

"Excuse me? Nigga, I got a phone!" I said while pulling out my Cricket cellular.

We exchanged numbers.

"Make sure you use it," I stated before hopping out of his car.

He was still parked outside when I walked into the building. While I was in the elevator, my phone began to vibrate. I received a text, which read, I don't know what it is 'bout u but I want u bad, Ma.

If only Zae knew that the feeling was mutual.

I had a feeling that someone was watching me. I looked over to find some weird old man staring at me from the corner of the elevator. I didn't think anything of it, because guys stared at me on a daily. I thought it was pretty normal.

The elevator stopped at my floor, so I stepped off, walked to my mother's door, and opened it. She was still gone. As I began to walk toward the back of the house, I heard the door open.

"That bitch be on the go, don't she?" I mumbled to myself while walking back up front, believing it was her coming through the door. To my surprise, it was the weird man from the elevator.

I turned back around and ran toward my mother's room, but he caught me by my ponytail and dragged me to the front room. He picked me up by my throat and threw me on the couch. I instantly started crying.

"Bitch, shut the fuck up before I kill you!" he yelled, spitting every word in my face. He started unbuckling my pants. In the back of my head, I prayed that I wouldn't lose my virginity by being raped.

The door popped open again, which scared both of us. It was Zae.

"Man, Jean, get the fuck off her! What you on, dude?" he said while pushing him off of me.

"Sorry, son! Man, I'm sorry. Please forgive me," the old man begged.

I gasped for air, holding my throat.

"Get yo' ass out, and don't come back!" Zae demanded.

Jean scurried out, and I ran to the bathroom. I locked the door. I sat on the floor and cried. I was embarrassed. Tears fell from my eyes.

I heard knocks at the door. "Open the door, Doll. It's cool. He gone!"

I didn't want to open it, but at the same time I didn't want to stay there. I opened the door and laid my head on his chest.

"It's cool, Ma. You can cry." He hugged me, and I just shed all the tears my soul had within.

"Grab your shit. You can't stay here tonight," he said, comforting me.

I got my stuff, and we left.

When we arrived at our destination, I didn't know where we were, but I knew it was at least an hour away from the Brands. The house we pulled up to was enormous. It was the biggest house I had ever seen.

"Whose house is this?" I asked with a raspy voice, as if I had been crying for days.

"My parents'. Mine's in the back. We got to cut through," he said while pointing to a walkway.

When we got to his house, it was definitely laid out. Big-screen TV, leather furniture, a big-ass fish tank . . . everything you could name. He showed me to his guest room and turned on the lights.

"You can just crash here. I'll take you home in the morning."

I wanted to sleep in a room with him because I didn't feel safe no matter how far we were from Jean. The expression on my face must have said it all.

"Or do you not feel secure?" He asked. "'Cause I want you to feel safe, specially if you with me. Feel me?"

I nodded.

He started walking to his bedroom, and I followed. His bed was beyond big. It had to be a king, because it was the size of Unc's bed and he had a king-size bed. It looked like a female had decorated it. There was no way a man could have put that shit together. His bed was tall and plush, and I sank deep into the mattress as I lay down. Once I took my shoes off, I was out.

I woke up to the smell of breakfast. I looked at the clock, which read 10:45 A.M.

Zae was no longer next to me, so I got up and walked to the front to see where he was.

He was in the kitchen, cooking with no shirt on. Boy, was he sexy.

"You hungry, Ma?"

"How did you know that I was up?" I asked with a smile as I took a seat at the table.

"Just had a feeling." He faced me and smiled back, revealing his six-pack. I had always loved a man that was in shape, and in shape he was.

Although I still felt disgusted by the events that took place yesterday, he made me feel so good.

"I'm sorry about what happened last night. He just been bucking. You know, doing the unthinkable," he tried to explain. I began to wonder how he even knew the guy.

"It's cool. I'm trying to forget about it. Thanks for saving me." I forced a smile. "By the way, how did you know him?"

"Everybody knows Jean. He's the neighborhood junkie," he explained.

"Oh, okay." I didn't have much to say about it. I was just glad to be out of harm's way.

He cooked us eggs, bacon, waffles, and hash browns. I must say, the boy could definitely cook. He told me a little bit about himself, and it appeared he was spoon-fed. You know, like, spoiled. His stepfather owned a construction company and a lot of houses. His mom was a nurse at the Toledo Hospital. He had an older half brother by the name of Julian, who lived in De-troit, Michigan. His status was single, and his last girl-friend was crazy.

He admitted to liking me and thought that I was cute and that my mouth was smart, but he liked that too. He wanted to get to know me, maybe even be with me, if it was going to be worth it. His real name was Markaylo Smith, and they got Zae from his middle name, Isaiah. We sat and talked for a little over two hours. I enjoyed every bit of it. I knew from that moment on that he would be a permanent person in my life. Hell, I owed him my life.

After we ate, I decided to take a shower. I stood by the bathroom sink as I watched his muscular body kneel down, getting the water going for me. I stood there imagining what would have happened if he hadn't come in and saved me. I got goose bumps at the thought of it.

Zae stood up and looked me in the eye. I tried to force a smile, but I was disgusted.

"Stop thinking about it," he said as he grabbed my hand. "You with me, so you safe." He kissed my hand and then exited the bathroom. This man was definitely something special.

I closed the door behind him, stood there for a minute, inhaled some fresh air. Looking in the mirror, I noticed Jean's handprint on my neck. I touched the red marks, and tears started welling up in my eyes. I wiped them away before they got a chance to drop. I refused to keep crying. *Life goes on.*

I removed all my clothes and stepped in the shower. The water was kind of hot on my soft skin, but it was needed, because I planned to scrub a whole layer of skin off. I grabbed the soap and the washcloth Zae had given me and scrubbed my skin until it turned red. I felt so disgusting, so worthless, and so filthy.

I scrubbed and I scrubbed until I felt that I was clean. When I was all done scrubbing, I just sat in the shower and cried. Deep inside I knew it wasn't my fault, but a part of me said it was. If I wasn't trying to always flaunt it and be so flashy, he wouldn't have even noticed me. I should have known he was too damn old to be eyeing me, anyway, but no, I thought it was cute. I could only fault myself.

After I was in the shower for, I guess, way too long, Zae knocked on the door.

"Ma, you okay in there?"

I cleared my throat. I didn't want to sound like I was crying. "I'm cool. I'll be out in a little," was my response. I turned the water off and got out of the shower. I stood there naked, staring at the off-white walls. I grabbed my towel and began drying off, constantly seeing Jean's old wrinkled face. I kept smelling his beer breath and feeling his sandpaper hands.

Zae walked in.

"Oh, I'm so sorry. I thought you was dressed," he said as he hurriedly left and closed the door. He stood on the other side of the door. "I was just seeing if you was okay. You been in there for over an hour, and with what happened last night, I was just tryin'a make sure you ain't try nothing," he said with worry in his voice.

I opened the door, fully dressed. "It's cool, and I'm okay. Thanks for worrying," I replied as I walked past him. I put my things in my bag and sat on the bed.

He came in and sat next to me. He just didn't understand. I was that close to being raped, and my virginity would have been out the door.

"I know you still thinking about Jean, but it's cool. He's gone," he said as he grabbed my hand once more.

"It's not something you can just forget, and I hear you telling me I'm safe"—I looked him in his eyes—"but am I really?" I searched his eyes for an answer. His eyes were so familiar, but I didn't know who I saw them on.

"Hell, yeah," he answered. "If I say you are, then you are. I'm a man of my word, so don't never doubt it, baby." He kissed me on my forehead.

I just sat there, hoping that what he said was the truth and nothing less. I did not want to return to the crime scene, but if Unc had to pick me up from here, there would be a whole 'nother crime scene. I told Zae that it was time for me to go back to the Brands, although I clearly didn't want to.

He dropped me off at my mother's house. I still had one more day to stay there, and due to my experience last night, I was dreading it. I didn't want the chaos that came with telling somebody what had happened to me. Zae assured me that I wouldn't see Jean for a long time, and I trusted him.

# Chapter 2

When I walked into my mother's house, she was sleeping on the couch. Why she never had her door locked, I hadn't the slightest idea. It was ironic that she hadn't called to see where I was, but I was glad that she hadn't.

I wasn't in the house for a good five minutes before Zae was already calling my phone.

"Yes, Markaylo?" was my answer.

"You cool?" he asked with a chuckle.

"Yeah, I'm cool."

"Yo' mom ain't ask you where you were?"

"Naw. She probably assumed I was at Mani's place."

"Oh, that's cool." There was a small pause in our conversation. Then he added, "Maybe we can go up to the Maumee theater to see a movie or something later."

I didn't hesitate. "Okay."

We hung up on both ends, and I walked to the back bedroom and closed the door behind me. I lay on the twin bed that was in there and daydreamed about Zae. He definitely had me sprung.

My mother was sitting on her bed when I came out of the bedroom to use the bathroom. It was pretty odd of her, so I went in there to see what her problem was.

"What's wrong with you?" I questioned her.

She just nodded her head. Well, whatever her problem was, if she wasn't telling, I for damn sure wasn't begging.

All of a sudden there was a loud bang at the door. It sounded like it was the police or something. A startled look came over my mother's face, and I assumed it was from the loud knocks on the door. She still remained seated, though.

"You going to get that?" I asked. I was confused as to why she still hadn't moved.

"No. Go out the window," she said immediately. "Call Unc and have him come get you. Run to Granny Franny's house. Go now," she whispered.

I was even more confused and startled. I didn't know what was going on. Before I could even put my leg out the windowsill, my mother's door was kicked in.

"Hide," she whispered and demanded at the same time.

I quickly dived underneath the bed. She remained sitting on the bed.

Next thing I knew, a deep voice said to her, "Bitch, you hiding now? You think you ain't needed on that track? I'm losing money in Flint!"

He grabbed my mother by her neck. I made sure to remain silent. Who was this man? What did he want from my mother? I listened and lay still.

"I'm sorry, Daddy!" she begged and pleaded.

Daddy? Was she a prostitute? If so, why would she allow me to stay here with her? What sick mother would do that to her child?

I remained under the bed, hot as hell. Sweat dripped from my brow.

My phone began to buzz in my pocket. My eyes grew big as I tried my hardest to shut it up before they heard it. I pulled it out of my pocket and saw that it was Zae. I silenced the vibration. The room grew quiet, so I laid my head on the floor so that I could see what was going on. At this point, the deep-voiced man had an even

tighter grip on my mother's hair, and he began drag-
ging her through the door.

I shed a tear for her. It hurt me that my mother
couldn't get her stuff together. Not for me, not for my
little sister, and not even for herself.

I waited an hour under that bed. I had to make sure
that the coast was completely clear. When it seemed
safe to come out of hiding, I ran out and headed to
Granny Franny's.

Granny Franny was an elderly woman whom everyone in the neighborhood respected. She lived in the
projects, across the street from the Brands. She was a
sweet individual who was always looking out for the
next. I knew that I could confide in her and that she
would accept me with open arms.

When I arrived at Granny Franny's, a smile spread
over her face as she opened the screen door. "Hey,
honey! Long time no see," she said as she approached
me with a hug.

"I know. I missed you a lot," I admitted.

I gave her the rundown about my mother and what
had just happened. She confessed to me that my mother had been a whore for a long time. She said she had
tried to talk some sense into my mother, but there are
some people that you just couldn't help. I guess she
was one of them.

I ended up falling asleep at Granny Franny's house.
When I woke up, all I could smell was soul food. She
encouraged me to make myself a plate once I was fully
awake. If I wasn't awake at first, I definitely was now.

Imani came over to keep me company once again. I
told her the entire story, from beginning to end. It had
all finally started to make sense the other day, when
Imani told me that my mother had gone with one of her
sugar daddies, better known as tricks.

"You knew she was a ho?" I questioned. I was angry.

"No! I swear I didn't!" she protested.

I knew the bitch was lying, but I knew it wasn't her fault that my mother was out there. I was debating if I should tell Unc and Auny what had happened. I knew if I told them, Zae and I would have to go out of our way in order to see one another. Besides, Unc wouldn't allow me to have a boyfriend, anyway, especially one who was Zae's age.

"You can tell them you're staying at my house," said Imani when I told her what I was thinking.

"Hmm, I don't know," I responded. "Maybe you should just stay at my house first so that they can see what type of person you are. Na' mean?"

"I see what you saying. Well, next weekend, then?"

"Okay, cool," I said. We had it all figured out.

Imani decided to call Malcolm. Apparently, he wanted us to go on a double date to the movies with him and Zae, but I had had enough adventures for the weekend. Instead, I let Zae come see me for a while, and then I called Unc to come and pick me up.

When Unc finally got there, his facial expression told me he wondered why I was even over Granny Franny's. Unc respected her, but he didn't care for her. She used to store his drugs and money, but one day his stuff came up missing. Granny Franny claimed her house had been broken into, but there wasn't any proof. Unc was convinced she had given his shit away to her grandson, Clyde. That gave him an everlasting dislike for her.

Now, Clyde was what you called a "so-called friend" to Unc. They were friends, but they didn't trust one another. Unc knew Clyde was jealous of him, especially after he got the girl whom Clyde had had his eyes on, Leslie Parker. She was the baddest young girl around, from what Unc told me. When they got married shortly after they got together, Clyde started hating even more.

When I saw Unc pull up, I grabbed my bags out of Granny Franny's house, said good-bye, and walked out. When I got inside his Lexus, the questions came.

"Why are you over here?" he quizzed. He still had the car in park.

"I just came to visit," I answered, hoping he didn't have a problem with it. He stared me down, making me uncomfortable.

"Well, where is April? What you over here with a niggar?" He asked, accusing me. I just looked dumbfounded. Why was he accusing me of shit? I explained to him that my mother had left with one of her female friends and I had decided to wait for him here. He squinted his eyes, letting me know he felt I was lying.

Imani was standing on the curb, staring at us. She probably could sense the tension.

"Doll, I don't want you over here. And is that that little fast girl that be having all the niggas over her house?" he said, looking at Imani. "Hell, naw, I know you up to something. It's gon' be a while before you visit again."

He finally pulled off. The entire car ride home he fumed about me being at Granny Franny's house when I knew he couldn't stand her. I just thought of Zae and the attempted rape as I tuned him out. I was so relieved when we pulled up to our house on Manchester Road.

I was staying with Unc and Auny in Ottawa Hills, a suburban area of Toledo. Our big, beautiful home consisted of four bedrooms, three bathrooms, and a basement, and there were three cars to choose from in their garage.

You see, Unc was a handsome man. He was in his midthirties and was dark skinned, with the smoothest skin you'd ever come across. He had a nice goatee and a clean fade, and he stayed fresh from his head to his feet. All the females wanted a piece of him. Unc was a drug dealer, no question about that, but he also owned a couple of businesses and homes. His belongings were legit, but he for damn sure wasn't.

No matter what, I considered Unc my hero. He had saved me from a very savage lifestyle. He had introduced me to the finer things in life. I wished he could have gotten custody of me and my sister, but I knew she was going to be well taken care of, even though she was hundreds of miles away.

I was greeted at the door by my Yorkie, Dora. She was adorable, and she loved me unconditionally. I went to my room and lay in my queen-size bed with Dora and daydreamed about Zae. He was a gentleman if I ever met one. He didn't give me the impression that all he wanted to do was have sex with me, but, then again, you never knew.

I jumped in the shower and got my clothes ready for an interesting Monday at Rogers High School. I was the youngest person in my class because I had gone to school in the summer so that I could get ahead. As I lay there, I kept replaying the events that took place in the projects. So much at once. I started to feel as if I was cursed.

# Chapter 3

I woke up to my phone playing the ringtone "Angel of Mine" by Monica. Of course, it was Zae.

"Hello?"

"Yeah, what up? Where you?" he asked.

"Home. Why?" I questioned.

It had been about six months, and Zae and I were rocking tough.

"I just miss you. Let me come get you. We can go by the water," he suggested.

To me, Zae was nothing like those other niggas. He was genuine, and he never rushed me to do anything. I had to admit, I was falling for him hard. I was trying to avoid falling, because what if I fell and he didn't catch me?

My best friend, Kola, had told me to stay away. Our age difference was her reason why. In my mind, I felt if he was playing games, I loved the way he played. He gave me the kind of love I had never had. Yeah, Unc and Auny loved me, but they showered me with material things. They weren't really there. Zae was only a phone call away whenever I needed him.

I was aware of his ex, Lakesha, and I was also aware of her crew, who called themselves the Get It Girls. They went to my school, so I knew them very well. Those females were known to jump anybody and everybody. You could never get a one-on-one fight out of any of the ten members of that self-made group. However, they had never been a threat or a worry to me and mine.

My friends and I didn't have a name. We just lived by the slogan "We all we got." Either you were my nigga or you were not. So you were either running with us or getting run over by us. The choice was yours.

I hopped up and got dressed. I decided a Baby Phat sweat suit with some Coach shoes would be okay. I heard the horn blow, and I grabbed my matching Coach purse and ran downstairs.

I opened the door to see a snow-white two-seater BMW sitting out front. Definitely my style. When I got in, it smelled brand new.

"This yours?" I asked. He kept me amazed.

"Yeah, my mom got it for me. You like it?" He smiled.

What kind of question was that? "Of course. It's nice," I replied while checking out the interior.

"You want to drive?" he asked.

Did I? Of course I did! I had driven plenty of cars plenty of times, but not any of his cars. I got behind that wheel and drove us to the Docks.

The Docks is a romantic spot downtown where one could take in the view of the water, go for a boat ride, partake in classy bars, or eat at a variety of expensive restaurants. It was the perfect place for couples to just sit and express themselves to one another. That was what Zae and I intended to do.

We found a bench to sit on, and he never let my hand go. Even when we sat down, our palms still rested in one another's. I knew he was about to spill his heart out to me about something. I could just tell by the way he was treating me. People went down to the Docks only to get emotional. I was hoping that whatever he was about to say was good, because bad news had been my friend for too long in my life. I didn't think I could handle any more bad news.

"Baby, this is nice, huh?" he said, smiling from ear to ear.

"Yeah, it's romantic," I responded. I took a deep breath and took in every moment.

"I ain't never been down here before. Malcolm suggested we go," he admitted.

I laughed. "I didn't know Malcolm knew anything about romancing."

We had a moment of calmness and silence. I had to admit the Docks was a place of refreshment. I gazed at the water, in deep thought, and then he grabbed my face and kissed me passionately.

Throughout our relationship, we had never French-kissed before. Hell, I didn't know if I actually knew how, but I received no complaints from him.

"Sommer, I love you," he finally said as he stared into my eyes.

I damn near choked. I knew I loved him too, but to say I was in love with him, um . . . no. I just refused to allow myself to be into someone that deep.

"I know you got yo' li'l wall up or whatever, but I'm willing to break it down. I want you to be my girl," he confessed.

I didn't know what to say. I mean, was I ready for all of this? This was too much for me to swallow. Here he was, seventeen years old, and I was only fourteen. I kept thinking and asking myself if this was all a game or if it was real.

I must have been thinking for a long time, because he made it his business to interrupt my thoughts.

"Babe, did you hear me?"

"Yeah, I did," I said, snapping out of my thoughts.

"So what up? You trying to be mine or not?"

I still didn't know how to answer him. My mind was racing. This *was* what I wanted, for us to be official . . . so why not?

"Yeah, I am," I said with a kiss.

He pulled out a box.

Oh, hell no! I knew this nigga was not about to propose!

He opened it, and there appeared a cute little diamond ring. MARKAYLO & SOMMER was imprinted on it.

"It's a promise ring. I promise to be true to you at all times," he said while handing it to me.

It was very cute, and he instantly stole my heart. I put it on, and it fit perfectly. We kissed for the remainder of that night.

I walked into Rogers High with my crew, Kola, Mari, and Ashley. We didn't have a single worry in the world. Word had got out on the streets that Lakesha wanted to fight me because Zae was dissing her for me. She just wasn't going to accept that a freshman like me had stolen her man. You know, the truth hurt.

I had been a fighter my entire life. That was your only option in the Brands, but fighting had come naturally to me.

At school there was this heater that everyone hung out on. People sat up there and skipped class or chit-chatted with the cool hall guards. My crew and I went upstairs to the heater to chill. We all got a spot on or around the heater and waited for the Get It Girls to arrive. We heard loudmouthed Tasha, and we knew it was them coming up the stairs.

When they reached us, Lakesha decided to speak.

"Rag doll," she said, looking at me, "I heard my man been hitting that! I hope you know he just hitting it to quit it, you dumb ho." She had too much attitude for me.

By this time a crowd of people had formed around us.

I began to laugh. I wasn't easily threatened. "See, dumb ass, that's where you wrong, because your man ain't so much as seen anything underneath these clothes, let alone fucked me! You wack-ass, wig-wearing, man-looking bitch!"

With that, I stole on her. Three punches to the face, and her nose instantly started to bleed. I can't recall it all. I must have blacked out or something, but with all the anger built up in me, her ass was grass.

All my girls started throwing blows. It was a royal rumble on the second floor at Rogers High that Wednesday. Security and teachers came to break it up, but couldn't anything or anyone get me off of Lakesha's loudmouthed ass.

When they finally pried me off of her, her face was bloody, my shirt was ripped, and there were scratches all over me.

Unfortunately, I was suspended and put out of school. Auny had to come pick me up, and I knew she would be pissed at me. As soon as I sat in the passenger seat of her Lexus, she started shaking her head.

"What's the deal, Sommer?"

"She started with me, Auny. I swear," I said convincingly.

"Over a boy, huh? That Zae character, right?" she said in her know-it-all voice.

I nodded my head, not wanting her to judge him.

"I know how it is when you got yourself somebody that everybody wants, but know if it's yours, you don't need to fight over it!" Auny was making perfect sense. "You're a lady and you're top-notch. Don't be messing up your nice shit on a bum bitch," she added and laughed.

I chuckled a little and looked out the window, replaying that ass whupping in my head. I must say, Auny was a fly bitch. She only rocked name-brand apparel. If it wasn't name brand, then it wasn't in her closet. I definitely looked up to her. She was younger than Unc, in her midtwenties. She kept her nails and her hair done at all times. She told me she didn't want any kids, because she had a figure that she adored and needed to retain. I respected it. I mean, she did have a nice body.

Unc adored her too. He gave her whatever she asked for. In return, she obeyed his every request. They had a beautiful relationship. I didn't recall them ever arguing, at least not in my presence. She told me she did what she was asked, not told. Her job was to keep Unc happy at all times. That she did.

"So, Miss Doll, tell me about this boy," she said with a smirk on her face.

"Well . . . ," I began. I smiled at the thought of him. "He's seventeen, and I know Unc ain't gon' have that. Besides that, he's a sweet person, and I'm falling for him," I said with confidence.

"Y'all do the deed?" she questioned.

I knew exactly what she meant. "No. He never tried to, either," I assured her.

"Sounds like a winner." She nodded her head.

We pulled up to the house, and she turned to me.

"Whatever you do, never give it up without getting in those pockets. He must pay to play. Nothing in life is free. Especially not the va jay jay," she told me, and I knew she meant it. I chuckled.

"I know, Auny," I said as I flaunted my ring so that she could see.

She grabbed my hand. "Hmm, a carat. Nice," she said, nodding her head with much approval.

I began to wonder how she knew, but being the materialistic person that she was, I knew she knew everything there was to know about jewelry.

We entered the house, and I went directly to my room. "Angel of Mine" sang through my phone. I knew it was Zae calling.

"What's up?" I asked dryly.

"Man, why the fuck you in school, fighting over me? Is you dumb? For what, Sommer?" he yelled.

See, me, I don't play the "getting dogged" role, so I handled mine. "First of all, don't call my phone to question me about anything! And fighting over you? I wouldn't roll my damn eyes at a bitch about you! Yo' tack-headed ho came at me with the bullshit, so I special delivered her an ass whupping. And how did you know, anyway? I thought you wasn't talking to her anymore, you lying-ass bastard!"

With that, I hung up my phone. I was completely heated and angered. Fuck Zae and everything he stood for! Next thing I knew, my phone rang again. This time it was "Lovers and Friends" by Lil Jon. Zae had sent me a text message, probably because he knew his phone calls would get ignored for the remainder of the night. It read:

> Baby, I'm sorry. I ain't tryin'a beef with you, but you ain't gotta fight over what's yours. I know you ain't gon' text back, but that's cool. Love you, anyway.

That man had my heart. He was so sweet. He knew exactly what to say and when to say it. Was I in love with him? Probably not, but I had a lot of love for Zae. He was always there for me, and that was something I was not used to. I had rules, and one of them was never to give in easily. This meant that he had to earn my time. So, no, Zae wasn't getting a text back from me, but in my mind I thought, *I love you too,* and that was enough for me.

I lay in my bed, staring at the ceiling, daydreaming about Zae. I was confused. Did I love him or didn't I? I knew it wasn't safe to love anybody, just because everyone I loved had disappeared on me. I wondered if it was possible to prevent yourself from loving another. I knew I wanted to be with him forever. I also knew I loved the way he treated me and how our relationship seemed so genuine. It was still too early to tell. All I knew was that Doll was taking no losses.

Sleep was nowhere on my agenda, so I decided to call Kola. Three rings and then it was, "What's up, bitch?"

"You really need to work on your phone skills," I replied.

"Whatever. This my phone, and I'll answer it however." She chuckled.

"And you wonder why you jobless."

"I'm not looking for a job."

We both shared a laugh.

"How about those ass whuppings we issued this morning?" I giggled.

"Man, what? We did the damn thang. I was upping the fuck out of Tasha. Ugh, I can't stand her loud ass," she said. You could tell by the sound of her voice that Tasha's name hit a nerve.

"Girl, you really hate her?" I asked.

"Bitch, if she was on fire, I wouldn't even spit on the bitch. That's just how much I can't stand her tacky ass."

"Wow. You wouldn't spit on her? I would piss on the bitch just to say I did the shit. Hell, she'd still be on fire."

We laughed again.

"You right, but damn, you beat the brakes off Lakesha. I bet she forgot Zae existed after that beat down. Man, the hall guard was so weak." She laughed.

I sat up on my bed and giggled. I had to admit, I did give homegirl the business, but she deserved so much more. I replayed Zae questioning me about it in my head and got annoyed all over again. Why was that bitch still calling him?

Kola and I decided to cut our conversation short and resume it after she got out of a school hearing that she and her mother had to attend about her role in the fight. I looked at the clock; it read 2:45 A.M. It was definitely time to go to bed. I got on my knees and said my prayers, then hopped back in bed. I wondered what I would do these ten days out of Rogers. I replayed the fight in my head one last time and laughed. *I may be a beauty, but I'm still a beast,* I thought.

# Chapter 4

The next morning I awoke to Unc coming in my room, questioning me.

"So why you not in school, Doll?" he asked as he stood over me.

Although I knew he knew the answer to that question, I still gave him one. "I got into a fight with Lakesha yesterday," I said in my innocent voice. I mean, it really wasn't my fault.

"So, in other words, you suspended. Am I right or wrong?"

I hated when he was in his serious mode. He would stare me in the eyes with a blank expression on his face. I wouldn't know if I was safe or in the danger zone. I already knew my school counselor had called and told him, but he just wanted to hear it from me.

"Yeah. For ten days," I replied, wanting to cover my face with my comforter.

He nodded his head and left my room. Unc had never put his hands on me, but with the looks he gave me, there was no need to. Hell, I'd whup my own ass if it meant he didn't have to. He wasn't very strict, but he put his foot down whenever he needed to.

Although he didn't say anything or do anything, I still felt as though I was in a world of trouble. I just lay there thinking, *What is Unc going to do? Put me on punishment, not pay my phone bill, or make me clean the house?* I prayed none of the above would happen, but only time would tell.

I decided to get up and start my day. I was praying I could go over to Imani's house, being that she was never in school. She would be my only available friend these ten days out. Unc would be either at his corner store or his barbershop damn near all day, so I would be able to escape. Auny wouldn't care as long as I took all the blame if I got caught, which I had no problem doing, because I had no intention of getting caught. Unc had never said I couldn't leave, although I knew I couldn't. But that would be my excuse, that I didn't know. I decided I would call Imani after I took a shower. So that was what I did: I got up and got fresh.

When I got done showering, I heard Auny on the phone. It sounded like it was a man she was talking to just by her tone of voice and her responses. I wasn't sure, so I decided to creep up on her. I stopped by her door.

She was in her and Unc's room, sitting on their cherrywood king-sized bed, all smiles. I found this beyond weird, because I knew it wasn't Unc she was lollygagging with, since he had a no phone call rule from 10:00 A.M. to 1:00 P.M. He was always at a meeting with his business partner, Mitch, at those times, and I knew it had to be at least eleven something.

"Baby, no, things would be so much better that way. That's really our only choice. You know I want to be with you just as bad as you want me, but you know shit will get ugly," she said.

I could tell she was smiling, but I wondered where that smile would go if I punched her in her damn mouth.

I was lost in my thoughts. *No, she is not creeping on my uncle.* I stood there with my feet sinking into our plush cream carpet, wondering if I should tell Unc. I must have been contemplating this for too long, because Auny was standing in her doorway when I was done collecting I looked up at her with a dumbfounded expression on my face. *Think quick,* I thought.

"I was wondering if I can go over Imani's?" I decided to act as if that was the reason I was outside her door.

"Yeah, but you know you on your own," she reminded me.

"Okay, cool," I said as I walked to my room. I decided I wasn't going to tell Unc about her little phone call, being that I didn't have any real evidence on her. I made a mental note to keep both eyes on her, though.

When Imani swung her door open, all I saw was niggas everywhere. Her house was definitely the kicking it spot. For as long as I could remember, her mother had never really been there. She was always at work, trying to make ends meet for her three kids. Imani was the oldest out of the three and was by far her worst child. Her other two kids lived with their father during the week. I didn't know where she went wrong with my homegirl, but I figured it was her not being around, which made Mani seek attention from any and every nigga she spotted.

All eyes were on me as I walked into the house. I noticed a few of the neighborhood hood rats were present. Justine was Imani's new best friend, and you know what they say. Birds of a feather flock together. She definitely was in the same bracket as Imani. Justine wasn't what I would call cute, but she wasn't ugly. She was dark skinned and bony. I figured if she ate as much as she fucked, she would weigh at least one hundred pounds, but since she didn't, she looked a sickly seventy-five.

I didn't know where to sit; there was shit all over the place. Imani's fling, Malcolm, and some boy with braids were playing an Xbox game, while five other dudes were gambling. Justine and the other two hood rats were on the couch, giggling and whispering like the kids they were. I started to question why I had even bothered to come over here.

I decided the safest place to sit was on the floor, so on the floor was where I sat. Imani sat down next to me.

"Zae coming over," she whispered.

"Oh, for real," I said. I acted as if I didn't care, although I clearly did. We had just got into it last night, so I had to remind myself to keep an attitude with him.

"Why you say it like that?"

"Say what like what?" I replied.

"Like y'all beefing or something. And why you got all them scratches on your neck?" she asked while touching my neck.

"Girl, I didn't tell you I fought Lakesha's bum ass yesterday?" I asked as her doorbell began to ring.

"Hell, naw," she said as she stood up and buzzed whoever it was in. Moments later in walked Zae, looking sexier than ever. He was rocking a gray velour Akademiks sweat suit with the matching gray Jordans on his feet. We made eye contact, but I rolled my eyes as I looked away. He walked over and grabbed my arm. I stood up. He led me to the back of the house, to Imani's bedroom.

Her room was the closest thing to clean, but it wasn't quite there. Her twin bed was made and it looked as if her comforter was clean, so I decided it was safe to sit down on it. He closed the door behind us. He stood in front of me, eyeing me.

"So I'm guessing you still mad at me?" He questioned.

"Naw, I'm not," I said nonchalantly.

"Doll, you lying. I don't see why you all upset, because I told you that you ain't have to fight over me. Where was I wrong at?"

"How you know we fought?" I quizzed him.

"I do know people who attend Rogers. Damn, 'cause I know I had to find out from her?" he asked.

"No, but I'm sure that's how you know with yo' lying ass." I crossed my arms. I didn't care what Zae said. I was convinced that Lakesha had told him about our fight. He swore up and down that he hadn't talked to her, but niggas lied, and he was obviously lying.

"So basically, you willing to let her break us up?" he asked me.

I sat there thinking, not realizing that this was reverse psychology he was using on me. I didn't want to break up, so I decided to let it go. "No, no one comes between us."

"Well, shut up," he said as he flopped down next to me, "and kiss me."

He didn't have to say that twice. I tongued him down, and he began feeling all over my body. My juices were surely flowing by this point.

He started unbuckling my pants, and I never stopped him. He got up and locked the door. He sat between my legs and started pulling my pants and panties off. I lay there wondering what he was about to do. He put his head down where it had no business being, spread my lips below, and began sucking and licking. I had never received head before, but Imani had told me all about it. She was so right. It was the best thing that happened to mankind.

I didn't know if Zae was doing it right or wrong, but however he was doing it, I was so into it. I didn't want to moan, being that there was a million people in the house. I decided to cover my mouth, but I still let out a moan here and there. It just felt that good. After about ten minutes Zae came up for air. He lay next to me and kissed me on my neck.

"You liked that?" he asked between kisses.

"Yeah," I responded, wondering if he expected me to return the favor. I lay on his chest, contemplating if I should return it. I didn't know a thing about sucking a dick. Hell, I had never even seen a dick, besides on TV. My eyes were glued to his pants. *Should I pull them down?* I thought.

I tugged at his pants, and he got the picture. He lifted his butt and pulled his pants and boxers down. When he whipped his dick out, it felt like I had whiplash. He was packing, and I didn't know what I was going to do with all that. It was too late to back out, so I opened my mouth and put it inside. I bobbed my head up and down, hoping I was doing it right.

"Move yo' teeth," he said. So I tried to move my teeth, but it was kind of difficult, being that his dick was so damn big. His manhood was dry, and it started hurting my lips, so I stopped. I was embarrassed. I already knew I had received a F for that task. I sat there, looking at the red Kool-Aid stains on the floor.

"What you thinking about?" Zae asked as he pulled his pants up.

"Nothing," I responded. He knew I was lying.

"You cool. I'm glad you ain't know what you was doing. That way I know you haven't suck nobody else up," he said, trying to make me feel better. "Next time slob on it more and keep yo' teeth out the way."

We both stood up and headed to the door.

"Don't worry, baby. I'm going to teach everything you need to know," he said as he kissed me on my forehead.

# Chapter 5

"You scared, Ma?" Zae asked me while I lay on his bed in the nude. We had been dating for a year now, and I was madly in love with him. There was no doubt in my mind about it. Still, we had never had sex, probably because he had never tried to have sex with me, and I, for damn sure, wasn't going to throw it at him.

I was a fifteen-year-old sophomore at Rogers now. Zae was eighteen and the co-owner of his dad's construction company. He was making real money and was no longer living in his parents' guesthouse in the backyard. He was now living in a big-ass home in Maumee, another suburban area of Toledo. He was the owner of his red, old-school Monte Carlo, his snow-white two-seater BMW and a midnight-black Range Rover. He was killing any eighteen-year-old I knew.

"A little," I said, being honest.

"It's going to hurt, dude . . . but I'll go slow," he told me. "If it hurt too bad, I'll stop," he said with the most assuring voice.

I was ready. He pulled his pants down and wow! I didn't think that I could handle all that he had to offer. He was already standing at attention. Hell, I was naked, so he had better be.

"I hope you about to put on a condom, 'cause I ain't tryin'a get pregnant, Markaylo!"

"Naw, I wasn't trying to. Come on, man. You mine, and this the first time you let me feel you," he begged.

Of course, my dumb ass agreed.

He was putting a little in at a time. That little was killing me. It felt like somebody had put a knife in there and was twisting it around. I must have been doing too much jerking, because he stopped.

"What are you doing?" I questioned.

"If it's hurting you, we can wait."

I felt bad. I mean, it did hurt like hell, but I didn't want to leave him hanging or, better yet, standing.

"Let's just get it over with." Then I grabbed his arm, and we were back at it again. It didn't hurt so bad after a while, but it still wasn't pleasurable.

He was in my ear, breathing like he had asthma.

"Baby, you don't know how good you feel," he whispered. "I swear, Doll, you fuck somebody else, I'ma kill you, on my mama," he said between moans.

"I'm not, Zae," I said, damn near dying.

When it was all over—I'd prayed for it to end the entire time—we lay there naked. He told me that he loved me and that when I graduated, he was going to get me pregnant. I just lay there and listened, because he had me fucked up. No kids for me. There was no way I was losing this figure.


"You gave him the goodies, Doll?" Kola asked.

"Kola, you are the nosiest friend I have. Damn, mind yo' business," I said while looking down at my geometry book. We were in Ms. Reese's class, not paying any attention to the lecture.

"Girl gone! You let him get in those jeans," she said, chuckling.

I laughed too. "Yeah, and it hurt like hell." I told her all the juicy details. I mean, she was my best friend. I even told her about the bittersweet threat.

"Kill you? You must got that snap back!"

"Shut up, Kola!" I shook my head.

"Hey, I'm just saying," she said through her laughter. Our class had been assigned twenty problems to solve, and we had the remainder of class to complete them. During class, I happened to gaze around the room, and I spotted a newbie.

"Who is he?" I asked Kola.

"Oh, that's Brian. He new. You remember Terrell? My guy friend?" she said, trying to refresh my memory.

"Oh, yeah, I remember. The one who plays on the football team." I made sure we were talking about the same Terrell, because Kola switched niggas like she switched her drawers.

Brian was definitely cute. He was dark skinned and had braids, and he had on an Enyce sweat suit with some all-white mid-tops.

"I think I want him," I said. I knew Zae and I were on good terms, but I figured what he didn't know wouldn't hurt him. It wasn't that I was trying to dis him. I just had this motto that you lived only once, and since I was young, I was just having fun.

"Uh, no, you don't! You're with Zae, and I'm pretty sure Brian's pockets ain't got nothing on Zae's," she said, as if I had lost my mind.

Deep down inside I knew that I wanted him, and no matter what, sooner or later I was going get him. Period.

Zae picked me up from school in his Range Rover. All the hoes were eyeing him, but they already knew what time it was, and they definitely didn't want me to clock out. We greeted each other with a kiss.

"How was school?" he asked, checking out my outfit.

"It was cool. Seemed long," I said while looking out my side of the windshield. My mind was on Brian. I was contemplating whether it was worth the risk. I looked at Zae, and my man was sexy and he was paid, so I wondered if I should risk my relationship with him over Brian. I was unsure of myself.

Zae took me to Penn Station for a steak sub. We had a great conversation over laughs, but eventually, he brought up that he had to go check on his employees. Then I had homework to do, so we both knew that our date would soon come to an end. He dropped me off in front of my house. We kissed, said our "I love yous," and I hopped out of the car.

Unc was sitting on the couch, watching TV, when I walked in the house.

"Nice ride," he said sarcastically. He never looked back at me. Instead, he stared straight at the television.

"Oh, yeah. That's my friend," I said nervously.

The entire year and a half that Zae and I had been messing around, I had never introduced him to Unc. Even though Zae had met Auny on the sly about six or seven months ago, I knew then that Unc wouldn't approve of our relationship.

"Yeah, I know. Zae, right?" he asked.

I assumed Auny must have told him about us. I should have known she couldn't hold water. I began to fume, but I didn't want to give myself away. "Yeah," I responded. I began to wonder where this conversation was headed.

"Come sit down, Sommer," he said. He patted the seat next to him on the couch.

I was nervous as hell. He called me Sommer only when shit was deep. I walked over to our leather chaise and sat down.

"Sommer, you know you ain't slick, right?" he said, not giving me any time to answer. "I know you been messing with Jerome's stepson, Markaylo, for some time now. I know all about it. I don't have a problem with it, 'cause he got a good head on his shoulders and the boy has money. I know he really loves you just by what Rome been telling me, but what I don't like is that you trying to be sneaky about it," he said, pausing in his speech.

I supposed he wanted me to respond, so I did. "Well, I—I—I just ain't think you'd approve, 'cause he's three years o-older than me," I stuttered. Unc intimidated me whenever he was in his serious mode.

"Doll, I understand all that, but how much do you think you can hide from me? I got little niggas all throughout Toledo. Now, tomorrow I want to meet the little nigga, so we all going to Red Lobster. Let him know, and don't do this shit again. . . ." He paused and gave me the eyebrow. "You dismissed," he said, laughing while fanning his hand.

He was watching *Martin,* his favorite TV show, so I knew it was a playful dismissal and not an irritated one. Thank God.

I texted Zae, letting him know that Unc wanted to meet him. He actually seemed excited. If I had Unc's approval, then I knew we were definitely unstoppable.

We established that we would do Red Lobster so that Unc and Zae could meet. I knew that meant we would all be riding with Unc. This meant there'd be no cuddling, kissing, or hugging with Unc around. I knew I had to get my license soon. Getting my license would grant me and Zae some privacy in our relationship. I instantly enrolled in driver's education.

\*\*\*

"So, Markaylo, you been dating my niece for quite some time now. Don't you think it's a little disrespectful not to meet her parents?" Unc asked.

I grabbed a cheddar biscuit from the tray and nibbled on it. I was nervous to hear what Zae was going to say. I knew from experience that Unc was a tough cookie, and I hadn't got the chance to prep Zae for this interview. Zae lifted his cup of Sprite and sipped on the straw. He sat the cup down and looked Unc in his eyes.

"Yeah, it is, being that Doll has met my parents, but she told me that she didn't think that you would approve of us, so I accepted that," he stated.

"So you knew I didn't approve of y'all, and you still continued a relationship with her?" Unc quizzed, with no expression on his face.

My palms began to sweat, so I put my cheddar biscuit down and looked at Auny. She too looked nervous.

"Yeah, I did. I'm in love with Doll, and if I have to sneak to give my heart what it desires, then that's what I'll do. I haven't disrespected you other than that." He paused for a moment. "We have never had sex," he lied, "and I'm more than willing to wait for that. I apologize for sneaking behind your back, sir, but that's the way love goes."

Unc leaned back in his chair and nodded his head. Everyone was silent as we watched to see what was to come next. When Unc cracked a smile, I knew that he approved of Zae. Unc loved people who didn't fold under pressure, and my baby had stood his ground like a man. After the interview, they talked to each other nonstop. They almost forgot Auny and I were even present. They talked for what seemed like hours about basketball and how the Lakers were going to win the finals.

From that day forward, Unc and Zae spent a lot of time together. They went to basketball games together and gambled together, and sometime I would come home from school or from one of my friends' house and Zae would be sitting on our couch, lollygagging with Unc. I became a little jealous that Unc was stealing my boyfriend away, but I guess that was why they said to be careful of what you asked for.

After I finished my homework, I called my girl Mari to come and pick me up and take me to my driving classes. I was finally going to get my license. Almost all my friends had their licenses, because they were all sixteen. I was the only one who didn't have a car or a license. I was pretty close, though. I had only one week left of my driving course, and then the only thing holding me back would be my sixteenth birthday, which was taking its time to come around.

The last day of school before spring break was beyond boring. All the exams had me drained, and I was definitely happy to see Zae when I exited the building. He picked me up in his two-seater, and we went over to his house. We sat in the car for a while so that we could talk.

"Hey, let's do something," he said, smiling. He was always spontaneous.

"Zae, what?" I knew he had something slick up his sleeve.

"Let me do something to you."

I also knew that it was something nasty, but I knew I would like it. "Okay," I agreed.

He pulled up in his garage. He told me to lie on top of his hood and take my pants off. I did what he said without hesitation. He climbed on top of me and put his stick where it belonged. It hurt a little, but after a few slow strokes it felt pretty damn good. I started getting into the motion, and he pulled it out and started licking and sucking all over me. I was in heaven the way he moved that tongue on my clit. I just knew I owed him one for this. I loved what he was doing and how it was being done.

I started to feel this feeling that was unexplainable. My whole body was shaking, and I was losing control. I moaned and screamed. I held his head hostage between my legs, and then my body collapsed.

I let go of his head, and he came up for air.

"You liked that, huh?" he asked while helping me get off the hood.

"You know I did." I smiled.

We got in his two-person shower. We washed one another. He was behind me, and he whispered, "Bend over."

I turned around to look into his hazel eyes, which made me weak. What made him think I was built for a round two?

"Just bend over, Doll," he demanded with a sexual voice.

I wasn't trying to do it again, so I just got on my knees and gave him some head. I wasn't an amateur at giving head. We had been giving one another oral sex way before we began having sex and going all the way. I felt he deserved it, anyway.

I sucked it like it was a Blow Pop and I was trying to get the gum. While I did this, I played with his balls, a trick he had taught me a while ago. I had him running a little, so I knew I was giving it to him something lovely.

He pulled his dick out of my mouth and lay down on the shower floor. I knew what that meant, so I climbed on top and rode it like a bike. He was moaning and bouncing my body up and down real hard.

"Go faster, Doll," he moaned. I went faster, and a minute after that he came in me. I felt the heat of his pistol run down in between my thighs, so I instantly hopped up. My mind started racing.

"Zae! You just came in me," I cried.

"Baby, it's cool. If you get pregnant, we can get rid of it if you don't want to keep it. But know that if you do, I'm here for you. You're not alone."

I made it home close to nine o'clock that night, and Auny was sitting at the table with her face in her palms. She was in tears. I went over to her.

"What's wrong, Auny?" I asked.

"They took him!" she cried. "Doll, they took him. Them damn crackers!" She sobbed. She got up and went over to the window, wiping the tears from her face.

Then it hit me like a ton of bricks. The only reason Unc would be in jail was drugs. I had to get more details, and I was hoping Auny would tell me.

"Why'd they take him?" I asked.

"Clyde set him up. They caught him with ten bricks, Doll. He ain't never getting out!" She ran upstairs, crying even louder than before.

I just stood there. What the fuck were we going to do? Unc was our world. He kept all of us together. Something told me Auny was going to lose it. Maybe even herself.

I called Kola, and she picked up after the first ring.

"Unc is in jail, Kola," I cried to her.

"What? Are you serious?" she questioned. There was a moment of silence. "So Unc is in jail?" Kola asked. She was obviously worried, almost to death.

"Yeah, I just walked in to find Auny crying, and she told me they just picked him up," I replied, barely mustering a response. "How fast can you get here?" I asked Kola.

"Twenty minutes," she said, and we hung up.

I needed some type of support. My mother had left me, and now Unc was gone. I was hurt. I didn't have anybody but Auny—but to me, she was nothing without Unc.

Kola arrived exactly twenty minutes later. I just needed somebody to be there with me. A little while after I got off the phone with Kola, Auny left. She said she needed air, and I understood that. Kola and I sat and talked until she fell asleep on me. We were like sisters.

She was born Kaliyah Harris, but everyone called her Kola. Why? No clue. I never asked, because it was never that important to me. She was caramel complected, with shoulder-length hair that she always kept dyed jet-black. She was one of the girls who lived in the Abercrombie & Fitch store. She told me that the white girls hated her because she outdid them in their own shit. Kola was a goofy individual, always laughing and being playful. She was my homie. If I swung on a female, I knew her hand was sure to follow, no matter what.

As usual, Kola and I were gossiping in our geometry class. Almost a month had passed since Unc got arrested, and this was the end of the school year, so everything was critical and would determine if I graduated. Like clockwork, Ms. Reese gave us our assignment and gave us the rest of class to complete it.

"Auny still ain't surfaced yet?" Kola asked in her concerned voice.

"Hell, no! I just hope CSB don't find out. There's no way I'm going into foster care." There was no way in hell I would be able to adapt to another family other than my own. I had no idea how I would handle that.

Brian and I had become kind of close at this point. So when Ms. Reese dismissed herself, he came over to me and Kola.

"What's good, Doll?" he asked, licking his lips like he normally did.

"This work," Kola said, interrupting our conversation.

He started to laugh. "Hey, we still on for tonight?" he asked me.

"Why wouldn't we be?" I asked back. He knew damn well that I wanted to chill with him.

Brian and I had reservations at my place. He was coming over to chill with me, and that was all. Nothing more, nothing less.

As soon as I had gotten my license, I started pushing Unc's Benz. After all, he was in jail, and I needed a ride to get around in. Auny was still out of the picture, so I was secretly doing things on my own. I was hiding from CSB, and the girls hating on me in school weren't making my situation any better, either.

I pulled up to my house and jumped straight into the shower. It was necessary that I had myself smelling extra good if I was going to be inviting a dude into my house. Brian was due to arrive at six o'clock, and I was anticipating his arrival.

My cucumber-melon-scented body slipped into a tank top and boy shorts. I wanted to look cute, but not as if I was trying to be cute for him.

Like an employee scheduled for work, he was there at six o'clock sharp. He texted my phone, telling me to open the door. When I opened it, there he stood, smiling from ear to ear. His gold grill was gleaming, and he was looking beyond fine.

"You going to let a nigga in, or are you going to just stand there drooling?" he asked.

"Shut up," I said as I moved to the side, allowing him to come in.

He sat down on the couch and began watching TV. I sat down next to him. We didn't say much, so I offered him something to drink.

"You thirsty?"

"No, I'm cool," he said.

We watched TV in complete silence for about a half an hour. Finally, he made his move and started kissing me on my neck. It felt good, and my Niagara started falling. We were kissing and feeling on one another, and then he proposed something that I wasn't expecting him to propose.

"Let me taste that," he whispered.

I definitely wasn't turning down no head. I took my pants off, and Brian started eating me alive . . . in a good way, that is.

After the head session, we relaxed, talked, and laughed about a lot of things. I had realized that Brian was down to earth after we started spending more time together. We were definitely more than friends now, and we had become really close.

We had started rocking a few weeks before Unc went to jail, so it had been going on for a month or so now. We were both in relationships with other people, but we had vowed to remain tight. What he did with her didn't bother me, and what I did with Zae didn't bother him, either. We were the best creeps, probably because we were both playing number two roles. Whatever the case, I didn't want anything to change.

I was sitting in the courtroom, waiting on the verdict from the jury. Auny was not present, and I knew it had to hurt Unc. I wanted to slap that stupid bitch for making my uncle go through more than what he had to. Unc knew that Auny had gone MIA, but he thought that I was staying at Kola's house and that her mother was looking after me. Although that was far from the truth, I just didn't want him to worry. Besides, I was damn near grown.

His lawyer came over to talk to me. Garcia was a sexy Mexican man in his late thirties. He was the best lawyer in Toledo when it came to drugs. He was also the most expensive. Shit, he cost us a pretty penny, from what Unc had told me.

"Hey, Sommer. How are you?" Garcia asked while shaking my hand.

"I'm fine. Just hoping they don't put my uncle under the jail." I was being honest. I didn't want Unc to spend the rest of his life like a caged animal.

"Well, we took the plea bargain so that he wouldn't get anything over ten years. He has a mandatory three-year sentence that he has to do, but if he behaves himself, he'll be out after that," Garcia assured me.

One year, two years, three! It was all a long-ass time for me.

They brought Unc out, and he looked like he hadn't gotten any sleep in a long time. He wasn't himself. When I looked at him, I saw a man who was down and out. I didn't know if it was the legal case or if it was Auny's disappearance. I figured it was more Auny than anything.

He didn't let the prosecutor or judge see him sweat, though. He held his head high and made eye contact with whoever was talking to him or about him. I smiled. Unc would be fine. I knew he had no choice but to do some time in jail, but at least it wouldn't be life, like Auny thought. I figured she was a gold-digging ho who had been in it for all the wrong reasons. Then again, I wanted to give her the benefit of the doubt. I mean, they had been together since she was seventeen.

Then the prosecuting attorney spoke.

"Jim Jones is a menace and should not be on the streets with the general public," the prosecutor said.

I sighed and dropped my head. It hurt me to hear those words coming from the prosecutor, even though we all knew it was going to happen.

Then the judge looked over the paperwork. He tilted his glasses and his long nose and put both eyes on Unc. "I sentence Jim Jones to five to ten years, with a mandatory three years served before he will be eligible for release. I also will take off the time you already served. Just behave in there and you'll be out before you know it," he said.

"Yes, Your Honor," Unc answered, then looked at me.

They made Unc stand up. He looked over and winked at me, then smiled. I discussed the trial with Garcia a little while longer, and then I was out of there.

For months, I made it my business to put money on Unc's books. Zae gave me a weekly allowance and extra money whenever I asked, which was quite often. Unc was allowed no more than fifty dollars at any one time. Every time I went to visit, I added enough money so that he had fifty dollars. My uncle had always been there for me, so I was making sure that I was there for him in every way possible. I just wished that Auny could have been doing the same. You know what they say. "Good things don't last forever."


It was Friday, and I had been over at Kola's since we got out of school. I hated going home when Zae had to work, because it was so boring. Besides, what was better than chilling with your best friend.

"So Auny's still MIA?" Kola asked as we sat on her couch, watching *106 & Park* on her big-screen TV.

"Yeah, she's still nowhere to be found. I been calling, leaving messages, and texting her almost every day," I replied, shaking my head. I didn't want to give up on Auny, but it didn't seem as if I had any other choice. "I think she was cheating," I added while sipping my Pepsi through a straw.

Kola turned to look at me. She had that "You lying" look on her face.

I shook my head no. "When I was suspended, I overheard her talking to somebody and it wasn't Unc. She was cheesy as hell, talking 'bout she wanna be with them and shit." I regretted saying nothing then.

"For real?" Kola was obviously astonished.

Auny had to have another man, because what loyal bitch would just up and dip when her man needed her the most? None that I knew. It was cool, though, because I had vowed that when I spotted her, I was going to let her ass have it. I decided to change the subject.

"So how you and Sean?" Sean was Kola's current fling. He played for Rogers's football team. He was cute, kind of cocky, and so full of himself. She thought him being conceited was cute, but I saw it as a turnoff. I guess you could say she had a thing for our football players.

"Girl, he plays today," she said, smiling.

"Really? I didn't know we played today." I never really kept up with our school activities. I figured it was because I didn't like anybody at Rogers, well, at least not until Brian came along.

She told me we were playing Scott, which was the school that had all the thugs, so I knew it was going to be a nice crowd.

"We should go," I said.

Although we made it there during the third quarter, we still saw the part of the game that mattered the most—the end. It was a little breezy out, and I regretted that I was trying to be cute and had not worn a jacket. When we walked onto the bleachers, we noticed the females were smirking and the niggas were eyeing us. We decided to sit all the way at the top. When we got up there, I noticed that Brian was sitting with this mixed chick, Janeen, who attended Scott. She was pretty and all, but she wasn't me, so she wasn't much. I rolled my eyes.

Kola must have caught the whole ordeal, because she spoke about it. "Jealous," she said and giggled.

"Who? Me? Girl, you know me better than I know myself, and if I want it, I'm going to get it," I said while pointing at my chest. "Act like you know." I wasn't worried about Janeen. I knew I was looking real good. I was rocking my powder-pink Baby Phat sweat suit with my all-white low-top Forces. My wrap was banging, and my eyebrows were arched. You couldn't tell me a thing, and, of course, the niggas to the side of us kept reminding us how good we looked.

"Let's go get something to drink," I said. I decided if we walked past Brian, maybe he would realize what he was missing. The concession stand was so far away, and I normally would not have walked all the way to it, but I had alternative plans. Kola already knew what I was up to, so she just giggled and followed my lead.

As we made our way down the bleachers and got farther and farther away, I noticed Brian watching. Mission accomplished. When we finally reached the concession stand, we saw Ashley and Mari in line. They let us cut in front of them, and I heard some lames smack their lips.

"Excuse you. I know yo' lips ain't pop," Mari said to the crowd of females behind us. They said nothing. Everyone knew Mari had a bad temper and was quick to lay her hands on anybody that asked for an ass whupping. We all giggled.

After getting my Coke and Skittles, I stood up against the fence and waited for the rest of my girls to get their stuff. Brian walked over to me. Tan was definitely his color, because that tan Carhartt with the matching Tims did him justice.

"I saw you watching me." He chuckled.

"Well, I guess you can't see, 'cause I wasn't paying you no mind," I lied.

"Damn, you harsh."

"Just being real." I smiled. He smiled too, and I noticed his teeth were perfect. I had this crazy fetish about straight pearly whites. I didn't know why, but it was a plus in my book.

"Well, if you wasn't watching me, I was watching you," he said in a sexy voice.

"You like what you see?" I asked, trying to run game and not let him see that I was loving everything that escaped his mouth.

"Yeah. I'd love to taste what I see again, too," he whispered in my ear as he licked my earlobe.

Whew, Brian had me going. My girls walked up and ended our conversation, but I promised myself that I would resume it in geometry class that Monday. They all had smiles on their faces as Brian got in line. We walked away, and I knew they were dying to know what we were talking about, but some things were better left unsaid.

# Chapter 6

Two years had passed by, and Auny had disappeared completely. I hadn't heard a single word from her. Unc had a few more months to do before he could be considered for an early release. The Feds couldn't take any of his property, because he could prove he had paid for it in a legit way. Unc was street, but he was ten times smarter. He had used his first couple of thousands to put himself and a few of his boys through college. He got a business management degree from the University of Toledo and his best friend, Mitch, got his degree in marketing.

After that, he started a marketing business, which he and Mitch ran together. Before anyone knew it, they had companies in four different states. He also had a barbershop and a clothing store. Many people didn't know about the marketing business, not even Auny. He purchased only things that the barbershop and the store could buy. So while he was in jail, he was still clocking in millions. My cousin Debo ran both of his businesses in Toledo, and Unc told him to put half of the profit up and to split the other half between him and me. He did that with no problems.

Unc eventually gave up on Auny. Besides, nobody knew what had become of her. For the past two years I had prayed that Auny would be sitting on the couch, watching TV, when I got home from school, or that she would walk through the front door, but it never happened. I just knew it was too much for me, but my broken heart was healing. I figured she had run off with some man, maybe the one whom I had caught her jonesing with when I was suspended.

I sat there reflecting on the day she told me Unc had been locked up. I wondered where she had got her info from. She said Clyde had set him up, but if that was true, how'd she know? Word on the street was that Clyde had fled town, which made perfect sense. I just couldn't imagine Unc doing any illegal activity with Clyde. He didn't trust him for shit, so them working together was unlikely to me. I knew all too well that the easiest way to set a man up was with a female. What if Auny had set him up? I wondered, but I quickly dismissed that thought. She wasn't that crazy.

At this point in my life I was getting ready to graduate from high school. I still remained close to Kola, but Imani and I had drifted apart a wee bit. We talked here and there, but not often. Why? I wasn't sure, but some people just grew up and grew apart. I also had to remain low key, dodging CSB investigators, in case they discovered Auny had abandoned me. I had raised myself during the past two and a half years of my life.

To my surprise, I got a call from Imani. It had been weeks since we had chopped it up. Before I could say hello, she spoke energetically into the phone.

"Hey, Doll! Quick question! How are you and Zae?"

"Umm . . . we're fine." I quickly changed the subject. "How's it in the PJs?" I was referring to the Brands.

"Oh, everybody cool, and by the way, I been meaning to tell you about Morgan. You know Morgan, right?" she asked.

"Yeah. What of her?" I asked dryly. I wasn't too much in the mood for being in anybody's business.

"Word on the street is she's been fucking yo' man." She said it very bluntly, and it pissed me off.

I almost dropped my phone. *Wait a minute.* No, my heart couldn't take this.

"What?" was all I could say.

"Yeah, I know this ain't the time, but you my bitch, and truthfully, he just picked her up in the Monte maybe twenty minutes before I called you."

She wasn't holding shit back, and I couldn't hold back my tears, either. I hung up with Imani and called Kola up. Kola and I decided to swing by Zae's house later that evening. I mean, he did wait patiently a whole year and a half before we had sex, so hell, he might have been cheating the whole time.

When we got down the street from his house, Kola turned the lights off to her 2001 Stratus coupe. Just like Imani had said, Zae's Monte Carlo was in the driveway, while the rest of his cars were put up in the garage. The lights were on in his upstairs bedroom, and then they cut off. I grew furious.

"I swear, if it's a bitch in there, we whupping her ass. No. Matter of fact, I'm whupping her ass!" I said. I could feel my blood boiling. I was ready to go in for the kill.

We got out of the car and went around to the back door. I knew it would be unlocked, because it always was. We snuck up the steps, and when we reached the top, it sounded as if they were making a movie or something.

The girl was moaning like she was receiving the best dick a man could give. I opened the door quietly, so quietly that they were still going at it. I could tell she was on top as they had sex under the covers. I had to admit she was riding the hell out of my dick, but that would soon come to an end.

Kola crept into the bathroom in Zae's room. I snatched the girl up by her hair so fast that she didn't know what hit her. I dragged her into the bathroom in his room. Kola was already in there, waiting for this moment. We locked the bathroom door and proceeded to beat the fuck out of Morgan with the lights off.

Zae beat on the door.

"Man, Morgan! Baby, you okay?"

*Baby? What the fuck?* How could he refer to this bitch as his baby? That hit me hard. I thought *I* was his baby. I hit her even harder. We whupped her ass for about five minutes, until Zae picked the lock open. He turned on the lights. My eyes were filled with tears, and his mouth dropped to the floor.

"Let's go, Doll! Our job is done!" Kola grabbed my arm, and Zae just watched.

He didn't utter a word. He never ran behind me, begging me to stay. I wanted so badly for him to beg for my mercy and tell me that she was just a nut . . . that he loved me and only me . . . and that we would be together and fix this. Kola and I were in the car before I knew it, and he never came out.

The car ride home was silent, except for when Kola tried to comfort me and convince me that I didn't need him. Then she told me she would stay over at my house to see that I was going to be okay. I just stared out the window, feeling so sick inside. Zae and I had just been together earlier that day. I began to question myself. Was I not good enough? My mind was running a mile a minute.

When we made it home, I ran into the bathroom and stared at myself in the mirror. I kept questioning myself in my mind, and then I managed to open the medicine cabinet. I grabbed a bottle of pills and shoved all the white tablets down my throat.

I couldn't do it. My mom didn't love me, Unc was in-carcerated, and the only person I thought really loved me had taken my love for granted. I promised myself that I would never get played again. Never.

I passed out.


When I woke up, I was hooked up to an IV, and I was lying in the Toledo Hospital. My vision was somewhat blurry, but I did know that my girls were at my bedside.

"She's waking up," I heard Mari say.

It took a minute before my vision actually cleared up. All I saw were smiles. Then I saw Zae coming through the door with a dozen white roses and a red one in the middle. Kola smacked her lips

"We'll give you guys a minute. We going to go to the mall and grab something to eat." She came over and kissed me on the forehead. Everybody took turns hugging me.

"Hey, baby." Zae sounded sad, like he wanted me to feel sorry for him and forgive him. I rolled my eyes. My heart couldn't take another heartbreak.

"Baby, I know you not fond of me right now. I know I fucked up. You may hate me, but I love you, Sommer. I really do."

He tried pouring out his heart to me, but in my mind I was done with him. He had never loved me, and he had showed me that.

"Sommer, I made a mistake. I'm human. If you leave me, my heart's going to die." His eyes were welling up with tears. "I don't know how to love. I never had it. My mom loved her husband more than me. My real dad is a crackhead. Listen, Sommer. I need you, baby. Please don't leave me."

By this time he was at the side of my bed. "You can't leave something you're not with!" I spat.

The nurse came in.

"Hi, Sommer Jones. I'm your nurse, Christina. You know you're in here because you took a whole lot of pills, missy. But you're recovering well. I also want you to know, if you aren't already aware, that you're three weeks pregnant. Were you aware of that?"

That was all I needed. I was only seventeen, and there was no way in hell that Zae was going to trap me with a baby. Sorry to say, but this pregnancy was getting terminated. Christina asked me a few more questions, and then she went to get my dinner.

I was in the hospital for two weeks due to the fact that I was pregnant, that they wanted to make sure I didn't try anything crazy. Zae was in the hospital with me the entire two weeks. I didn't understand why, because I barely said anything to his ass. My girls came and went throughout the two weeks to keep an eye on me.

Before they released me from the hospital, they gave me an ultrasound. I didn't see anything but a little alien-looking figure, but I made a connection with my unborn child. Zae insisted on taking me home, but I wasn't having that.

"Doll, I'm taking you home. I'm not trying to hear all that mouth," he stated.

Who the hell did he think he was? I didn't know, but what I did know was that he was about to snap back into reality. In the end, however, I relented, and he drove me home.

"You really hate me, don't you?" he quizzed on the way to my house.

"Zae, I really don't feel up to all yo' questions. I'm tired, okay?" I begged him to leave it all alone.

"Okay, baby."

For the remainder of the car ride there was silence. I was debating whether I was going to keep this child or not. My graduation was a month away, and I was only five weeks pregnant. This meant that I would be eighteen when I actually had the baby. I wasn't trying to be tied to Zae's lousy ass.

We pulled up to my house, and he insisted on walking me in. When I got settled in my nice comfy bed, he sat at the foot of it and just stared at me. I didn't pay him any attention. Instead, I fell asleep.

I woke up to find Zae next to me, asleep. His phone was on my dresser. Now, I was a woman, so you already know I went through the phone. There were a lot of numbers with no names, and the phone calls didn't say too much, either, so I went through his text messages. There really wasn't anything in there that caught my eye until I spotted Morgan's name.

"He still messing with this bum bitch?" I said aloud. The messages read:

> Morgan: So what was that? A one-night stand?
> Zae: Man, Morgan, u knew it was nothing like that.
> Morgan: What? I get a piece of u every five years or something?
> Zae: I really ain't tryin'a mess with you at all, so I don't think you'll be hearing from me in five years. Take care, though.
> Morgan: What? So you gon' dis me for that young bitch?
> Zae: Watch yo' mouth, and you already knew what it was. I love her, and I'm not leaving her for no bitch. Sorry about the ass whupping I caused you, but other than that, I'm happy where I'm at.
> Morgan: Fuck you.

I smiled, but at the same time I was still hurt that he had given what was rightfully mine to someone else.

"Quit going through my phone!" he said with a dry tone of voice.

"Shut up." I rolled my eyes and crossed my arms.

"So what you going to do about the baby?" he asked.

"I really don't know at this point. I just got a lot on my plate right now, okay?"

He nodded his head as if he understood.

"Well, whatever you decide to do, just know that I got your back," he said, kissing me on the forehead.

It just didn't feel right. Things felt different. I was starting to believe that the love that was once there wasn't as strong as it was before.


I had my first ob-gyn visit two days after I was released from the hospital. Christina, the nurse, had scheduled it for me. I was still unsure if I was going to keep the baby. I figured a doctor's visit wouldn't hurt, just in case I was going to keep it. Zae wanted to go, but I didn't feel like being bothered by him, so I ignored his text messages and phone calls until I made it home from the ob-gyn.

Since I was feeling better, I decided to invite Zae over to my house. When he came through the door, he had a box of pizza and Gatorade for us. As we sat down at the dining room table, with little to say, I thought it would be the perfect time to talk about what we had discussed in the hospital. I was in the mood to hear what he had to say.

"So tell me what you were talking about while I was in the hospital." I looked directly at him as I folded my feet underneath my chair.

"What you mean? I said a lot while you were in there," he said between swallows of Gatorade.

"Well, elaborate about everything, then, 'cause I want to know," I said with a serious voice. By this time I was rolling my neck. I could tell he was frustrated.

"Like what, Sommer?" He was definitely annoyed.

"Tell me your story, Zae. It's starting to seem like you're a stranger to me all of a sudden!"

"I'm the same me. But what I was saying at the hospital is I been through a lot too. I may not show it, but I have. Okay? I don't really know how to love anybody, but I do know I love you. Yeah, I fucked up! But I'm human, and we all make mistakes!"

I saw the truth in his eyes. I started to feel for him. He was beginning to tell me his life story.

"I don't know why I fucked Morgan. I really can't tell you. I just know she begged to suck my dick, and after a while I decided to let her. Yeah, I was wrong. I know that," he proclaimed.

"Well, why you ain't chase me or explain yourself to me when I ran out of there?" Tears began to form in my eyes. "Zae! You were supposed to chase me." I hardly got it out.

"I don't know, man. I wanted to, but I just seen the hurt in your eyes. I knew I fucked up." He got teary eyed with me. He had this embarrassed look on his face.

"What?" I asked.

"Do you remember Jean?" He looked away and then looked back at me, dead in my eyes.

I almost threw up at the thought of the name, but I faced him and whatever words he was getting ready to say.

"How could I forget?" I became angry. I remembered that Jean was the man who had tried to rape me years ago in my mother's apartment.

"Well . . . that's my biological father."

"What the fuck are you talking about, Zae?" I stood up. I was disgusted.

"When I was a young buck, he got hooked on heroine. My mom kind of fell off until she met my stepdad, Rome. She ain't really pay me much attention when he came along, so I fell into the streets. I went to CSI for about thirty days, and when I got out, they started spoiling me." He took a break, then added, "Sit down, Doll." He gently grabbed my arm, and I sat down to feel his pain and to focus on his story.

"So after all that, they gave a nigga whatever he wanted, but still my mom ain't pay me no attention. So growing up, I ain't have love. You feel me? That's why I'm so much on trying to be with you and having a seed with you."

I looked at him with teary eyes.

"But if you not ready, I ain't tripping," he stated.

I just looked at him in amazement. I had thought he was living the life. I guess even though he had been showered with material things, there was still an emptiness in his heart . . . and I was planning to fill that void.

I decided I was going to keep our baby.


The next day at school I replayed Zae's story to Kola.

"Word? I would have never guessed that about him. That's really fucked up," she said, shaking her head. "I guess he won you back with that one."

I laughed. My girl knew me oh too well. I gave her a sarcastic response, anyway. "No, we've just been working on us, if you must know." I looked up at the teacher and began listening to the lecture.

As usual, Zae picked me up from school, and he told me we had to make a run in the city. We drove down to

Junction Avenue and parked. He told me he was going to be right back, and he hopped out of the car. Usher's "Let it Burn" played on the radio, so I turned it up a notch.

It was taking Zae a little while to return, so I looked out the window. Through it, my eyes saw the unthinkable. There was my mom in a zebra-print catsuit and a twisted blond wig, her face full of messy makeup and scars. She looked like she was strung out on the worst drugs made by mankind.

My heart dropped. My mom had hit rock bottom. I knew things were bad for her and that she was turning tricks, but damn, I didn't think it would be like this. I didn't expect to see her in this condition.

Some man walked up behind her, yanked her, and pushed her into the car that was in the driveway. When the car rolled past, I saw a familiar face. It was the same pimp from two years ago, when I was in her apartment.

Tears surfaced; then they fell. I fixed my face before Zae returned. I had a lot on my mind now. The rest of our ride together was silent.


"So, you're fifteen weeks pregnant. Everything looks wonderful, and your baby is healthy. Continue taking your prenatal vitamins, and you'll be fine. See you in two weeks, Sommer and Markaylo," my blond-haired ob-gyn said before she stepped out.

"I hope it's a girl," Zae said, smiling.

"I want whatever my baby wants," I said while giggling and rubbing my tummy.

"You trying to go make love on that table?" He pointed to a table in the room.

"Zae, hell naw! Quit being so damn trifling and hand me my clothes," I said while extending my arm.

He hugged me and kissed me on my lips. I had to admit, Zae was beyond loving, and I loved it.

When we pulled up to my house, there was a red Hummer sitting in the driveway with a red bow on it.

"Is that mine!" I asked, sounding like a happy kid.

"Yeah, that's yours." He handed me the keys.

I got out of the car and ran to the driver's side of the Hummer. I rolled the window down. I couldn't wait to drive this baby.

"Come on. Let's test-drive it!" I said. Zae got in with me, and I pulled off. We drove it around for about ten minutes. I was in love with this Hummer already.

We pulled back up to the house, and to my surprise, Morgan was sitting on Zae's car. I looked at him in confusion. I was getting ready to say something and hop out of my brand-new gift, but he held my arms down.

"I got this, baby." He jumped out of the car and walked over to Morgan.

I sat there and listened. Morgan stood up to face him.

"You know I'm pregnant, right?" were the first words that flew out of her mouth.

I took a deep breath. I anticipated hearing his response.

"Man gone, Morgan. Why the hell you here? You gon' show up to my baby mama house, though? That's what you on?" he asked.

I decided that Zae didn't know how to handle this situation, so I jumped out of the car.

"Excuse me, Morgan, but if you have anything to tell him, please call first. You don't have any business showing up to my shit! That is so disrespectful." I was trying my hardest to be and sound nice. It never worked for me.

"Oh! No disrespect! But your man got me pregnant," she said. It was as if she was boasting about it—like a smack in the face.

"Hmm, well, that's nice . . . but like you said, *my man,* so me and *my man* are about to go in the house. And, like I said, either you call or you can bring your ass here again and leave with more than what you came with."

Somebody had to let the bitch know. I grabbed Zae's arm, and we proceeded to go into the house. He gave me the "I already know" look when we got in the house, 'cause he already knew there was no need to remind him. I went upstairs and hopped in the shower. I had school the next day, and I had plenty of homework to do.

As I sat in my room, finishing up my final project, I thought of Morgan. I couldn't stand the filthy bitch. Yeah, she was very pretty, but she was a ho. She was cool with Imani. They hung out here and there, but only when it came to boosting and boys. I was disgusted that he would even mess with her kind. She had more miles on her than Greyhound. I shook my head. Boys fucked anything walking, I thought.

Since my graduation was approaching fast, Imani, Kola, and I decided to go look for something to wear on the special day. I was four months pregnant, and you couldn't even tell. We were in New York Collection, chopping it up, when Brian and his boys walked in. I was watching, but not too hard. Brian and I had chilled together a few times in the past, but that had faded away. He was looking so good to me, and I wanted to relight those flames.

"Sup, Doll?" he said while licking his lips, like always. I loved it when he did that. I think he knew.

"Oh, nothing. You?" I asked, trying to keep it non-chalant.

"I'm straight. Take my number," he said while putting it in my phone. How he got my phone out of my hands, I didn't know.

"We lost touch," I responded, which was true, and I definitely missed the way we touched.

When Kola and I got in my Hummer, I just knew Kola's mouth would run nonstop.

"Bitch, now you know," she said, referring to me taking Brian's number when things were going good between me and Zae.

"Kola, shut it! I ain't trying to hear it." I had to shut her down before she started. Hey! You got to live only once, and that was what I intended to do. There were some things that I just couldn't resist.

Zae was at my house when I got there. When I walked in, he was sitting on the couch, watching ESPN. He was so glued to the TV that I doubted if he knew I had come in.

"Babe!" I called out.

"Yeah. Come here. I got to tell you something," he said, never taking his eyes off the TV.

"What's up?" I flopped down on the love seat.

"I got to go out of town tonight on a little business trip. Just for the weekend. I'll be back by Monday, though."

He still was staring at the TV. He didn't even look my way. Was he bluffing?

"Aww, man. Well, okay. I guess I'll have Kola and Imani stay here with me, then." I knew damn well what I really was going to do while he was away.

"Cool, 'cause I don't want you to be bored without me," he said, finally looking up at me.

"Yeah, I'll be fine. Go ahead and handle your business, baby," I said, assuring him.

"All right. Come give me some loving before I go."
He stood up, grabbed my arm, and walked me upstairs.

When we reached my room, I began taking off his
clothes, and he did the same to me. He lay down on
the bed, and I began to give him head. I didn't want to
do it, because I had alternative plans. I was sucking so
good that Zae was running for his dear life. While I was
giving him something he wouldn't forget, I caught myself thinking about Brian. Those thoughts were erased
quickly when Zae came in my mouth.

I hopped up and spit it out in the toilet. Zae wanted
to lie there and have pillow talk, so we did. He told me
how much he loved me and that we would get married
sooner than later. I couldn't wait, either. Zae was definitely a charmer and a sweetheart.

Zae and I kissed before he left and said our "I love
yous," and then his car disappeared down the street.

When he left, I was happy and sad at the same time.
Sad because it was Friday and Monday was so far away.
Then again, I was happy because that gave me and
Brian more playtime.

I went to brush my teeth and called Brian.

"Shit, you want me to come through?" he asked me,
as if he didn't know the answer.

"Yeah, you can." I felt a little uncomfortable answering a question he knew the answer to.

"Give me an hour," he said. Then we hung up.

I was wet just thinking about Brian. Word around
the way was that Brian had a great pipe game, and I
was trying to test the waters, pregnant and all.

In a little over an hour, Brian was at my door, all
smiles, like he always was, licking his lips. I led him
into the house.

"Man, I missed you, girl," he said while holding me
from behind.

"Missed you too. You disappeared on me." I turned around to face him.

"Hell no. I knew you had a lot going on and you had to distance yourself, so I respected it. You know I wouldn't leave you hanging like that."

He started licking his lips again, just how I liked it. We sat down and cuddled up, watching *Friday After Next*. We shared plenty of laughs, but after the movie went off, we sat there in silence. One thing was on my mind.

"Shit, we supposed to go to sleep or something?" he asked.

I laughed. "No, silly."

"Oh! You must want to do something nasty," he said as he leaned in and began kissing me on my neck.

I never said yes, but I never said no, either.

He began undressing me. Hell, I helped him. First, he played with me, placing two fingers in, and then he started licking me down there too. I definitely didn't want him to stop by this point. I pulled his head up.

"Let's try something new," I suggested.

He whipped out his dick with those horny sex eyes. It was a facial expression that said he was getting ready to tear me up.

"Like what?"

Those rumors couldn't have been any less true, because he was definitely blessed. He put a condom on and flipped my little ass over. I moaned.

First, the strokes were slow, and then he sped it up. He grabbed a handful of my hair and started smacking my ass. I was loving it.

He lay down, and I hurried up and climbed on top of his thick muscle. I started riding him backward. He was tossing me in the air, or at least that was what it felt like. We tried so many different positions, and I fell in love with Brian's sex. I gave it two thumbs-ups.

He asked if he could stay the night with me, and there was no way in hell I was saying no. We lay in my bed, naked, and talked each other to sleep.

That weekend Brian basically lived with me, and we had sex at all hours every day. When Sunday came, I was sad our love nest was getting ready to go out of business. Zae would be coming home, and it was almost time for Brian to go.

It was Sunday night, and we had just got done going at it like rabbits. We were lying on the couch, watching ESPN. The Lakers were whupping ass. Brian loved them. We made a bet that whoever's team lost had to give the other head. That was fine with me. After my team lost, I proceeded to give Brian some head that I knew his main bitch couldn't top. He was moaning, and it made me wet. I slipped my panties off and climbed on top of him. I knew his dick too well by now.

Brian decided to do the work, because he placed himself on top instead. He was going nice and slow, putting his dick all the way inside me. I pulled his body closer to mine. The way we got it on, no porno could top us.

After our session, Brian told me he had to go. After all, we had school in the morning. We kissed, and he jumped in his old-school and drove off. I kind of felt disgusted with myself that I had had sex with him while I was pregnant with Zae's baby. I just felt like I had to get Zae back for fucking Morgan. I didn't know why; it just felt like it was something I had to do. After I shut the door, my cell phone began to ring. I went to retrieve it.

Aunt Sasha had called to check up on me. She told me she missed me and hadn't talked to me in a while. She asked about Auny. She thought that Auny was here taking care of me. I allowed her to believe that as we continued our conversation.

"Um . . . she's fine. She's not here right now," I said, just in case she asked to speak to her.

"I really think you need to come down here with us. I don't too much care for Leslie, and I don't want you to be a burden on her," she explained.

"Why don't you like Auny?" I asked.

"She just isn't for Jim. She's an opportunist," Aunt Sasha began. "I just don't think she has his best interests in mind. Well, that's how I read her."

She definitely had hit it on the nose, because Auny was MIA. We ended our call with me telling her I would consider moving in with her. Something kept telling me Auny had something to do with Unc's arrest. No matter how I tried to sugarcoat the situation, I couldn't fight this gut feeling.

# Chapter 7

"Graduation rehearsal was stressful," I complained.

Almost the entire class of 2007 was sitting in T.G.I. Friday's. Brian was buying my food for me, so you already knew I was ordering up some shit. We kept a low profile, though. We didn't want everybody knowing we were messing around.

Zae surprised me and showed up at Friday's with Malcolm.

"Hey, baby," I said, irritated that he was there. I knew that Brian and I wouldn't be able to flirt.

"What's up, y'all?" Zae said as he sat down in the booth with us.

I could tell that Malcolm and Kola were feeling each other, because they kept staring at one another. I was hoping like hell they didn't, because that was Imani's "old thing." I didn't want any part in them hooking up, even though something kept telling me that I was going to play a major role in it.

When the waitress came over to take our order, I stole a look at Brian. He rolled his eyes. I couldn't understand why he was angry when he already knew that I had a man. I turned away. If he was mad, then so be it. Sommer was going to enjoy her day regardless.

"So, Kola, where's your man at?" Malcolm asked. I knew it was coming sooner or later.

"Well, I don't have one. I'm reserving myself," she proclaimed.

"For who?" He just had to know.

Brian's attitude was still on my mind, but I listened to Malcolm and Kola's conversation.

"Someone who's worth giving myself to. I'm tired of all these lames and liars," she replied.

I knew my girl had experienced some serious heartbreaks in her lifetime and she was just tired of it. I had to admit, I was tired of seeing her cry. I also knew that Malcolm wouldn't be any different. Besides that, he had messed with Imani. He didn't need any more of my friends.

Once the waitress brought us our food, it got quiet in our booth. We ate good, we laughed hard, and then it was time to leave. Almost every female had a hair appointment the next morning, so it was definitely time to go home. I needed to get myself together for graduation.

Zae and I decided to go to his house, and Kola and Malcolm decided to join us. I so didn't want them to hook up . . . like, not at all. I didn't want Imani to find out about them two, either. I knew she would assume that I had hooked them up, and it was true that I hadn't tried hard enough to stop them. Although Kola was my current BFF, Imani was still my ace, no matter what.

The guys went down into the basement to play on the PlayStation 3, while Kola and I sat on the living room couch. I immediately brought up Malcolm's name.

"So you and Malcolm are really about to talk?" I was secretly praying that she would say no.

"I don't know, girl . . . but he *is* sexy."

"Ugh! Now, you know that was Mani's man first," I hurried to say.

"Yeah, but that's your friend. Not mines," she reminded me.

I gasped and got up. I went upstairs, because she obviously didn't understand. I had done my part in letting her know the deal.

"Do you hear that?" Zae asked while we lay in bed.

I lifted my head up. "Hear what?" I asked.

We got completely quiet to listen, and that was when I heard Kola moaning.

"I know she ain't fucking him!" I got irritated and sat up in the bed.

"Why are you tripping?" Zae questioned.

I rolled my eyes and went back to sleep. I had a hair appointment to get to in the morning, and if Kola wanted to fuck Malcolm, so be it.

The next morning Kola and I headed to Master's Touch to get done up by the lovely Sherrie, my beautician.

Now, Sherrie was gifted when it came to doing some hair, and she put God first, so you already knew her shit was on point. She had me under the dryer, and Kola was in the chair, getting color, when a disturbing text came through my phone.

Oh, so, bitch, you hooking people up with Malcolm? It was from Imani.

How did this bitch know already?

I tried to explain to her that they had hooked up on their own terms, but homegirl wasn't trying to hear that. I'm not the type to try to convince anyone, so I left it where it was. I knew I had lost a good friend due to Kola's carelessness, but life went on.

When we left the shop, we were the baddest thangs walking up out of there. We were definitely going to turn heads later that night at Club Shadow.

"I can't wait till we step off in that club, Doll!" Kola was excited.

"I can't, either! Hoes better put they man up." We laughed and got in my Hummer.

Graduation was both long and touching. The speeches were taking forever, and I was so ready for my row to get up and walk across the stage. This moment was classic. After all I had been through, here I was at the Stranahan Theater, getting ready to take the same steps as everyone who had graduated from high school before me. I was graduating early *and* with honors. I couldn't have painted a better picture.

Finally, it was my row's turn to get up and shake the administrators' hands and walk across the stage. I became nervous as hell.

"We got this," Mari whispered in my ear while we waited for our turn to go across.

I handed Mrs. Neely my paper and began to strut my stuff.

"Graduating with a four-point-oh, Miss Sommer Jones."

I couldn't have said it any better.

My feet were killing me, but the pain was well worth it. Everyone in the Stranahan was very loud and proud. I couldn't stop smiling. I finally did it. Mother on drugs, Unc in jail, Auny missing, and I was pregnant. Yeah, you couldn't tell me a thing.

After the graduation ceremony, Zae and I took numerous pictures outside with everyone else and their families. We had all decided to have our graduation dinner at Mancy's, one of the most expensive restaurants in Toledo. We smashed, and then my posse and I went straight to Club Shadow. We couldn't wait to kick it.

The line of people at the club wrapped around the building, and we were going to stand there to get in that club. All the niggas were trying to holler at us, but we didn't really pay them any mind.

Brian and his crew got in line behind us. He licked the back of my ear.

"Ugh, nasty," I said, turning around to face him.

"You going to save a dance for me, right?" he asked.

I whispered in his ear, "You can get more than a dance if you act right."

"Promise I will," he said while kissing on my neck.

The club was jam-packed when we finally got in there. We were at the picture booth, sweating bricks.

"I think we need to bounce," Mari said while wiping the sweat off of her forehead.

"I agree," Kola said and nodded.

We took our picture and left. I instantly called Brian's phone.

"What's up, baby?"

"I just left the club . . . so you should too," I informed him.

"I'm going to call you in a sec."

I already knew he was going to leave the club, because we had that type of understanding with one another.

He called me ten minutes after we hung up, and I met him at his hotel room. All his boys were in the club, and all my girls had gone to IHOP.

I had him alone.

He played Usher's "Love in This Club, Part II" on the CD player. That was definitely my song, so I was certain that we were about to make love in this room.

He slid my Baby Phat dress up and slid his tongue in my treasures. I lay down so that he could get a better view and angle. We sixty-nined, and then I made sure to ride him. As usual, we were having the time of our lives.

If I ever decided to leave Zae for anyone, it would definitely be for Brian. We had never been in a relationship, yet it felt like we were together.

"You know I love you, right?" he said while he was hitting it from the back.

"Love you too," I moaned, gripping the sheets.

I came first, and he came shortly after. We lay in the bed and did a little bit of talking and a whole lot of kissing.

I jumped in the shower and threw my dress back on without my panties. When I stepped out of the bathroom, there stood Brian.

"Where you going?" he asked.

"Home." As if he didn't already know.

"Well, I want to see you tomorrow. Let's go by the water," he said while getting in the shower.

"All right. We can do that," I agreed as I shut the door.

When I got in the car, all my girls had something to say.

"Now, how in the hell are you about to pull this one off? You look like you been fucking." My friend Mari laughed.

"Man, what? Girl, Zae's going to kill your ass!" Ashley was laughing her ass off.

"Whatever. Just drop me off at home please," I said, staring out the window.

They pulled up to my house, and no one was there. That was a good thing. I got out of the car.

"Bye, y'all!" I said as I closed the car door behind me.

"I want all the juicy details!" Kola laughed. Then they pulled off.

When I got in the house, my phone started to ring and it was Zae.

"How was the club?" he wanted to know.

"It was cool. Where are you?" I questioned.

"I'm at home. I got to get up early. I just called to check up on you and make sure you made it home safe. I love you, baby," he said, making it short and sweet.

"I love you too."
We hung up, and I fell asleep.


I decided to go and show Granny Franny my diploma. I was proud of myself, and I knew she would be so proud of me too. I pulled into her driveway in Unc's Benz. As always, Granny Franny's door was open, an invitation to visit, and I walked right on in.

"Hey, Granny!" I embraced her, and she wrapped her arms around me.

"Hey, honey!" She kissed me on the forehead.

I showed her my diploma, and then we chatted for a little while before I left. On my way out, I spotted Imani and a few nobodies sitting on Unc's Benz.

"Excuse all of you bitches," I said with much attitude. I was steaming with heat.

"What's up, Doll?" Imani asked. It sounded like she was ready to fight me at any moment. I knew exactly what it was. I put my diploma down and squared up with her. I already knew I was going to get jumped by her and her group of nobodies, but I was sure I was gon' whup Imani's shit if I couldn't tag anyone else there.

By this time, there was a crowd of people surrounding us, goading us to fight and throw the first punch.

Imani and I began going at it, and as I had expected, I was beating the living daylights out of her. Her girls jumped in and wore my little ass out. They were stomping the hell out of my stomach. All I could think about was my poor little baby. Malcolm and his friends got them hoes up off of me. I knew Imani had started a war.

They rushed me to the hospital, and I already knew that the news would be bad. The doctor came in and told me my little one was gone. They gave me some-

thing like an abortion. Zae came in after the procedure.
He looked angry.

"I'm sorry, Zae. I really am," I pleaded.

He just looked at me with disgust.

"How long you been fucking him, Sommer? Huh?"
he asked.

"Fucking who, Zae? What are you talking about?" I
tried to lie and play dumb.

"Tell me that bitch lying!" he screamed.

*Okay.*

"She's lying!" I cried.

I could tell his heart was broken. I could see the look
in his eyes.

No, this bitch didn't try to take the white picket fence
from around our happy home. Oh, yeah! Imani was
as good as dead. First, she jumped me—and killed my
baby with no remorse—and then she went and told my
man I was cheating on him.

He sat down in the blue chair that was at the foot of
my bed. I sat up, watching him cry with his face in his
hands.

"Zae, I know you don't believe her, do you?" I hoped
like hell he didn't.

He looked up at me with an evil look in his eyes.

The look told me he did. My heart sank, and I could
feel it in my toes. I wondered if he was going to leave
me. I lay back down, praying that he didn't leave my
side. What was I supposed to do? I had no one but him.

"Doll, if you fucked him . . ." He took a deep breath
and shook his head. "If you fucked him, just know that
we're done. While you pregnant with my seed, you gon'
fuck another nigga, you nasty bitch!" he yelled.

The words cut like a knife. I knew he was hurt, because I was too.

He stood up and walked to the door. "And you ain't
got shit to say." He walked up to me.

Tears started forming in my eyes. I knew that I had fucked up and that everything we had built was destroyed.

He stood on the side of my bed, looking at me with hate in his eyes. "Trifling bitch," he said as he mugged me. He turned toward the door, walked out, and slammed the door behind him.

I cried even harder. I had to charge it to the game, because it was obvious I had lost. I was hurt. I couldn't imagine my life without him, but I knew I would have to learn to live without him, because he was gone.


When I was released from the hospital two days later, I had no one there waiting for me and no one to drive me home. I could have called Kola or Mari, but I didn't feel like hearing all the questions about why Zae wasn't picking me up instead. I was lonely. I got my discharge papers, put on the outfit I got jumped in, and bolted out of the hospital in tears. I hopped in Unc's Benz , started the ignition, and drove off.

I decided to drive past Zae's house. Although it was out of my way, I still felt as though I needed to. When I finally reached his street, I grew nervous. I wondered if I should go to the door or just ride past. His Range was in the driveway, so I assumed he was there.

I parked the Benz and left it running. I opened my car door, wished myself luck, and began walking to his door. When I reached the door, I got butterflies. I prayed he didn't curse me out or a bitch didn't answer the door.

I knocked.

Then I waited.

He opened the door with no shirt on, looking sexy. He stared me in the eyes. His eyes told me the sight of me hurt him.

"What's up, Doll?" he asked in a calm voice.

"Zae, I . . . I . . . I'm sorry," was all I could think to say.

"I know you are."

"So you don't hate me?"

"Naw, but I gotta go, baby."

Then I heard a female's voice. "Zae, baby."

"Who is that?" I questioned.

"Doll, I'll call you," he said as he moved out of the doorway and shut the door.

I stood there looking dumbfounded, but I couldn't get my feet to move. After about twenty minutes, I decided to go back to my running car. I got in and put my face in my hands and cried. *Why don't he love me anymore?* I thought. I also wondered who the bitch in the house was, the one he had dissed me for.

I wanted to hide under a rock and die. Now I saw that Brian wasn't worth losing Zae for. I could blame only myself for losing Zae, but this was too much for my heart to take. I went home and climbed in my bed. I needed to take a shower, but I didn't feel like moving. I cried myself to sleep, a sleep I never wanted to wake up from.

My heart was in so many pieces, and I had no one to help me put it back together. I guess I had finally met karma up close and personal. She was definitely kicking my ass. I was left to face the world alone.

# Chapter 8

After listening to the two voice-mail messages that Kola had left me, asking about what had happened and telling me how worried she was about me, I decided to call her up and tell her all that had happened. Inside, I believed this was all her fault. She was the reason for Imani hating my guts. If only she hadn't slept with Malcolm, all this shit could have been avoided. Now I was sitting up with bruises all over my gorgeous face, and I'd lost my unborn child, over some bullshit that I had tried my hardest to prevent from happening. Maybe I didn't really need a baby at such a young age, but the fact that I had carried it that long and had lost it to someone else's carelessness hurt my soul.

"Man, that's fucked up. Why she hating on you that hard?" Kola asked me.

"Because you're fucking her man and she thinks that I hooked y'all up!" Kola was beginning to irritate my nerves at this point. "I'm gon' call you back." I hung up on her.

I lay in my bed, recapping all my life events. Whew! This had really been a trip. Zae hadn't talked to me since the hospital deal, which was over two weeks. I hadn't called him or anything. No need to push when all he was going to do was run. Brian and I had exchanged a few phone calls, but no visits.

I had my back against the wall once again. I lay there wondering if I should retaliate or let things go. God knew I didn't want to beef with Imani. She was still like a sister to me, and that made my love for her stronger than ever. I was lost in my thoughts until the doorbell started to ring.

I looked through the peephole, and there stood Justine, the hood rat from the Brands. We weren't very tight—we hung out only because of Imani—so I really questioned why she was standing at my door. I barely opened the door. I didn't want her ass looking all up in my place.

"What's up?" I asked. I eyed her up and down.

"Girl, I'm so sorry for what happened to you with Imani and all them other bitches. That was fucked up, and them bitches knew that," she admitted.

I could see from the look on her face that the lumps and bumps on my face were awful.

"Yeah, that was, and they knew I was pregnant, but it's cool. I ain't tripping." I didn't want her to see me sweat at all. I wanted her and everyone else to know that I bounced back easily.

"I know it ain't my place to be telling you this, but Imani's been fucking Zae. She's been pregnant by him at least twice. I know you're wondering why I'm telling you this. . . .Well, I think you're cool peoples and you deserve to know."

Honestly, that hit like a brick. I couldn't swallow any of what she had just told me. It was too much all at once. I finally invited her in, and we chopped it up for a few hours.

She told me that they had been messing around for at least a year. She also told me that they were seen together the night of graduation. That explained the nice and sweet phone conversation he had with me that night—and his rushing me off the phone and shit. I also wondered if Imani was the one at his house when

I stopped by. Damn! They had slid that one right past me.

After she left, I cried enough tears to fill up the entire Gulf of Mexico. Love was definitely a kind of pain, and I felt every bit of it.

I turned my phone off and didn't eat for days. I just couldn't. Everyone called: Zae, Kola, Mari, Brian, and Justine. I couldn't talk to them. My heart was too weak. I couldn't win for losing, and this was a real loss. All I could think was, *Why me?* I wanted to fall asleep and never wake up. I had lost everybody I loved, and now I was losing my heart and my mind.

I remained cooped up in my house for almost two weeks. When Brian stopped by to check on me, I didn't want to answer the door . . . but I did. I knew I was looking threw and tired. My head was wrapped in a scarf, and I had on pajamas, with no makeup. I just wasn't my normal fly self. I opened the door to see Brian standing there with roses.

"How sweet," I said while grabbing them.

"Damn, what's going on with you? You look dead, baby," he said, chuckling.

"Hush, and come in or stay out," I said, rushing him.

He came in. I explained to him all that I'd been through. He had never known what was going on in my life, and I thought that this was the perfect time to let him know. He listened, never interrupting me or judging me. I needed to let all that out. It had built up in me for too long.

By the time I finished telling him my story, I was in tears. I figured he would no longer want to be bothered with me, being that I had been pregnant and fucking him. He probably thought I was a ho now. I mean, I would think that.

"Naw, it's nothing like that. I care about you. I told you that, and yeah, that was fucked up . . . but shit happens."

I was so happy to find that he was calm. Brian and I had built a strong connection, which I appreciated. He gave me the company I needed. Kola didn't even bother to come and visit me, but I heard from Justine that she was wrapped up with Malcolm and that Zae was wrapped up with Imani. Brian told me not to worry and not to let those things bother me. I was beautiful and could get any man that I wanted if I liked, but I didn't feel that way.

"So where is Janeen at?" I asked. I wondered if he and his ex were still in touch, since my relationship with my Zae was completely ruined.

"She's at work," he said, looking at his watch. "I got to go and pick her up pretty soon."

I didn't want him to leave, but I knew he had to go. I walked him to the door.

"I'll try to come back by," he said sincerely.

I just nodded my head and shut the door behind him. I was lonely.


It had been a whole month since Zae and I had spoken or had seen each other. I decided to cope with what I was going through, and I couldn't let it stress me out too much longer. I didn't want to go crazy. I called up my girls Justine and Mari. We all decided to go to Famous Dave's together for some rib tips. We needed to catch up with one another, anyway. This would also be my first time leaving the house. I had been off the scene for too long.

"My eighteenth birthday is coming up," I said excitedly after we sat down at a table.

"Girl, I know. What the hell are you going to do?" Justine asked me.

I'd been wondering the same thing. That was why I brought it to their attention. We put our heads together but couldn't come up with anything.

"Have you talked to Kola?" Mari asked. It was like she was on the edge of her seat and couldn't wait to ask me.

"Um, no. She's probably booed up with Malcolm. I can respect it." From the tone of my voice, you could tell that I didn't want to talk about her. We all sat and enjoyed a few laughs, until the crew themselves rolled in.

Zae, Malcolm, Kola, and Imani sat at a booth together. They walked in like they had been walking in restaurants together like that for years. They couldn't see us at our table, but we definitely saw them.

"What the fuck?" Justine spat out.

"Now, that's foul as hell! I'll help you beat them bitches' ass!" Mari was ready for whatever, but I just couldn't move. As hard as I had tried to get over the whole ordeal, hiding myself for a month, I learned that one month of staying away didn't help at all. My heart was still weak.

"Get up, bitch!" Mari grabbed my arm. She was ready for war.

I took a deep breath and got up. The three of us marched over to them. I must admit, I was nervous. Just the thought of having to whup both of my best friends' ass was a bit too much for me.

When we got close to them, Imani spotted us. She tapped Kola.

"Oh, bitch, don't ring the alarm now!" Mari was really hot and bothered.

Before I could say anything, my arms had already be-
gun to swing. I know for a fact I had Imani by the hair
and I was uppercutting the shit out of that fake bitch. I
didn't stop until I saw blood, and after I saw it, I let her
drop. My next victim was Kola. Mari was stomping on
her, and I pushed her. I stood Kola up and proceeded
to beat that bitch down. I gave her that "every bitch I
ever wanted to fight" type of ass whupping. After that
bitch was lifeless, I spit in Zae's face. I'll never forget
the dumb look on his and Malcolm's face. Before he
could react, the security got a hold of me, Justine, and
Mari and carried us up out of the restaurant. Hell, I
should have kicked him in the nuts.

"Y'all crazy!" Justine yelled, laughing, once we got
inside of Mari's Mustang and sped off.

"I can't believe that bitch." Mari was highly upset. I
think she was madder than the rest of us.

I just sat in the backseat, looking out the window.
This was the last straw. I was ready to go to Atlanta and
join my sister and aunt. I had been thinking about it for
a while, and now was the perfect time to go.

We dropped Justine off in the Brands first. As she
was hopping out of the car, Mari looked back at me.
She had noticed I was quiet.

"What you back there thinking about?" Mari questioned. I got in the front seat and closed the door, and
we pulled off.

"I'm leaving, Mari. I'm going to Atlanta," I replied.

"Do what you got to do, Sommer. I already know
these last couple of years have been a lot, and I think
you need a break from here too. Just don't get down
there and never come back." She gave me a look that
said she wasn't playing.

I chuckled. "Never that. I just need a mini vacation
away. Besides, I haven't seen my younger sister in a
minute."

She dropped me off at home, and I landed on the couch. I woke up hours later, my body sticking to the leather. My bones were sore, and I could barely move. My phone was vibrating on the coffee table. Luckily, my arms were pretty long and I could reach it. It was a text message from Kola, trying to explain the situation, but the obvious doesn't need an explanation. I was completely done with her trifling ass. She was a snake, and I could no longer trust her.

Another text message came in, but this time it was from Brian. He said he was outside my house and told me to open the door. I had to use damn near every muscle in my body to get up and get the door.

When I opened it, there he was, smiling from ear to ear, as always. He was looking mighty sexy. I moved out of the way so that he could enter my house. He went straight to my kitchen.

"Excuse me, but who the hell told you to go in there?" I had a bit of an attitude.

"Chill, Ma. A nigga hungry," he said while grabbing the necessities to make a sandwich.

I just laughed, because this boy was too comfortable for me. I sat down at the kitchen table, gazing at him while he fixed up his turkey, ham, and cheese sandwich.

"Heard you got yo' ass whupped." He laughed.

"Boy, please! That's what you'll never hear about me," I said, smirking.

"I'm just playing, baby. I heard you was doing people in at Famous Dave's," he replied while throwing a Doritos in his mouth.

It never took Toledo a long time to circulate a story. We sat at the table for about an hour, and I told him I had plans to move to Atlanta.

"I think that's a good idea," he said. "There ain't nothing but drama here. Plus, you've been through so much shit here." I was glad he understood my situation, and I was happy that he was encouraging me to go.

"By the time you get back, I'll be ready to be with you on a serious level." He was throwing hints that he wanted to be with me. There was no man in this city worthy enough to make me want to stay.

"Yeah, I'll be ready too. I just need a break. You know, clear my head." I rubbed my sore knuckles.

After we got up from the table, Brian decided to give me a massage. God knows I needed it. He oiled me up and rubbed my body down, from my head to my toes. It was so soothing. While lying there, I replayed a lot of important events that had taken place in my life. Toledo definitely would be the death of me if I stayed here.

The next morning I called my aunt Sasha.

"Fall speaking!" my sister said, sounding like a receptionist or something.

"Fall, this is Doll. Is Aunt Sasha around?" I asked.

"Girl, no. She's at her office. Do you know the number?"

"Yeah, I got it."

"I heard you was coming down here. I got so many people I want you to meet," she said excitedly.

"No ugly people. I have standards," I told her.

We conversed a little while longer, and then I called my aunt Sasha's office number. She told me my flight would be leaving in two days. I was so ready to go.

Brian came back to visit me. I didn't mind, because I enjoyed his company. We sat and talked all night. He told me that he might have gotten his ex-girlfriend pregnant and that she claimed the baby was his, but he didn't believe it was.

"And why not?" I questioned.

"Because I don't understand how she just ended up pregnant after I dumped her. That girl trying to trap a nigga, and I'm not on that." He was serious.

He was lying down on the couch, and I was sitting on his legs. I began to play with him. I mean, my days in Toledo were numbered. Why not enjoy them?

I pulled his penis out and began jacking him off. He was moaning and grabbing my thighs. I was getting turned on just by seeing how excited he was. I put his dick in my mouth and began giving him head . . . slowly. He started going crazy. He couldn't handle it.

"Yeah, Doll . . . right there," he moaned.

Using the technique that Zae had taught me, I started playing with his balls while speeding up my pace.

"Baby, I swear you the best," he said while gripping my hair. When he let go, I climbed on top and began riding him. I wasn't done with him just yet.

I rode him pretty slowly at first; then I got in the motion and sped up the ride. We started kissing, and then I began sucking on his neck while he fondled my breasts. He moved me under him, and then he started sucking all over while fingering me at the same time. I'm not a big fan of the finger, but I wasn't going to stop what we had started. He put his head down there, and I melted.

Brian was definitely a professional when it came to giving head. He was sucking the life out of me, or at least that was what it felt like. He had given me a natural high. . . . He had taken me to ecstasy, and I was totally ready for the ultimate prize.

He looked up at me. His face was covered with my juices. "Baby, I ain't got no condoms," he said with disappointment. I wanted him in me so badly. Did I let him go bareback, or should I be a lady and just keep doing foreplay? I didn't know. I mean, I had ridden him without a condom already.

"I'll pull out . . . but it's up to you," he said.

I guess he was thinking the same thing I was. Sounded like a good idea to me.

He put it in, and it was the perfect fit. I loved the way he sexed me. He was in my ear, telling me how he loved me and how when I got back from Atlanta we were going to be together. It all sounded good, but what didn't sound good when you were in the middle of fucking?

We came together, and then we fell asleep.


I had one more day until I would depart from this cold city, so Mari and I decided to go get dolled up. We started by getting our fingernails and toenails done. We were getting a pedicure when Kola walked in.

"I should hop up and slap that fake bitch." Mari really disliked her.

"No, just be cool. Let's get pretty and let that bitch slide. I'm not trying to go to Atlanta all sore." I was serious.

"You're right." She sat back in her seat.

Kola came to the back, where we were seated, and sat two seats away from me. This bitch was doing this on purpose, but I didn't even look her way.

"So y'all really don't like me anymore, huh?" she asked both of us.

"That had to be a rhetorical question, 'cause you already know we ain't fans of your fake ass," I said. Now she had given me a reason to want to slap her.

"But why not? What did I do?" she asked.

"Now, you know we don't do that fake shit, Kola! Yo' dumb ass knew the whole time that Imani was fucking Doll's man, and you never said shit!" Mari explained to her.

Kola sat there in silence.

"All up in Famous Dave's, eating with that bitch and everything. You know you foul, Kola!" Mari was not playing. She was ready to break her new nails on Kola's face, and Kola already knew not to get too fly with Mari, because everybody knew Mari was a force to be reckoned with.

"I swear I didn't know that they was creeping. Malcolm picked me up, and when we got there, they were already in the parking lot, waiting for us." She was trying hard to convince us.

"Okay, and that's when you were supposed to call or text my phone. You did neither of the two. Therefore, to us you're fake, and we don't do fake bitches," I told her. I didn't care what anybody had to say. Kola was foul and could no longer be a friend of mine.

The remainder of the time we were there, she kept quiet. It was indeed her best bet. When we were done, we got up, and I laughed at that miserable bitch. I was so ready to leave this dead city.


The doorbell was ringing, so I rushed down the stairs with my iPod playing "Year of the Lover" by Lloyd. I opened the door without asking who it was, and to my surprise, it was Zae. I tried to hurry and shut the door, but he was stronger than me, so he made his way in. I was shaken.

"How rude, Sommer," he said, shaking his head while walking past me.

"What the hell do you want is the question," I said, as calm as could be. I didn't want him to sense any fear.

"So you leaving? You running away now?" he asked.

"Markaylo, I'm getting a fresh start, and there is absolutely nothing here that I care about," I said nonchalantly.

He stared me up and down.

"I don't think you should feel that way. I care about you, and I know you care for me."

Little did Zae know, I was so over him. It had been months since we had spent time together or done anything. Brian had replaced him. If he knew better, he would use Imani as my replacement, although that tack-headed ho could never fill my shoes.

"I came here to tell you something," he said while playing with his phone.

"Well, go tell the next bitch, because I don't care to hear anything you have to say!" I was fed up with the bullshit, and I wanted him to leave.

"So you tough now, Doll?" Zae asked.

"It's not about being tough. It's about y'all crossing me and me cutting y'all off. Zae, you already knew I was over here, going through it. I had just lost my baby, and you fucking Mani!" I just shook my head. He already knew he was foul.

I walked to the door and opened it, hoping he got the hint. He got up from the couch and proceeded to the door. He stopped in front of me.

"I know I've made many mistakes when it comes to us, but know that I love you, and no matter what, you have my heart. I wish you the best of luck, and I hope you find that man that makes you happy."

He kissed me on the forehead and walked out. Without any response, I shut the door behind him.

I didn't know what Zae thought. All the shit he had put me through, and then for him to think he could just pop up and things would be back to normal? He was a damn fool!

I decided to call Mari and tell her how he had popped up here, trying to apologize. "Doll, what the hell do you want?" she asked when she picked up.

"Don't ever answer yo' phone like that when I'm calling," I said.

We both laughed.

"Girl, guess who just popped up to my house?" I was hoping she would guess right.

"Zae?" She didn't sound so sure, even though she hit it dead on the nail.

"Yes."

"What did he want? Ugh! Why would he do that?" She was disgusted.

"Girl talking 'bout he had something to tell me. I let his ass know and showed him to the door." I was proud of myself.

"I know that's right. Fuck that nigga," she said, laughing.

Mari was my girl. She had my back to the fullest. If somebody made me mad or hurt me, she wouldn't like them. She was the definition of a true friend. I had thought that about Kola, but sad to say, I'd been so wrong. I didn't understand why our friendship had to be destroyed the way it was, but things always happened with little or no explanation. I prayed that Mari would be different from the two best friends I had had. Only time would tell.

Mari stood at five feet three, pretty short if you asked me. Her weave stayed fresh and her nails stayed done. She rocked only urban clothes. Baby Phat was her favorite. She had a caramel skin tone and pretty light brown eyes. Guys loved her, but she was the type of girl who didn't take bullshit from anybody. If a nigga acted up, he was sure to get the boot with no hesitation. Maybe even a sliced tire.

She lived in Outhill, where the grass was green. It was considered the middle class of Toledo. "Make money" was the motto out there. That was exactly what Mari was about. She helped to pay her bills by doing manicures and pedicures, and I must admit, she was the coldest when it came to designs.

After Kola started hanging with Malcolm much more than with me, Mari and I started to hang tougher. She was the only one who popped up and blew my phone up to make sure that I was okay. She wanted only the best for me, and to me that was what a real friend would do. She would catch a case and take a bullet for me. I would do the same for her. The word *friend* didn't do her justice. *Sister* was a better word to use for her.

"I hope you like it. You for damn sure wasting all my gas, going to this airport in Detroit." Mari chuckled.

Mari was taking me to my flight, and Ashley had decided to accompany her.

"I'm sure I will," I said while reading my book.

"What's not to like? That's where all the real ballers are at," Ashley said. She had just come back from a two-week vacation in Atlanta. I figured it had to be much better than Toledo. It was worth a try.

"You gon' get you a dread-wearing, chain-slanging, grill-gleaming, twenty-three-inch-riding thug, Doll?" Mari asked.

"Girl, ugh! No! Now, the grill and the rims, I can do. Dreads have never been my taste." I laughed. Mari had watched one too many music videos.

"Well, know that I'm coming to visit. My future husband may be there." Mari looked at me to make sure I had heard her. I just shook my head. She was definitely coming to visit.

"I wonder if my cousin Jasmine is in town. It's going to be boring if she's not," I said. I was beginning to have second thoughts.

"Ain't yo' sister there?" Ashley asked.

My sister was much younger than me, and I wasn't going to want to hang with her.

"Yeah, but she's fifteen. What the hell am I going to do with her? Jasmine's eighteen. That's more in my ballpark." I wanted to hit the scene and go to a few nightclubs. What scene was I gon' hit with a fifteen-year-old, besides some Boys and Girls Club?

"I'm sure your cousin is there. I mean, it's summer vacation. She's in college, right?" Mari was looking at me, waiting for an answer.

"Yeah," I said.

"Okay, so stop making excuses, doll face," Mari told me. "You just scared of this change, but I honestly believe it's going to be for the best. So go and enjoy yourself. What's the worst that can happen?"

"You got a point," I said. I was kind of scared, but I would never know until I tried.

My phone beeped, letting me know that I had received a text message. I looked down at my phone, which was sitting on my lap. It was Zae. He was telling me that even these thousands of miles couldn't keep us apart. Chills went down my spine. The text scared me.

We pulled up to the terminal at Detroit Metro Airport, and we all sighed.

"Well, here goes nothing," I said and opened my door. I got my luggage out of the trunk and gave them both a hug. "See you ladies," I said before entering the terminal.

"Sommer!" Mari yelled.

I turned around, thinking maybe I had forgot something.

"Knock 'em dead, bitch." She smiled. I smiled back.

You had to love Mari. She always made what was difficult easy. I checked in and waited patiently to board my flight.

# Chapter 9

When I stepped foot in Atlanta, I already knew I was going to take this city by storm. My aunt Sasha was waiting for me in the lobby at the airport. She looked nice in her Aeropostale sweat suit. I guess she was aiming for a young look, and it definitely was working for her. She had blond hair that was cut short.

"Hey, Aunt Sasha!"

She gave me a warm hug.

We walked out to her Benz truck and loaded my luggage and proceeded to Buckhead.

"So what made you want to come to Atlanta? I've been trying to get you here for years," she proclaimed as we drove.

"I just needed a break from home." I didn't want to go into why I felt that way, and I prayed she wouldn't ask.

"Well, congrats on graduating from high school. . . . Maybe you should look into some of the colleges down here. They're historically black, so you'll have a lot of our people there," she explained to me.

"What schools are here?" I really didn't have a clue.

"Well, there's Spelman. It's an all-girls school. Then we have Clark Atlanta and Georgia Tech. You could choose one of those too. There are a lot of schools that aren't in Georgia but are really close to the area. I'll have my assistant help you with that."

In Buckhead we pulled up to a house that was much bigger than Zae's family home. When I walked inside, I was in total awe. Her house was beautiful. It was something you would see on *MTV Cribs*. I knew Aunt Sasha had to be rolling in that dough just because she was a celebrity attorney, and we all knew that celebrities were where all the money was.

After I got a full tour of the downstairs, Aunt Sasha told me that Fall was upstairs and she would show me where my bedroom was. I ran upstairs like an excited kid in a candy store.

Fall's bedroom was the first room on the left, and when I entered, she was lying on her bed, talking on the phone.

"Fall," I sang.

She popped her head up and told whoever was on the phone that she would call them back.

I must admit, my younger sister, Fall, was very pretty. She favored me, but something about her was different. She had hazel eyes, hanging black hair with red streaks in it, and a light skin tone that was pretty. However, her shape didn't take after mine. She was quite skinny. She had that Southern accent, but it wasn't a very thick one. It was enough to let you know that she was definitely from the South. She wore plain black leggings with a black shirt that had EXPRESS written on it in silver letters. Her silver accessories complimented her shirt.

If she ever decided to live in Toledo, she was sure to have a lot of dudes flocking to her just as much as they flocked to me. She was just that damn pretty.

"Doll, it's about damn time you got here," she said while extending her arms to me. I gave her a hug.

It had been way too long since we had seen each other. We had spoken on the phone from time to time, but nothing compared to having your sister's company. We sat in her room and talked for hours. I told her most of the things that had happened . . . but not everything.

She told me what she had going on in her life. She had a boyfriend whom she'd been with for six months, but to her, it wasn't anything serious. She had two best friends who were like sisters to her. She had had sex once with a previous boyfriend, but he was a jerk, so she had dismissed him.

Aunt Sasha was planning a very big sweet sixteen birthday party for her at Justin's, which was P. Diddy's restaurant. Her birthday was the 16th of July, less than a month away.

"So what do you want to do for the Fourth of July?" she asked.

"Um, I don't know. What do y'all normally do?" I questioned. This was all new to me.

"Well, Jasmine and I normally go to Miami. They have a lot of events around that time, but if you want to do something else besides that, I'm sure Aunt Sasha won't mind," she assured me.

I was beginning to think that Aunt Sasha was running things sort of like Auny had, which was a good thing to me. I wasn't going to complain one bit.

I loved the Southern hospitality, and I hadn't even been there for a whole twenty-four hours yet. Fall showed me to my room, which I immediately fell in love with. It had a royalty look to it, and I felt like I was indeed a royal being in that house. I unpacked my things and then lay down on the plush bed and fell into a deep sleep. I slept for hours, but I was awakened by their maid, Rudy.

"I apologize for waking you up, dear, but Jeff, the chef, wants to know if you eat seafood or not. I believe shrimp, crab legs, lobster, and steak are on the menu this evening," she said properly.

"No, I don't have a problem with that. Thanks for asking."

I tried to resume my nap, but it was impossible for me to fall asleep again. I grabbed my cell phone and saw that I had five missed calls. One was from Brian, one was from Mari, and three were from Zae. I decided to call Mari first.

"So how is it?" she asked when she picked up the phone. She was more excited than me!

"I like it. Girl, my aunt is paid! They got a maid and a chef. Like, her house is huge! My sister is the prettiest thing walking, and everyone around here is extra nice."

"Have you seen your cousin you were telling me about?"

"Naw, I haven't seen Jasmine yet," I told her. "But I'm going to try to get into one of these colleges this fall." I went on and on, bragging my ass off, because I was so excited to be making a change. I just couldn't stop talking.

"Well, I can tell you really like it there. That's good, Doll." She chuckled.

"Maybe you can come and go to school here with me."

"Yeah, that'll be cool. I always wanted to go to Clark Atlanta. And maybe we can pledge a sorority or something!" She was growing just as excited as I was.

"Yeah, we could. Okay, I'm going to talk to my aunt some more about it, and then I'll keep you posted about everything," I said before we hung up.

My next call was to Brian. He had become more than a cuddy buddy. He had been upgraded to a lover and friend.

"What's up, Ma?" he answered.

"Nothing. Just woke up," I said through yawns.

"You sound like you're still sleepy. I was just calling to make sure you made it safely and to let you know that I was thinking about you," he said.

"Well, yeah, I landed safely, and I miss you already." Might as well run a little game.

"I miss you too, baby. I hope you don't try to stay there forever," he added.

"Well, you never know. My aunt is putting me through college down here, so it may not be forever, but it's going to be for a while." I knew I wasn't going to be able to see him much.

"You said a vacation. You ain't said nothing about college, Sommer." He sounded disappointed.

"I can always come visit you during breaks, or you could even come here with me," I assured him.

"We'll come up with something, 'cause a nigga ain't about to have his heart that many miles away. But I'll get up with you a little later. Love you, Doll." His voice still sounded sexy.

"I love you too." I hung up and decided Zae was not getting a call back from me.

There was absolutely no need for him in my life. He had hurt me too bad, and I was clear across the map. What was I going to do with that excess trash besides throw it away? I was moving on, and Atlanta was a new chapter in my life. I planned to make my stay here one I wouldn't regret and one that I would recall happily time and time again.

Then I kept replaying what had happened when he popped up at my house. Despite all the shit we had been through, I found myself missing him. I wanted him. It was crazy how the one that hurt you was the one you wanted to be under. I really wanted to call Zae, but my mind told me that I knew way better than that.

\*\*\*

When it was time for dinner, my aunt Sasha, Fall, and my cousin Jasmine sat at the table. Jasmine was Aunt Sasha's only child. She was spoiled, no question about it, but she wasn't all stuck up. She was humble. She was a year older than me. We were really close when they lived in Toledo, but after the whole custody thing that took place with me and my sister, they moved to Atlanta and we lost touch.

Jasmine was what you called a "white black girl." She was proper, and she dressed as if she were one of the white girls. She could fit right on in with them. Even though she had the swag of a white girl, she was still very hood when she needed to be. She was dark skinned and had shoulder-length black hair. She was pretty and always had a glow to her. I had plans to mend our long-lost friendship. How else was I going to meet people?

"Long time no see, Doll," Jasmine said and laughed.

"I know! It's been forever," I said, sitting in the seat across from her. Jeff, the chef, brought us our entrées, and we passed the dishes around until our plates were full. I thought we had all the money in Toledo, but we were broke compared to the way they were living.

Aunt Sasha's phone rang.

"Excuse me, ladies," she said while getting up from the table. She picked up the phone and was on it for a while. Then she told us she had to run up to her office. She rushed upstairs.

"So what's been up?" Jasmine asked me.

"Not much. Just sick of Toledo. I see y'all living lavished," I said while looking around.

"Can't complain," Jasmine declared.

After dinner Jasmine told me that she wanted me to join her at this party that was being thrown at a nearby club. I had never really gone out in Toledo, just because the clubs there didn't excite me much, but Atlanta seemed to have caught my attention.

We got up from the table and went to our rooms to get dressed for the night. I slipped on a little black Bebe dress with matching shoes, clutch, and accessories. I curled my hair, making spirals, and I was ready to go.

When I walked out of my room, Jasmine was coming down the hall in her Dolce & Gabbana tube-top dress. Her hair was in an updo. She was simple, but cute. We went outside and hopped in her hot pink Range Rover. They definitely had money, and I wasn't mad at them.

"We have to pick my girl Tionna up. She lives over in Decatur."

I didn't know what Decatur was, and I didn't really care. I was just happy I was going to be meeting this city my first day here.

By just riding through Decatur, I noticed it was totally different from Buckhead. I could tell that this was going to be one of those places where I would spend most of my free time.

When we pulled up to Tionna's place, she told us the door was unlocked and to just come inside. Her home was a little old-fashioned. . . . It was nice, though. Everything looked expensive.

We hurried up to her bedroom. There she was. Short and caramel complected and what most people would consider thick. Her hair hung a little past her shoulders, and she was rocking a red and gold Coogi dress. It was cute, I guess.

"Tionna, this is my cousin Doll. She's from Ohio. Doll, this is my girl Tionna," Jasmine said, introducing us.

"Hey, I know the niggas are going to love her here!" Tionna laughed.

I was thinking, *Duh. What nigga doesn't?*

On our way out the door, her brother pulled up in his 1977 Chevy. It was clean, and I was a sucker for old-schools.

"There goes Mally," Jasmine said.

Tionna looked over at me. "Girl, come on before he be all down Doll's throat," she said, hurrying us. They already knew I looked good and was sure to get attention.

While I was getting in the passenger side of the car, I made eye contact with him. Shit, I couldn't stop looking at him. Normally, I didn't pay too much attention to the light-skinned brothers, but he was definitely fine.

He nodded his head, as if to say, "What up?" He came over to the car as we were about to pull off.

"Hi," he and I said in unison.

"Where y'all headed to?" he asked. He never took his eyes off of me.

"The club. Damn! You're asking way too many questions." Tionna was obviously annoyed.

"I only asked one." He gave her the "Shut up" look, and then he turned his attention back to me. "So what's your name? You aren't from here, are you? I ain't ever seen you before."

Now he was asking too many questions.

"I'm Doll, and no, I'm not from here. I'm from Toledo," I replied.

He was pretty cute, but as he opened his mouth to speak, I noticed he had a chipped tooth. Eww. I loved all types of guys, but if your smile wasn't together, I just couldn't do it. Too bad for him. I was actually thinking about giving him a chance, but now I couldn't do it.

"He's so damn thirsty," Tionna complained in the backseat.

I thought to myself, *He's probably going to get dehydrated, because he's not going to drink a glass of me!*

We pulled off and made our way to Club 112. It was a twenty-one and up club. To us, it meant we wouldn't have to worry about any kids being there. Jasmine and Tionna must have been on the VIP list, because we didn't have to stand in any lines. We were able to walk right into the club.

There were ballers everywhere we turned. There were so many men grabbing at my arm, begging for my attention, as we walked over to the bar. I knew I was the baddest bitch in there.

"Doll, do you drink?" Tionna asked.

"No, not really," I replied. She looked back over to the Asian bartender.

"Let me get a Long Island Iced Tea and two Blue Muthafuckas on Gip's tab," Jasmine told the bartender.

*Who the hell is Gip?*

As we waited for our drinks, a gang of guys walked in. There was one who stood out from the others and instantly caught my attention. He had on a red Pelle outfit with red Mauri gators. An iced-out chain hung around his neck, and a blinging grill was in his mouth. He had waves that made me seasick. He was definitely a far cry from the dudes in Toledo.

"Who is that?" I asked Jasmine as I sipped on my Long Island Iced Tea. I almost fell out of my chair. For one, my drink was strong, and secondly, I was drooling over Mr. Pelle.

"Oh, girl, that's Money. His name speaks for itself," Jasmine said. She giggled.

Money and his crew made their way over to the bar, where we were, and started ordering up some drinks. Money was standing next to me, and he smelled just like Unforgivable by P. Diddy.

"You need another drink, shawty?" Money asked me, with a wad of money in his hand.

"I'm cool. I really don't drink," I replied while scooting my empty glass over to the side.

Yes, he was definitely looking mighty edible. He had
a nice clean cut. He was lined up perfectly. He was just
how I liked them, caramel. He was a little taller than
me, and he had a light accent. I was getting wet just by
being in his presence. I had to adjust myself in my seat.

I watched as different girls took turns approaching
him and his entourage. Money engaged in little conversation with the many females. Then they would go
over to one of his boys. He wasn't on any of these girls,
and that was what made me want him even more. He
turned back toward the bar.

"Hey, Ma," he yelled, trying to get the attention of
one of the bartenders.

The Asian bartender turned to him.

"I'm buying the bar! Announce that shit," he said
while taking out his bankrolls.

Shortly after, the DJ stopped the music and said, "I
just got word that it's drinks free all night. Shout-out to
Big Money for buying out the bar."

Money put his cup in the air, and then the music was
put back on.

Tionna tapped me and signaled me to join them on
the dance floor. As much as I wanted to stay where I
was so that I could continue to sniff Money's scent, being thirsty was against my life rules. With that in mind,
I went to show them what I was working with on the
dance floor, because dancing was definitely my thing.

"Love in This Club" was playing loudly, and it sounded as if Beyoncé was right there in the club with us. I
was rolling my hips and just rocking in my own little
world. When I turned around, I saw Money and two of
his boys watching me like hawks. That made me really
start doing my thing, and I could feel all types of eyes
on me.

After a few songs I was ready to sit down, so my girls and I decided to make our way over to the VIP section. There were glasses and two bottles of Cristal on our table, waiting for us.

"You ever had Cristal?" Jasmine asked me.

"No. I want to try it," I said anxiously. She immediately poured me a glass, and I watched it bubble.

A clean-cut dude with dreads came over to us and sat next to Jasmine. From their conversation, I could tell that was her man, Gip, the one she'd been talking about earlier. After a while, niggas kept stopping at our table to chop it up, asking who I was, and then moving on. When Keyshia Cole's "Let It Go" came on, I immediately hopped up.

"I'll be back. This my song!" I pulled my dress down, then headed to the dance floor, with Tionna following behind me.

When we got to the middle of the floor, we rocked it out. I was falling in love with Atlanta, until gunshots got to flying all over the damn place. We all dropped like roaches, scattering all over the place. *Atlanta ain't no damn better than Toledo,* I thought.

I lost Tionna, and someone grabbed me and rushed me to the exit with them. I went along with the flow because I felt safe with this mysterious guide. When I turned to see who it was, it was one of the dudes from Money's crew. He led me to an all-white Escalade, and without hesitation, I climbed in the backseat once he hurried to open the back door.

"I need to find my cousin!" I yelled, panicking.

"You cool?" he asked, making sure I didn't have a scratch on me.

"Yeah, I just really need to call my cousin Jasmine," I said as I fidgeted with my phone. I could barely dial the number.

When I finally got through to her, I calmed down. "Jasmine, where are y'all at?"

"We over at this McDonald's. It's down the street from the club. Can you meet us over here, or do you need me to come get you? Where are you?" she asked.

I moved my mouth away from the phone. "Can you take me to that McDonald's down the street?" I asked the guy from Money's crew.

"Yeah." He nodded.

I got back on the phone with Jasmine. "Give me a minute. I'm on the way," I told her before hanging up.

When we pulled up to McDonald's, a familiar face hopped in the backseat with me. To my surprise, it was Money.

"Man, them niggas wild," he said while shutting the door.

This man was the definition of *sexy,* and I definitely had to have him.

He looked over at me seconds later. "You cool, Ma?" He nudged me.

"Oh, yeah, I'm cool," I answered shyly, and then I looked out my window for my girls.

"You ain't from here, huh?" he asked.

"I'm from Toledo. It's a small city in Ohio," I answered, betting he had never heard of it.

"Oh, word? I got peoples that stay there. X-block," he said.

"Oh yeah? Yeah, that's the north side," I replied.

He nodded.

He was giving me this look that made me want to drop my panties at that very moment. Damn, he had some type of spell on me, because I wanted him badly.

"I'm glad you made it out safe," he said, shaking his head. He was breathing heavily.

"Yeah, me too. Y'all are crazy down here." I laughed.

"Not crazy, just gun happy. But besides that, I saw you watching a nigga in the club," he said, referring to himself. Somehow, he had switched the subject.

"No. Obviously, you were watching me."

He had me fucked up! He had been staring me down in the club.

"Naw. You had to be watching me to even know I was watching you." He smiled.

That grill was shining as if it had just gotten cleaned. We continued to make seductive eye contact with one another. It was too much for me to handle, so I kept looking away. I couldn't stare too long, or else I would have grabbed him up and tongued him down.

I noticed Jasmine's car. She and Tionna were standing in front of it.

"You should try to look people in the eye when you talk to them. It shows you have confidence. You too badd to be shy," he told me while staring me dead in the eyes. He had made a good point, but I couldn't help myself. I couldn't look at him too much longer, or I'd have a sex attack!

"My cousin is over there," I said and pointed. I wanted to get out of that discussion about my shyness.

"You got a number?" Money asked before I could get out of the car.

"Mmm-hmm," I responded with a sexy grin on my face.

He handed me his phone, and I typed in my ten digits. I said good-bye in the sexiest voice I could find, and then I opened the car door and stepped out. I walked over to Jasmine's Range like a model out of a magazine. In my mind, I knew Money was going to be mine in due time.

We all hopped in the Range, and both girls had smiles on their faces.

"What y'all smiling for?" I asked them as we all sat in the car.

"You know whose shit you just stepped out of?" Tionna turned to me, awaiting my answer.

Money had to be someone of importance, because everybody was treating him like he was a celebrity or something.

"That was Money, right?" I had to make sure, even though I knew.

"Yes, girl, and Money is that boy!" Jasmine laughed.

"Oh, well, he seems like a cool cat, so we'll see." I enjoyed keeping those two puzzled.

"Now, he don't be on bitches like that, and that's what make these hoes buck after him. Don't none of them understand why he don't be checking for them. He ain't got no kids or no bitch, and plus, he paid! Girl, don't mess that one up," Tionna said, schooling and warning me.

Then Jasmine added, "He hangs with Gip. The only person he's crazy about in this world is his little brother, Cash. If you fuck with him, then you done fucked up!"

I was in the backseat, soaking it all in. He sounded like a must-have, so I was going to do all the things that I had to in order to get him. In the midst of this, I was going to act like a lady as well.

We dropped Tionna off at her house first and then made our way back to Buckhead. When we got home, I went straight to my room. I peeled my dress off and got into bed in just my panties and bra.

I tried to force myself to fall asleep, but I couldn't stop thinking about Money. How he could please me, what it would be like if he was around, and how well he would treat his woman. I also wondered what his mom was like and if his brother was sexy like him.

All these thoughts soaked my panties. Damn! How could someone who I had just met, hardly, have so much control over my thoughts this soon? It didn't make sense, but Tionna's ass was right. He had the girls bucking over him, and I was a part of that bunch. Maybe it was the liquor talking. . . . I didn't know. My thoughts wore me out, and then I finally drifted off into a deep sleep.

# Chapter 10

"Doll, your car is here!" Fall yelled at the top of her lungs from the bottom of the steps. I had been in Atlanta for a week without a car, and I was so tired of it. I ran outside like it was the first time I had seen my Hummer. I climbed inside and rubbed the dashboard and popped in a Keyshia Cole album. It felt so good to have my baby back. Yes, this car had been missed. I started it up and moved it from in front of the house. I parked it in a nice spot and went back in the house. I found Fall in the entertainment room watching BET.

"So what you and Jas doing for the holiday?" she asked me, referring to the Fourth of July.

"I don't know. We haven't discussed anything yet. Why? What you doing?"

"Aunt Sasha and me and my friends are planning a trip to Miami. It's always a whole lot of fun," she said with joy. It sounded like fun, but I was not interested at all.

The doorbell rang.

"Can you get that, Sommer?" she asked. "They're my friends."

I dragged myself to the door. When I opened it, there stood two little well-kept-looking girls.

"Hey!" they both said. "Fall's expecting us."

I smiled at them and said hello to them too. "She's in the entertainment room," I told them, directing them to her, and then I headed upstairs. When I reached my room, a call came in from Money. Now, this was the first time he had called since he had gotten my number. I had damn near forgotten about him.

"Hello." I tried not to sound too excited. I lay down on my bed and stared at the ceiling.

"What's up?"

"Nothing. I almost forgot about your existence," I said sarcastically.

He laughed. "I've just been real busy. So what you doing for the holiday?"

"Everyone keeps asking me, but I don't know. I guess I'm going to do whatever my cousin is doing. What about you?" Little did he know, I was trying to do whatever he was doing.

"I don't know. I'm trying to stay away from the club scene, especially after that little shoot-out. I might just sit at home. . . ." Then he added, "Can I take you out to eat later?"

"Um . . . sure," I replied. "We could meet up somewhere. I push my own whip," I told him.

"Oh, is that right, shawty?" He laughed.

After all, I did like him, but I didn't know him that well.

We decided to meet up at McCormick & Schmick's Seafood & Steaks. I wore brown leggings and a gold and white shirt with some gold and white Coach shoes and a matching Coach purse. Fly ole me.

When I walked in, he was already seated, awaiting my company. He was wearing a Polo shirt with matching shorts and shoes. I was loving this conservative look he had going on. I sat down and crossed my legs.

"You look nice," I admitted, barely looking at him. Deep down, I was admiring how he had transformed himself from the thug I had seen at the club.

"Thanks, shawty. You looking nice too," he said, returning the compliment.

I smiled while looking over the menu. I had never been to McCormick & Schmick's Seafood & Steaks, so I just let him order for me. After the waitress took our orders, we sat there in silence.

"So what's your name?" he asked to break the silence, chuckling. It was a trip that we hadn't even discussed those things, yet we were on a date.

"Well, my government name is Sommer, but everyone calls me Doll. You?" I said, as if I ain't already know his name.

"Deneiro, but people call me Money," he responded.

Then I told him I was seventeen and that I would soon be eighteen. He told me he was twenty-two and he didn't really do underage girls. He told me he had no girl or kids, but he wanted some soon. He liked the fact that I was about to start college. I mean, what guy didn't like a smart girl? It seemed like we had known each other our entire lives, the way the chemistry sparked. We were really having a good time, even though I was still feeling a little nervous.

"Loosen up," he told me. He could read me well.

"What do you mean?" I already knew he was referring to my shyness.

"You acting like . . . uptight. You know, being all scary and shit." He grabbed my hand. I was hoping like hell my hand wasn't wet from sweating so damn much that evening. He was making me hot.

"I can't help it," I said while looking down.

"Come here." He wanted me to sit next to him. I slid my curvy body from where I was sitting. Shit, I was even scared to do that. I got up and sat on his side of the booth with him.

"How you going to be my ole lady if you scared of me?" he asked.

I didn't have the answer to that question. Luckily, the waitress came with our food, and so I sat back in my original seat.

After we ate, I told him I had to leave. Not that I really wanted to, but I enjoyed the feeling of making him want more of me.

He walked me to my car. He started checking out my Hummer as he opened the door for me.

"Damn, this you?" He smiled with his perfect white teeth. His smile was perfect with or without the golds. That was a plus.

"Yeah, this my baby. Where's yours?" I was curious as hell.

"That's me," he said, pointing. My eyes followed his finger.

Sparkling like it had just run through the car wash was an all-black Aston Martin.

"Okay then," I said and laughed while stepping in my ride.

He grabbed my hand and kissed it. "Stay in touch," he said before closing my door.

A thug and a gentleman! Yeah, I was beginning to like him.

When I got in the house, Jasmine and Tionna were sitting on my bed.

"Yeah, girl, we been waiting on you," Jasmine said and laughed. She patted the bed, signaling for me to come take a seat.

"For what?" I chuckled. I sat on my bed and took my shoes off.

"Gip told me that you and Money hooked up today," she replied, letting me know that she wanted to know what went down.

"Oh, yeah. He took me to McCormick & Schmick's. Nothing too big," I said in a nonchalant way. I mean, it wasn't anything worth telling the next chick about. I gave them the little rundown, and then I hopped in the shower. I was drained and ready to make my way to dreamland.


Fourth of July morning Jasmine and I were in the shop, getting our hair done. Aunt Sasha and Fall had left for Miami two days before, so we had the house to ourselves. I was getting my hair colored brown and honey blond with a roller wrap. I always looked good with that. Jasmine got a sew in, and it did her justice as well. We had our hair, fingernails, and toenails done, so you know you couldn't tell us we weren't badd.

We made our way to the mall to get a few items for the night. While shopping for accessories, we spotted Gip and Money coming out of Underground Station with bags in each of their hands. In front of the store, they stopped to converse with two hoochies.

"Look at them niggas," Jasmine muttered, glimpsing them first.

Her entire mood changed. Money wasn't my man or my concern, so it didn't bother me.

"Let's go over there. That's your man," I said as I led the way to them.

We made our way over there, and the hoes must have sensed the tension, because they dipped before we reached them.

"So, um . . . who was that, Lance?" Jasmine asked with attitude in her voice as soon as we walked up. He immediately began explaining himself. It tickled me inside, so I laughed as quietly as I could.

"Jas, I'm going to go in here," I said while giving Money the head-to-toe look as I walked past him and into Underground Station. He obviously couldn't help himself, because he walked in right behind me. I added an extra swish to my walk.

"Damn, you ain't speaking?" he asked. He grabbed my arm and turned me around.

"Hi," I said. I turned back around to check out a pair of heels on a shelf.

He smiled. "Get what you want. I'm buying," he said.

My face lit up like a lightbulb. That was all I needed to hear. Freebies never got turned down in my world. Hell, I didn't care if I didn't have any intentions on wearing anything in that store that night, but I did know that I was leaving with something.

He ended up buying me a clutch and two pairs of heels.

"Thanks, sweetie." I smiled at him as we stood at the register. I noticed a group of females whispering to one another. He grabbed my bags off the counter.

"No problem. I take care of mine," he said and handed me my bags. I heard one of the females gasp.

"Yours, huh?" I said loudly, making sure that they heard me loud and clear.

"Mine, Doll," he said while patting his chest. He had definitely made it clear. "After the club I want to see you," he said as we made our exit out of the store.

I assured him that he would be seeing me afterward.

As we walked over to Jasmine and Gip, they were hugged up. I assumed they had set aside their differences. I hugged Money as she shared one last sweet kiss with Gip, and then we walked off.

"Girl, Money got long money. You hear me? There are so many bitches that really want a piece of that man, but he don't even be on it! I can tell he really likes you, Doll!" Jasmine told me as soon as we got in the car.

"And you know what? I really like him too. He real cool."

My mind began to wander. I already knew that Money was not going to get too close to me at all. I was not going to allow myself to get played to the left anymore. I was definitely going to make him my Atlanta man and maybe even my dick source, but nothing more . . . or so I thought.

Tionna was at our house at 11:30 P.M. sharp. We got our last touches in while getting ourselves together and then headed out the door.

Club Crucial was definitely crucial, because the line was wrapped around the building. Once again there was no standing in line for us. We walked straight through. The niggas were looking good and the hoes were looking mad once we stepped foot in the club.

"Get Silly" by V.I.C. was playing, and we hit the dance floor and got silly, all right. I had no plans to leave Atlanta. This was definitely the place to be.

Not spending a penny in the club was definitely something I could get used to. Guys were buying drinks for us left and right. I felt my phone vibrating inside my clutch, making it move all around the VIP table.

It was a text from Mari. I know you probably in the club, rocking, but Brian in this club, all in Janeen face, like they a couple, and word is she knocked up by him, but don't trip. Enjoy yo' nite, Doll.

If it wasn't one thing, it was definitely another. I caught a feeling, but I refused to let that ruin my night. I was in Atlanta. I wasn't even trying to think about what was going on in Toledo.

"Lollipop" by Lil Wayne came on, and I made my way to the dance floor.

Plenty and many were checking for me, and there were some I was checking for myself. By the end of the night, my wrap was threw. I told Jasmine it was time for me to go home. There was no way in hell that I was going over to Money's house looking like I did. She agreed that we both needed to freshen up.

As soon as we made it home, I ran upstairs, kicked off my BCBG heels, threw my clutch on the bed, and slipped out of my dress. I went into the bathroom, got the water at the right temperature, and hopped my tail in the shower. I had the entire bathroom smelling like Love Spell body wash by Victoria's Secret. I knew that scent was going to erase that club smell off of me.

After my long shower, I decided to throw on some Victoria's Secret Pink booty shorts with a matching beater. I slid on the matching sandals and put my wipes and extra panties in my Gucci bag and headed downstairs.

"I invited Gip and Money over," Jasmine said while spraying on her Victoria's Secret Pure Seduction body spray.

"Oh, that's cool!" I said.

That was better for me because I didn't know Atlanta or Money well, so this would be safer for me. I went back upstairs and lay down until their arrival. Shortly after, Money was creep walking through my door.

He was rocking a navy blue Coogi outfit with some all-white Forces and a matching fitted hat. The middle of my booty shorts grew moist.

"You going to sleep?" he asked while sitting on my bed. He took his shoes off and got under the covers with me.

*Oh, he shouldn't do that,* I thought to myself.

"Naw, I was just waiting on you," I said in all honesty.

"Waiting on me, huh? You ain't have to wait too long, did you?" He asked seductively.

"No, or else your access would have been denied. Time waits for no man, and neither do I," I told him as I scooted closer to him.

"I like you. You too much," he said and laughed. He held me tight.

I could get used to this.

We watched *Bad Boys II,* his favorite movie. I kept thinking about sex, knowing it was way too early to give up the goodies, even though I wanted him to have them so badly. I didn't want to be the one to make the first move, but it didn't look like he was going to bust one first.

"What you thinking about?" He asked.

"Nothing," I responded quickly.

Then he slid his hand in my panties, and that warmth made me even wetter.

"Oh, I know what you thinking now." He laughed, but he still didn't try anything. "See, I would do some things to you, but you ain't legal yet. Besides, I want to get to know you before I get to know your body," he said while staring me in the eyes.

I could tell he was being sincere, and for that, I respected his wishes. He was talking good things, but at the same time, bad things . . . because it left me horny.

After the movie went off, we wrestled a little. The positions he was putting me in made me visualize the sexual positions he could put me in. After our wrestling match, we began talking about our lives.

"So, you got a man, shawty?" He turned over to lie on his back.

"I'm single. What about you?"

"Same, or else I wouldn't be here." He looked at me.

"When was the last time you had a girl?" I stared back at him. I wanted to turn away, but I was trying to get rid of all the shyness I had built up around him.

"It's been a good minute since I had a shawty," he said as he sat up. "I don't tend to date people unless I really like them. I can fuck whoever I like, so I feel like, why should I date somebody that's only good for a fuck? That's what most of these hoes are good for."

I sat there, speechless. This man was smart, and a lot of the shit he said, I didn't have a comeback for.

"So why did you break up with your last girlfriend?" I wanted to know.

"She was too damn insecure. Always thought a nigga was cheating. All that complaining, nagging, and arguing is annoying. So I had to let her go. You got to have confidence to be with me, and you got to know that none of these females out here are capable of replacing you."

I could tell he was giving me hints about what he wanted me to be, so I took mental notes.

"That's how I see my woman, so that's how I want her to see herself."

The more he had to say, the wetter my pussy got. This man was good.

"What about your ex?" He asked.

"Well, me and my ex broke up after I had a miscarriage and he started creeping with my friend."

His eyes got big.

"Pretty fucked up, I know. And there's more to it, but that's just the outline of it." I caught a feeling just recapping the situation.

"See, that's why you can't fuck with these little boys. And quit fucking people without a condom, unless you want a kid and you know they mature enough to take care of one."

He made me feel younger than I was. *Damn.*

He went on. "I ain't trying to boss you around. I'm just trying to get you on my level, you know. Like, ready

for me." He smiled while placing his hand on my face. I
wanted to rape him by this point.

We got under the covers, and he held me close to
him. All I remembered was smelling that Unforgivable.
I had to admit that cologne was definitely a panty drop-
per. Too bad I didn't get to.

When I woke up, Money was not in the bed with
me. I was hoping he was somewhere in the house, like
cooking breakfast or something.

I got up and looked outside, and sure enough, his
Aston Martin was gone too. I went to the bathroom to
freshen up, and then I headed downstairs to find Jasmine, who was eating at the table.

"Food's in the warmer," she said while cutting up a
waffle. I made my plate and sat across from her.

"So when did they leave?" I asked her.

"Money left like an hour ago," she replied. "He told
me to tell you that he want to hang with you today."

Just the thought of him made me smile, but I had to
remind myself that I shouldn't fall so fast so soon. He
was so much older than me in age and mentality wise.
I knew I had to grow up a little faster in order to get on
his latitude.

"Hmm." I smiled. "Hell, yeah, I want to hang with
him! So did you have fun last night?"

"Yes, girl. I had a good time with my baby."

"Girl, Money is too much for me." I couldn't stop
talking or thinking about him.

"Girl, isn't he? He's on some whole other shit. The
man a genius, though," she said as she sipped on her
orange juice.

"I just don't know, Jas. He's been really making me
feel so . . . dumb." I was not sure if I was ready for him
. . . or if I had just used the correct term for how he
made me feel.

"Girl, he wouldn't have came over here if he wasn't trying to make anything out of y'all. Trust me, Money don't be wasting his time in no shape or form. Plus, you're younger than him! I'm sure he knows that he's got to work on you. Like, he's probably going to try to school you 'cause you fresh in Atlanta. You're like a new face around here!"

Jasmine was right. I was probably right on time for Money.

"Just play that badd bitch role, but don't do too much. Girl, you'll do fine," she told me.

I trusted what Jasmine had to say because she had to do the same thing when she hooked up with Gip. That was what I was going to do. I knew I had to step my game up. I enjoyed Money's money and company, and I knew if I didn't get it together soon, my time with him would come to an end.

# Chapter 11

Mari and I sat in our advisor's office at Clark Atlanta. We planned to stay on campus and be roommates. I already knew my girl would love "the A," because I did and we had the same taste.

"So it appears you both will be in the school of nursing," our orientation director said while reviewing our papers.

She then took us to a room where we would make up our class schedules and get room assignments. The orientation director opened the door, and we saw that there were multiple computers inside the room. She handed us both a few papers.

"The directions to log on to the computers and the steps to make up your schedule are on the pink paper. The other paper lists the general classes you will need to take. When you're all done, you're free to leave."

We sat down at two computers and looked over the log-on paper. After we logged on to the computer, we began picking classes to add to our schedules.

Since this was Mari's first day in Atlanta, Jasmine, Tionna, and I planned to show her a good time, even though she did have family in Atlanta.

"You're going to love it here, Mari. I'm so excited my bitch came!" I told her while creating my schedule.

"I know! It's definitely way better than Toledo," she said as she kept her eyes on the computer screen. Since we were both majoring in nursing, we decided to have the same exact schedule so that we could be study buddies.

There were three other girls in the room with us, whispering among themselves. Then one asked, "Are y'all from here?'

Mari and I looked at each other. I knew we were thinking the same thing. Were them bitches whispering about us the whole time?

"Naw, we from Ohio," Mari responded.

The girls looked as if they were from here. The girl in the middle, who appeared to be the ring leader, was dark skinned and had a wet and wavy sew in. She was pretty and had some expensive taste, because her Louie handbag was screaming "Big money." The girl to her left wasn't as pretty, but she kept them giggling, so I assumed she was the life of their party. She was also dark skinned and had a cute little bob. The one to her right was a white girl, who acted very black. She was pretty and seemed to be very urban. Her hair was to her shoulders, and she had false eyelashes, which attracted you to her gray eyes.

"Oh, that's what's up! I'm Kita," the ring leader said.

"And I'm Ona," the life of the party said. "And this is Faith," she added, pointing to the white girl.

"I'm Mari, and this my girl, Doll," Mari said, introducing us.

After a little more conversation, we realized we were all going for nursing and our rooms were in the same dorm.

After we finished making our schedules, I dropped Mari off at her cousin's house in Bankhead. I was due to meet Money at a restaurant called Justin's, so that was where I headed.

When I walked inside, he was already seated. This nigga was always on time.

"How long have you been here?" I asked him as I took my seat across from him.

"Not too long," he said, with his menu in his hands.

Money and I had been dating for damn near three months now. The longer we kept in touch and hung out, the more I fell for him.

"So your birthday's coming up. What do you plan to do?" he asked while setting his menu down on the table.

My eighteenth birthday was quickly approaching. September eighteenth couldn't come any slower. I couldn't wait to be legal.

"I really don't know yet." I didn't have the slightest clue. I just knew I wanted to do something.

"You got to come up with something, shawty. Anyway, how did your orientation go?" He gently massaged my hand.

"It went well. I got my schedule made and everything."

School began next week, and I was so ready for it. I couldn't wait for my first day of classes.

"You trying to go skating today?" he asked excitedly while letting go of my hand.

"Yeah, sure!"

Back in junior high in Toledo, skating was the popular thing to do . . . but that was years ago. I didn't know if I still had it in me.

We finished eating, and then we hopped in his fabulous Aston Martin and drove to Cascade Family Skating, a skating rink. After riding in his car, I realized that I really wanted one of those, because that baby was smooth and fast at the same time.

Cascade was full of older people . . . which was okay with me. When there were too many younger folks, drama always erupted.

"What size you wear? A twelve?" he joked.

"No, a seven, sweetie." I laughed as I handed my shoe and ticket to him.

When he went to get our skates, I sat on a bench. Soon he came back with our skates in hand, swinging them lightly.

"You know how to skate, don't you?" he asked, chuckling as he sat next to me.

"Don't you think it's a little too late to be asking me that?" I laughed. "It's been a while for me." I laughed again. "You going to help me?" I was so serious.

Lord knows I didn't want to bust my ass in front of him or, better yet, in front of everybody on the rink.

"I got you, shawty," he assured me, grabbing my hand. We made our way to the rink.

They were playing Young Jeezy's "Soul Survivor," and Money and I skated away. Surprisingly, I still had it! I was doing my thing, until I tripped over this man who was lying on the floor and I landed on my ass. I was so embarrassed.

Money made his way over to help me up, laughing his ass off.

"You all right?" he asked.

I got up and dusted myself off. "Yeah, and embarrassed," I said, looking around, hoping that no one saw me.

"It's cool. When you fall, you got to just get back up." He was speaking the real.

"We gon' slow it down a bit. Grab yourself someone special for the couple skate!" announced the man in the DJ booth.

They slowed it down, all right, playing "Cater 2 U," one of my old-time favorite Destiny's Child jams.

Money grabbed my hands and started skating backward while I skated forward, facing him.

A thug that was hood, sweet, and could skate, yeah, he was definitely one of a kind.

"You going to let me cater to you?" He asked, taking me out of my train of thought.

"You already are," I replied. I didn't know what more the man could do for me.

"This ain't shit," he said. Hell, if this wasn't shit, then I was excited to see what was next.

"I'll accept." I smiled.

"Smart choice," he said. He leaned in and kissed me on my neck.

I kept my phone on vibrate the entire night. I didn't want to be bothered by any ringing. When I finally decided to answer my phone, I looked at the screen to see who it was and it was Brian.

"Brian, it is two in the morning. Are you crazy?" I was irritated.

"I couldn't sleep, so I wanted to talk to you." He sounded upset.

"Well, why can't you sleep? Ain't Janeen there to hold you?" I guess he didn't think I knew what was going on.

He got very quiet.

"Yeah, Brian. I know you up there fucking her, and that's cool. Enjoy your life." I hung up and fell back to sleep.

When I woke up in the morning, Fall had planted her tail at the foot of my bed. She was watching the *America's Next Top Model* marathon.

"What's up?" I asked while making my way to my bathroom.

"Nothing. Just seeing if you wanted to go for some ice cream at Sno-Flake. You know, maybe talk a little." She was throwing hints, which I definitely caught.

"Yeah, sure." I immediately jumped in the shower and got dressed. My sister and I hadn't hung out together yet, so I figured this would be a good time.

We got in her new Benz, which Aunt Sasha bought her for her sweet sixteen birthday, and we headed to her favorite ice cream shop.

We sat in a booth, and I ordered a strawberry milkshake, while she ordered a banana split.

"This is a nice little shop," I said. I wanted to start a discussion of some sort to break the ice. She smiled.

"Yeah, me and my friends come here all the time to have girl talk and just chill."

"So what did you want to talk about?" I questioned.

"Nothing in particular. I just wanted to talk to you." She fiddled with the napkin holder.

"Oh, well, okay," I said as I sipped on my shake. "So what's up with you? How's the boyfriend?" I started off with something basic.

"We're good. How are you and Money?" She laughed. I laughed with her.

How did she know about us?

"We're fine." I smiled.

"How's Mom?" she asked and continued to fiddle with the napkin holder.

The waitress came over to us. "Can I get you young ladies anything else?"

"No, thanks," I said. I knew I still had to answer Fall's question about our mother. I didn't know how to break it to her in the nicest way possible. I didn't want to just say, "Well, Momma's a ho, and she strung out on drugs!" I decided to keep it simple.

"She's not doing so good," I said while stirring up my shake with my straw.

Fall changed the subject quickly and spilled the beans. "I'm pregnant," she stated. I figured that was the subject she had wanted to discuss in the first place.

"Oh, wow," was my response.

She looked over at the customers sitting behind us. Then she focused on her banana split. Her eyes were filled with tears, which she was trying to hold back.

I scratched my head. "So what are you going to do? I know you're not going to keep the baby. I mean, you're just a baby yourself!"

I was pissed. I could have sworn the girl had told me she had had sex only once in her life. How on earth could she be pregnant if she wasn't having sex anymore?

"Of course I can't keep it, Doll." She leaned in closer. "I want you to take me to get rid of it," she whispered.

I was definitely down with that. She was way too young to be having anybody's baby. Her life was just beginning, and having a child would put a hold on her life. I wanted so much for my younger sister to have the life our mom could never give us.

Fall wasted no time. While I finished my milk shake, she set up her appointment to have the abortion procedure, and she made me promise not to tell Aunt Sasha. I didn't have any intention of saying a word.

After the ice cream, I dropped her off at her best friend's house and made my way to Bankhead to see my bestie. I parked Fall's Benz in the driveway and walked up to the door. Before I could even knock, Mari opened the door.

"Hey, Doll!" She was excited to see me. I walked in and sat on the couch.

"We move on campus tomorrow! I can't wait!" She took a seat on the floor.

"Did you get some dick or something?" I laughed, wondering what had her so damn happy-go-lucky.

"No, nasty. I'm just happy we're doing something with our lives." She chuckled. I had to agree we were making the best out of our lives. "Well, have you decided what you are going to do for your birthday?" she asked.

"No, and it seems like we been questioning this situation forever." We both laughed.

"Yeah, the last time we brainstormed, I think we whupped a bitch or two's ass!" She was laughing so hard. I replayed in my mind our fight at Famous Dave's. That night was extremely crazy.

As we both fell over in laughter, I realized how much I really enjoyed spending time with Mari, because we always had a great time. I was at her house for hours, helping her pack up her things, and then it was time for me to pick up Fall and head home.

"Well, pumpkin, I have to go . . . but I'll be back in the morning to get you," I said while opening the front door.

"Well, let me walk you to your car, 'cause there's some goons out here." She laughed as she walked me to my car.

Mari and I decorated our dorm room in hot pink everything. Aunt Sasha bought us a thirty-two-inch flat-screen TV, a laptop, and a printer. We had our dorm laid out. Mirrors were everywhere, maybe because we were conceited and needed to know if we were cute at all times.

When we finished unpacking, we headed to the cafeteria to get something to eat. We saw a lot of fine guys who we both planned to meet. We also got a lot of mean mugs from the females, but that was cool too. We were used to it.

The cafeteria didn't have anything exciting to eat. There was a Pizza Hut there, so we decided to order that and call it a day. We found a nearby table by a window where we could sit down across from one another.

My phone rang. It was Money.

"What's up?" he asked.

"Nothing. At this cafeteria. What you doing?" I asked.

"Just thinking about you. I kind of miss you." He chuckled. I was happy to hear that and to know that I was going through his mind.

"Kind of?" I laughed.

"Yeah, not too much!" he told me. "But, hey, I want to see you." He got straight to the point.

"Well, I got my friend here with me, and it's our first day here. I can't just leave her." Even though I wanted to for him, I couldn't.

"That's cool. Maybe I'll come through later." He sounded so sexy.

"I'd like that." We exchanged a few more words, and then we hung up.

"So who was that? Who has my girl smiling from ear to ear?" Mari asked. She was blowing on her slice of pizza, which was obviously hot.

"That was Money. Girl, he is the man," I said and laughed. The thought of him put me on cloud nine.

"I can tell." She shook her head.

We finished our pizza and made our way back to our dorm. When we walked into the building, some light-skinned boy was handing out flyers.

"Hey, we're having an icebreaker tonight. Y'all should come out and meet the school," he said. He handed us both a flyer.

We grabbed the flyers and made our way to our dorm room. We decided we were going to attend the party. We didn't have anything else to do. I called Jasmine and told her about the party. She said she and Tionna were going to get dressed and meet us at our dorm later that night.

When ten o'clock came around, we started to get dressed. I decided to wear a plain black fitted dress with red heels and accessories. Mari wore brown leggings, a leopard vest, and leopard heels with the matching clutch. We were looking like a million bucks. We were definitely about to turn heads.

By eleven, the girls were calling, telling us to meet them outside the dorm. When we pulled up to the party, the parking lot was beyond packed.

"Aww, yeah! We about to rock out!" Tionna was excited.

I pulled my personal mirror out of my clutch to make sure everything was in place. We all stepped out of the car and made our way into the party once we assured each other that we were all intact.

As we made our way into the party, all eyes were on us. Plies's "#1 Fan" was tearing the speakers up. We rushed to the dance floor and started singing Keyshia Cole's part on that song. We were rocking out and sweating our wraps out as well. A lot of the dudes there kept flocking our way, but we were just there to have fun. We didn't want them to think we were easy.

The party came to an abrupt stop when the sororities and fraternities got in the middle of the dance floor and starting doing their thing. We watched in awe and vowed that we were going to join either the Delta Sigma Theta Sorority or the Alpha Kappa Alpha Sorority. After they finished doing their thing and taking over the dance floor, we resumed partying. They all walked off, throwing up their sorority signs and shout-outs.When the clock struck 2:00 A.M., it was about time to go. Once we got in the car, we replayed all the interesting things that had occurred that night.

We made it back to our dorm, and I noticed I had three missed calls from Money. I called him back.

"Damn, what were you doing?" He asked.

"We went to the school's icebreaker. What you into?" I was trying to see if he still wanted to come over.

"Nothing. Trying to be in you." He laughed. He knew damn well he wasn't going to let me put no water to that pipe.

"Yeah, right. Well, do you remember what dorm I'm in?"

"You know I do," he replied. With that, we hung up, and I rushed into the shower and put on a pair of cute pajamas and awaited his arrival.

When he got to the dorm, he called me, because I had to sneak him in, being that guests weren't allowed in after 11:30 P.M. I made Mari go and do it. As he walked into our room, I looked him up and down. He had on a Pelle shorts outfit with matching mid-tops. He was looking good, as always. Mari decided to go next door to the neighbors that we had met during orientation to give us privacy.

Money sat on my bed, smelling like the smell I loved. I stood in front of him, inhaling every bit of it.

"I missed you," he said. He didn't waste any time. He grabbed me and sat me on his lap.

"I missed you too," I confessed.

It had been a while since we chilled because I was so busy with school. He kissed me on the lips. We stood up, and I pulled my hot pink covers back. He kicked his shoes off, and we climb onto the bed. As we lay there cuddling, I thought of how I was dying to fuck him. I couldn't wait until my eighteenth birthday, because I was going to be getting a piece of that dick. He stayed with me until I fell asleep, and then he left.

I woke up to Mari smiling from ear to ear.

"So did you get you any?" she asked.

"Girl, no. He won't fuck me until I'm grown," I said sadly.

"Well, that is smart. Just in case somebody try to get him for rape, but, damn, can a bitch get a sample?" She giggled.

"Man, I'll settle for a dry hump." We both laughed.


"Today is your first day to a new beginning. Here in Math for Allied Health, you'll learn everything you need to know about the percentages and amounts of medication to give a patient," said our math teacher.

This was our very first day of school, and I already knew that I was not feeling this class. It was an hour and a half long, but it was beginning to feel like forever. Mari and I sat next to the three girls we met during orientation.

"I already can see myself skipping this class," Ona said.

We all agreed. The teacher was too boring for me. His voice had the same tone no matter what he was saying. He just had no energy. He told us that during the twenty minutes that were left, we could get acquainted with one another.

"So how's Ohio?" Faith asked.

"It's cool and a lot different from here," I answered.

Ona and Kita were engaged in their own conversation. I wasn't being nosy, but when I heard "Money," and not the kind you spent, my ears tuned in.

"Girl, I hope Money pay for my nails to get redone and that dress I saw," Kita said.

Mari and I exchanged looks, but I didn't want to go off on Kita. If I did that, how would I get any information?

"Girl, you know he will. What won't he do for you?"
Ona giggled.

I was getting pissed off by the minute. I had to keep
reminding myself to keep my cool.

"She got him so open," Faith added.

I looked at the clock on the wall and saw that it was
time to go. I grabbed Mari's arm as I stood up.

"See you, ladies," I said as I led Mari out the door.
She shook her head when I finally let her arm go. She
told me just to call Money and ask him if what Kita had
said was in fact true.

I felt sick. My heart was hurt. I prayed that this shit
wasn't true. I mean, how much could I take? I was feeling Money, and if he was splurging on Kita, like she
claimed he was, I would be so torn.

We went back to our dorm, and I decided to see what
his side of the story was.

"What's up, baby? How was school?" were the first
words he said.

"It was cool up until some chick named Kita claimed
you checking for her," I said, wasting no time.

"Kita?" He repeated.

"Yes, Kita," I replied. I was irritated. All he had to
say was yes or no; there was no need to beat around the
bush about it.

"Man, she ain't nobody," was his response, which
didn't make me feel any better. So I asked him what
"She ain't nobody" meant.

"She's nothing. She ain't you. Yeah, I fucked her a
few times in the past, but that's the past. Why? What
she say?"

"You be tricking on her."

"Not true. Don't let her make us fall out. Fuck her,
and I'm coming to get you in an hour, so get dressed."

When I hung up, Mari asked me what he said, but I told her he didn't say anything. I grabbed my towel and headed to the shower room to do as I was told. The whole walk there, I wondered if I had gone about things the wrong way. Maybe I should have cursed him out or not given in so easily. Hopefully, this would be the last encounter with one of his hoes, but only time would tell.

# Chapter 12

"Wake up, Sommer!" Mari was all up on my bed.

It was Saturday, and it was also my birthday! *At last!* Finally, I was eighteen. I was happy, but I was still sleepy.

"You know we got to go and get fly for your day!" She was right, so I got up and freshened myself up.

First stop was to get dolled up, so we right on over to the Glambar Hair Salon. My cousin Jasmine was already there. Jasmine never played any games when it came to getting her hair done. She was always up early.

We walked in, and the beauticians with whom we had set up our appointments directed us to sit in their chairs. We sat, and they began to make us over.

I had decided that I was going to have my party at Cascade. Money was throwing it for me since I didn't know too many people in Atlanta. I was nervous about how it was going to turn out, but I knew Money would know how to make my birthday beyond special. He had paid for everything.

Unc sent three thousand dollars for me to enjoy my birthday. I just put it in the bank, because Money had me covered. He had sent me an Armani dress that complimented my curves, with matching accessories and shoes to go with it.

While I sat under the dryer, Money sent me a text. I hope you enjoying your day. I'm gon' make sure you enjoy your night.

I was hoping that he meant I was getting some dick. It had been three whole months since I had gotten laid, and I was going through it at this point.

After our hair was done, I took Mari back to our dorm. Then I met up with Money at Mr. Chow's. When I walked in, he was looking better than ever. He was already seated, as usual, so I just sat down across from him.

"You look so handsome," I told him. He was rocking a brown Gucci shorts set.

"Thank you, baby," he said as he flagged down the waitress. He ordered for both of us. I guess he knew I wouldn't know what was good, since I had never been to this restaurant before.

"You ready for tonight?" he asked. He sipped on the drink the waitress had just brought him.

"Yeah, I'm ready if that means I can get a piece of you," I joked. In the back of my head, I knew I was as serious as a heart attack.

"You can have all of me." He licked his lips.

I knew this was going to be a birthday that I would never forget. We ate, and then we made our way to the exit. He walked me to my car. I got in and started the engine, and he leaned in and kissed me gently. I was shocked. I guess he couldn't wait for this day, either, or maybe I was just looking way too good for him.

"See you in a little," he said before shutting my door.

It was a little past nine, so it was about that time to start getting dressed and head to *my* party. Mari had on a nice fitted yellow Bebe dress and I put my cream Armani dress on and we were out the door. When we walked outside, there was a pearly white Charger limo parked in front of our dorm. A driver wearing a black-and-white tuxedo was standing in front of the door.

"Are you Doll?" he asked me. My eyes got big. I was about to scream.

"Yeah!" I said, looking at Mari.

When he opened the limo door, I saw that Jasmine, Tionna, Fall, and a few others were already inside. Mari and I exchanged glances, and then we walked over to the limo. We climbed in, and the driver shut the door behind us.

"Money loves you, girl!" Tionna said while pouring her Cristal. There were so many different drinks to choose from. I wasn't really a drinker, so I didn't choose to drink anything. I just let my girls pour.

Jasmine handed me an off-white envelope. I opened it up, and the note inside read: *I don't know if now's the perfect time or not, but I love you and I hope you feel the same. See you soon. Money.*

I was definitely in love with him, but I was in denial. How could I be in love with anyone after all the things I had been through with these niggas?

We pulled up to Cascade, and the parking lot was jam packed. *All for me?*

"I bet all the ballers going to be up in here," Jasmine said while looking out her window. She rolled her window up.

We made sure we were all cute before we got out of the limo. When we walked in, it seemed like all eyes were on us. They had turned the rink into a dance floor, and there were so many people on it, having a good time. The party was definitely packed, and that took a burden off my chest.

Everybody kept telling me "Happy birthday" as I walked past them. When we finally made our way to the dance floor, Money grabbed me up and wrapped me in his arms. He was in a Crown Holder outfit, looking better than he had earlier.

"You having fun?" he asked. He kissed my lips.

"Well, I just got here, and so far, yeah. Thanks for everything, baby," I said while kissing him back on the lips.

He told me he wanted me to meet a few people. He grabbed my hand, and I followed his lead. We stopped at a group of guys. They appeared to be the same group he was with on the very first day I laid eyes on him. He introduced me to his crew and to his younger brother, Cash, who I had heard so much about already.

I understood why he and his brother had money names: they actually had money. Cash was a miniature Money. He was fine. He was a little darker than Money, and he was shorter.

"This my heart, Cash." Money pointed to him.

Cash and I shook hands.

"This my ole lady, Doll," Money told Cash. I liked the sound of that.

"Oh! So this is Doll," Cash said with a big smile on his face. "I heard a lot about you." He rubbed his hands together.

"Good or bad things?" I asked.

"Nothing major. Just that you was a badd young thang." Cash shook his head while he looked me up and down. "Yeah, Money, I think she's a keeper," he said.

I smiled. Cash definitely had good taste. I was honored in a way. I remembered Jasmine telling me that Cash was Money's everything and that meeting him meant I was "somebody" in Money's life. I looked over at Money, who was also smiling.

"Tonight is our night," Money told me before I went to find my girls on the dance floor. I smiled, and then I walked away.

When I finally found my girls, they were dripping sweat, and I planned on being in the same condition as they were soon. We danced until it was time to sing the "Happy Birthday" song. After the song, we enjoyed and smashed on the big-ass birthday cake Money had got for me. Before I knew it, the party was over.

"I just want to thank everybody for coming out to celebrate my lady's birthday. We appreciate it," Money announced on the microphone.

I was smiling from ear to ear. Money made me feel so special. He was being very generous to me, and there was nothing that I could do to stop myself from falling in love with this man. Honestly, I didn't even want to stop myself from falling.

I climbed in the limo with my girls and Money, and the driver dropped my girls off first and then took me and Money to a five-star hotel. I knew I was about to get the business. I was happy I was wearing my Victoria's Secret lace panties with a matching bra.

Our room was all the way at the top of the hotel, the penthouse. The bed was decorated with rose petals in the shape of a heart. There was also a Jacuzzi and a fireplace in the room.

"Baby, this is nice!" I had never been in a hotel room quite like this one. I gave myself a quick tour. I was in complete awe.

"Let's get in the Jacuzzi," he said.

He took off all his clothes. Now, I had thought Zae had a nice dick, but boy, was I mistaken! I hurried to take off my clothes and hopped in with him. He got between my legs and began sucking on my neck. I melted. It had been way too long.

We kissed for a while and then we decided to go to the bed. We stepped out of the warmth of the Jacuzzi and into the coolness of the room. We made wet footprints to the bed. I pulled the covers back. I lay down on the bed.

He rolled the Magnum condom down on his manhood. He got between my legs and stuck it in. He had a little trouble getting it in, but before I knew it, he was in and I was loving it. He was taking his time with me, doing slow strokes while playing with my clit. I was making all types of noises.

"You want to ride it?" he whispered.

Sure I did.

I had to let him know that I knew what to do with it and how to do it. I climbed my soft body right on top of his and began riding him. He moaned a tiny bit, with very little heavy breathing. Every time I humped, he would hump with me. He was a little too much for me.

"Roll your hips when you ride. Like this," he demanded as he grabbed my hips and tried to show me. I went fast, and then I slowed down. I was beginning to get the hang of it.

He laid me down and started eating me out, flicking his tongue back and forth. Now, he was better than I had ever had. I figured he knew what he was doing because he was older. He inserted his tongue into my vagina, and my juices started flowing. He then fingered me while he sucked on my clit. I was grasping the sheets as I eased closer and closer to the headboard.

He turned me around, lifted my ass up, and started eating my pussy from the back. I couldn't take it as I jerked toward the headboard. He grabbed my hips and put his dick in from the back. Now, normally I would throw it back, but with him I had some trouble.

"Quit running," he said, but I couldn't help it.

He was too advanced for me. He started going faster while grabbing a handful of my ass. At this time, he had total control over my body. I took all of it and clenched the sheets. I even bit the sheets and moaned loudly.

I came first, and he came after. We couldn't do any-thing but lie there. We were both naked, and sweat dripped from every inch of my body and his too.

I was wondering if we were ever going to do it again. He was probably annoyed that I didn't know what I was doing. Even though I had thought I did, he had proved me wrong.

"What you thinking about?" he asked, and then he smacked me on my ass.

"Nothing," I responded quickly. Shit, I had a lot on my mind.

"Why you lying?" he asked me, pulling me closer to him.

"I bet you think I suck in the bed," I blurted out. I was so embarrassed.

"No, you cool. I can teach you some things. It's not your fault that you was fucking with them rookies be-fore me," he said while kissing me on my neck. "Come on." He sat up and pulled me up with him. "Let's go take a bath."

The bubble-filled bathtub had candles lit all around it. This was beyond romantic. We got in and took turns washing each other's back. When we were finished bathing, we got out and dried each other off. We didn't put any clothes on; we just got in the bed.

"Look, Money, you really made my day." I meant it.

"That's what I was aiming to do," he said as he posi-tioned himself to lie on his back.

"You did a great job," I told him. I placed my head on his chest. "Thank you."

"You don't have to thank me, baby. I told you, I take care of mine," he reminded me as he wrapped his arm around me. I put my arms around him also. I never wanted to let go.

"I'm yours, huh?" I said as I lifted my head up to look him in the eyes. I was holding him tight.

"Mine." He kissed me on the forehead and said, "I love you."

"I love you too." Surprisingly, I meant it.

We lay there silently, and he suddenly fell asleep before I did. He was even fine while he slept. I watched him sleep for a while. I couldn't believe that I had fallen in love with him so quickly. No matter how hard I had tried not to love him, he treated me so good that I didn't have much of a choice. He was perfect for me.

In Toledo, Doll's mom was on her normal stroll, doing anything for a hit. Her pimp was fed up with her poor performances and the little money she was bringing in. She couldn't help the fact that she was no longer the beautiful yellow bone she once was. She was now a twisted-face, wig-wearing junkie.

April Jones used to be a badd bitch back in her prime. The niggas in Scott High School loved her. She was thick and light skinned, and she had that long hair that niggas saw as sexy since it was her own. Most guys were afraid to approach her because she had her big brother, Jim, and his best friend, Mitch, who were very protective of her and her older sister, Sasha.

That didn't stop Derrick Rogers from trying his luck. He was the best player on the football team, taking the Scott Bulldogs far in many play-offs. He saw April walking down the hall with her books close to her chest, and he saw the perfect opportunity. April remembered their conversation.

*"April!" he yelled.*

*She turned around, smiling. "Yes, Derrick?" she responded, still all smiles.*

*"You doing anything later?" he asked.*

*"No, not really. I have to put a perm in my sister's hair, but other than that, I have no plans." She knew*

*he was going to ask her for a date, and she didn't want
anything to get in the way of that.*

*"Okay. How about you let me come pick you up at
eight, then?" he asked, hoping she would agree.*

*"It's a date," she said before walking to her locker.*

*Derrick arrived at her house at eight sharp. They
decided to go see a movie that they both would enjoy.
After the movie was over, they went to get something
to eat. While they were sitting in the car, eating their
food, Derrick pulled out a small bag containing a substance that was as white as snow.*

*"What's that?" April had never seen anything like it
before.*

*"Sniff it," he said while taking a sniff himself.*

April, not wanting to be considered lame or stuck-
up, took a sniff, and her life went downhill from there.
She and Derrick made two kids together, Sommer and
Autumn. Derrick was never really around, being that
he was so hooked on drugs. His football scholarship
was taken away, and there was no way in hell he would
pass anybody's drug test.

He blamed April for ruining his life by entrapping
him with those two kids. He made sure to beat on her
every night. He was good with the kids, and he never
harmed them. He was always nice to his daughters. All
his anger and frustrations were taken out on April.

Derrick died from an overdose when Autumn turned
two. His family blamed April for the bad things that
happened to Derrick. Of course, they concentrated on
the things he would tell them. However, April's family could help her only so much. That so much wasn't
enough, though.

April became stressed. She had no job at all and had
two mouths to feed along with her own. She went back
to the drugs because it was only thing that seemed to

take her stress away. She returned to coke. The day she returned to coke was the day she lost it all.

April was now on Junction, looking and searching for a hit.

"You come back with anything less than five hundred dollars, and I'm going to kill your ass!" her pimp threatened.

She only laughed at him. There was nothing he could do without her. She was his very first ho. When she finally found what she was looking for, she was ready to go home.

She opened the door, and there were two other hoes lying out on the floor, higher than a kite. She looked around to see where her pimp was. She found him upstairs, sitting on the bed.

"Daddy, I'm home," she said, slurring.

"How much you got for me, ho?" He was fed up with her.

"You count it." She threw the money on the bed.

That answer made his blood boil over. He got up from the bed and backhand slapped her. She fell to the floor. He got down there with her and began to choke her. After she began to turn purple, he stopped choking her and got up to count the money as she had told him to do, anyway. She was two hundred dollars short of what he'd asked her to bring.

He grabbed her by the neck. "April! If you don't get yo' ass back out there and come up with my two hundred, I promise you'll be dead."

He pushed her up against the dresser. The glass mirror broke, and everything on it fell.

"Go!" he yelled.

She was startled. She got up and headed out the door.

"Ana, Jane, and Lisa! All you hoes, come clean this mess up!" he yelled as he lit a cigarette and sat back down on the bed. He looked out the window, down at April, who was stumbling along the brick street.

She stood on the corner, hooting and hollering, for over two hours before she caught a trick. He pulled over and rolled his window down. She pranced over to his car and leaned inside.

"What you trying to get?" she asked in her sexy voice. It was a white man who appeared to be in his late twenties. He looked like he hadn't shaved in ages, but she didn't care. She needed the money, and white men always had all the money.

"I want a blow job and sex," he said. That was just what she needed. A quick one hundred dollars would make her night easy.

"That'll be one hundred," she replied. He demanded that she get in the car, and that was exactly what she did.

"I got a motel," he said. April knew that most guys wanted it instantly and inside their car. The easy white guys always had to get special and get rooms and shit.

They arrived at a Motel 6, where the john checked them in. After he got the key, they went inside the room. She went straight to the bathroom to get herself together. She stepped out, and he was lying on the bed. She made her way over to where he was, and she unbuckled his pants.

She began giving him the blow job he'd requested. He tasted just like salt, and he had a foul smell to him. She gagged almost every time she sucked. After almost an hour of giving him a blow job, she decided that screwing the man would be less tormenting.

He demanded that she lie down. He put a condom on and jammed his penis inside her. She jerked because it was so painful. He grabbed her neck to help bounce her on his penis. She was cringing from the pain, but she made her cries sound like moans. He didn't care when he flipped her around and began pulling her hair so hard, it started coming out of her scalp.

"Daddy, you're being too rough," she cried.

It seemed as if he didn't hear her, because he got even rougher than he was before. Tears began to form in April's eyes. When he finally reached his peak, April slid out from under him and put her one piece of clothing back on. She collected her dues and tried to stumble her way out the door.

He grabbed at her waist. She turned around and faced him. She was obviously in pain.

"Wait. Where do you think you're going? The fun is just getting started," he said as he stood tall in front of the door.

"I have to get back home." She began to get scared, because nothing like this had ever happened to her in her years of hooking. There were always the aggressive losers who wanted more than enough, but something about this man was different and scary. He was absolutely serious.

"Well, I want to get my money's worth."

He grabbed her. She struggled to get away from him. He slammed the door, and as she tried to run, he pushed her onto the bed. She tried to scramble away once again, but he grabbed her by the throat and began choking her.

He whispered in her ear, "I get a kick out of watching whores like you die slow."

April couldn't breathe, but she could still cry. She knew she wasn't going to make it out of that room alive. No one knew where she was or who she was with. She was doomed.

He grasped her neck tighter and tighter, until she was no longer moving. After she lay there, lifeless, he again jammed his penis in her and had his way with her dead corpse.

When I got home, I found Fall crying in the entertainment room.

"What's wrong, Fall?" I asked.

"Mama's dead," she said, her face full of tears.

I couldn't even find tears to cry for her. I mean, for what? My mom was in a much better place, because Toledo had definitely done her wrong. I held Fall on the floor.

Aunt Sasha came in next.

"Are you girls all right?" she asked with sincerity.

I was numb. Damn, that meant I had to make a trip back to the place I had had no intention of going back to. Aunt Sasha told us she was getting two plane tickets for us so that we could go to Toledo the very next day. She then told us that she would come next week. I didn't want to go, but I knew I had to.

The next morning Fall and I were on our way to Toledo. When we touched down, Debo drove us to Unc's house. It was still how I had left it. We were both extremely tired, so we decided to take a nap. It had been a long day.

Money's phone call woke me up.

"Hello?" I answered dryly.

"Baby, I heard what happened to your moms. Are you cool?" He asked.

"Yeah, I'm cool. I'm just trying to get myself ready to see her." I knew I wasn't prepared for this.

"Well, if you need anything, let me know," he said before we hung up.

***

The day of the funeral was more than I could bear.
Fall and I sat in the front row, along with Aunt Sasha
and Jasmine. The church was filled with people who
wanted to pay their respects.

There were hoes in the back row with some familiar-
looking guy. I stared at him to see if he was the man
that I thought he was. Indeed, it was my mom's pimp.
He wasn't there very long, either.

I had plans to spit in his face.

Fall cried rivers, while I sat there numb. I wasn't as
sad as she was, but I wasn't my normal self, either. I
knew my mother was better dead than alive, because
she didn't know what to do with herself.

We all walked up to the casket to get one last view
of her. She was very skinny and delicate . . . fragile. I
couldn't see anymore. I quickly turned away. The sight
of her made me shiver.

Moments later the church doors flew open. There
stood Unc, cocky as ever. He was chained up and ac-
companied by two sheriffs. I could tell he was embarrassed about his late arrival and appearance, but at
least they were letting him say good-bye to his younger
sister.

I jumped up out of my seat and ran to give him a hug.
I instantly started crying. "You don't know how much I
miss you, Unc!"

I had tried writing Unc many times, but my letters
kept returning to me. I called Stryker, where he was
located, and they told me that he had been shipped
someplace else. Unc never called or wrote me back,
and I had no clue where he was. That made me feel
like nothing. People would ask me where he was, and
I couldn't even tell them. Although he paid my bills, it
was through my cousin Debo, and when I asked him
about Unc, he'd brush me off.

Unc sat down between me and Aunt Sasha. He held my hand through the entire service. When the service ended, he gave me a piece of paper with his address on it. "Thanks, Unc. I really miss you. Why didn't you tell me where you were moving to?" I questioned him.

"Doll, if I had told you, you wouldn't have gone off to Atlanta. You would've stayed in Toledo so that you could still be close to me. I don't want to be a burden on you," he said while touching my face.

Tears began to drop down my face again.

"Don't cry, Doll." He held me tightly. "My time is coming. I want you to visit me before you go back to Atlanta. I have to go now." He kissed me on the forehead, and the guards walked him out.

The reception was held at the Octagon Hall. That too was filled with a lot of people. I spotted Zae walking through the door, and I didn't want to see his face at all. He was looking good, as usual. A Polo outfit with matching shoes. I had always loved him in that. He noticed me from afar and immediately approached our table.

"Can I talk to you, Sommer?"

I wanted to tell his ass no, but he was looking too good for rejection. I got up, and we went outside.

"Zae, what the hell do you want?" I asked in a very annoyed way.

"I just wanted to tell you that I'm sorry. I know your life hasn't been the best for you, and I know the shit I did didn't help better your situation—"

I interrupted him. "Zae, I'm sick of all your damn sob stories. Yeah, you're right! You did me wrong! But you know what? Life goes on!" I stated.

"I love you, Doll. I really do. All that shit was a lie. I never fucked Imani. I would never do that to you. We planned that because I wanted you to feel how I felt.

Why do you think Justine was always around?" he declared.

*What? If they did plan that, why is he just now coming clean with this?*

"I tried going to your house to tell you, but you was so pissed at me. I ain't think you would believe me," he continued to explain as he stared me in my eyes.

Was it too late to give him another chance? I was so into Atlanta and Money that there was no need for me to make a U-turn.

"Look, this isn't the right time to be discussing this. My mom just died, Zae! How selfish could you be to come here and try to talk to me about you and me after all this time?"

"Doll, it's 'cause I care!" he explained.

"Whatever," I said and walked off. I had no plans to finish that conversation. He was too late.

I went back inside and conversed with the rest of my family until the reception ended. Then Fall went with Aunt Sasha to visit a few of our family members, while Jasmine and I decided to chill at Unc's. When we pulled up to the house, Kola was parked there in her Stratus.

I was beyond irritated. I got out of the car and walked up to her driver's side. Jasmine went up to the front door of the house and watched from afar.

Kola rolled down her window.

"What are you doing here?" I asked.

"I just wanted to let you know that I was praying for you. I'm sorry about your mom." She sounded down and out.

"Thanks," I said.

"I wanted to go to your mom's funeral, but I just didn't think it would be safe," She sniffled.

"So do you think that being in front of my house is any safer?" The girl sounded dumb. I didn't feel the least bit sorry for her, and I wanted her to leave, so I walked away and went into the house, closing the door behind me and Jasmine. It had been months since Kola and I were knit tight, and the love I had for her had disappeared.

The doorbell rang.

"I'll get it," Jasmine yelled while opening the door. Seconds later she yelled, "Doll, it's Brian!"

I just didn't get it. Why was everybody popping up at Unc's house?

I headed downstairs. There he was, smiling ear to ear while doing his usual licking of the lips.

"What's up, Doll?" he asked.

I responded with the rolling of my eyes. I really wasn't in the mood to be bothered with him.

We sat and talked for a little while. He told me that Janeen was pregnant with his baby, and surprisingly, I wasn't hurt or anything. I already knew the truth, so there was no reason for me to feel hurt. I was cool.

After our little chat I walked Brian to the door. That chapter in my life was over as well, and I had no plans to rekindle that flame.

"Who was that?" Jasmine asked me after he left.

I gave her the little rundown about both Brian and Zae.

"I guess you had all the fine dudes," she said.

I laughed. "Girl, everything that look good ain't good for you," I told her.

I made sure to go see Unc, and the bus ride there was a hectic one. When I finally got there, I felt like a convict myself. They patted me down, checked my purse, and told me to take a seat. I waited a good fifteen minutes before they called my name. I sat down at a table and waited for him to come out.

Unc was buffer than ever. He came out with a smile on his face. A tear dropped from my eye just from looking at him. I missed my hero, but I understood that because he did the crime, he had to do the time. He understood that too.

We embraced. We sat and talked about everything we could in the couple of hours they gave us. During our conversation he mentioned that he still hadn't seen or heard from Auny.

"At this point in time, I don't even want to see her," he told me.

I agreed that that would be best for him.

"Hey, Doll?" He looked confused.

"Yeah, Unc?"

"Lately, I've been seeing strange faces," he told me. I was confused.

"What? Unc, you'll be okay. You just need to get out of here."

"Yeah, I'll be all right, Doll," he said. He smiled. He then went on to tell me how he wanted me to help him sell his house and put the money up for him. He gave me all the contacts that I needed.

We ended the visitation with "I love yous" and him letting me know that he would be getting out in a year on good behavior.

The next day, I made it my business to set up an appointment with a real estate agent so that I could immediately have the house put on the market. In the course of three weeks, I sold everything in the house, and I put the lump sum of money I made in the bank, as Unc had told me to do.

After I got a great offer on the house, I knew Unc would be more than financially set once he got out. I just hoped that him seeing faces wasn't something that could harm him. . . . You just never knew with Unc.

# Chapter 13

I was so ready to put the year behind me, but I had to get to Christmas first. Zae had become a serious pest, calling and texting me nonstop. I decided to get my number changed and to leave him in the past with the rest of the trash I had already thrown out.

It was exactly one week before Christmas, and Fall and I were out looking for a gift for Money. You never went wrong with jewelry, so we went to Jared.

"What about a nice watch? I noticed his wrist was naked," Fall said as we walked into Jared. The jeweler was ready to help us as soon as the door closed behind us.

"Anything in particular that you're looking for?" the man asked.

"A nice blingy watch." Fall laughed.

He directed us to the Rolex watches. There were some pretty nice, expensive watches, but there was only one that caught my full attention.

"How much is that one?" I pointed at one that had a diamond band.

"Oh, this?" His eyes lit up as he pulled it out of the case. "Fifteen thousand."

"Fifteen grand?" Fall repeated.

"Yes, ma'am," he responded, assuring her that she had heard correctly.

"I want it." I pulled my platinum card out of my Coach bag and handed it to him. He blinked at me twice.

"Well . . ." He paused. "I'll just get this wrapped for you, then."

As he went to wrap the watch, Fall and I kept our eyes glued on the engagement ring section.

"This one is so cute," I said, drooling over a big purple diamond that sat on a ring. Fall agreed.

The jeweler walked over to us as we admired the purple diamond. "Oh, yeah. A lot of women fall in love with that ring!" He placed my box, card, and receipt on the counter. "You're all set," he said with a smile on his face, probably happy that he had made a sale.

"Thanks." I returned the smile as we headed toward the door.


It was Christmas Eve, and Money and I were at his house, relaxing by the fireplace. He constantly told me how convenient it would be if I just moved in with him, but I wanted to finish my freshman year on campus. After all, I had dragged Mari all the way down here. It would be rude of me to just leave her on campus alone.

"I like that you're loyal to your friends," he said while placing his lips against mine. "But I want to go to sleep with you every night and wake up next to you every morning."

"I want the same, but that's my girl, Money," I told him. There was no way that I could just dis her like that.

"How about we introduce her to my brother, Cash?" Money was going to have Cash keep her occupied.

It sounded like a great idea to me, so I made a mental note to hook it up.

Money and I exchanged gifts. He handed me a red gift-wrapped box. It was long, so I knew it was jewelry. I opened it up. It was a beautiful diamond tennis bracelet. I handed him my gift. He took his time opening it up. He took the lid off, and his eyes got wide.

"Doll, I swear Cash and I were peeping a watch like this out!" He was excited. "I got one more gift for you," he said while going to retrieve whatever it was.

He came back in the room with a basket. There was a Yorkie puppy inside it. He knew I loved Yorkies. Sadly, I had to get rid of Dora when I came to Atlanta, and it had broken my heart. Money knew how to mend it.

"What's its name?" I asked him while playing with my newfound love.

"It's a girl, and her name is Lovie." I fell in love with my dog instantly. She was going to live at his house, since no pets were allowed on campus.

Everything was falling into place, and something told me that Money would be in my life for a while. With those thoughts in mind, I cooked us dinner, which consisted of steak, potatoes, shrimp, and a fresh garden salad. I wasn't the best chef, but I could cook. Since Money loved me, I was the best chef ever in his eyes. He enjoyed every bit of dinner.

After we finished cleaning our plates, we cuddled up and watched the game. I wasn't in any rush for winter break to be over. Being under Money all the time was like heaven to me. I noticed that his phone kept ringing throughout our romantic night. I wondered who it was.

"Why aren't you answering your phone?" I questioned.

"No reason. It's just Cash and Gip. I'm trying to give you my undivided attention. Is that a problem?" he asked while pressing IGNORE on his phone.

I decided to let it go and not let that ruin our day. I ignored the situation and continued to watch the game, even though I could care less about either team. Money started nibbling on my ear, and I already knew what he wanted.

"Sorry, babes. It's that time of the month," I said, shutting him down early. He looked upset, and I had to admit he was sexy when he was sad. I decided I would give him some head instead. I unzipped his pants and pulled out his penis.

I jacked him off until he got rock hard. When he finally stood at attention, I began sucking the life out of him. This was the first time I had given him a blow job. I wanted to show him that even though I didn't know how to fuck as well as he thought I could, I could definitely give a nice blow job in place of it.

I put the whole thing in my mouth and started off slowly; then I sped it up. After doing that for a few minutes, I started sucking the head only. I was whirling my tongue around the head and tip. Money was on the go, and I knew I was doing my thing. After twenty minutes of complete satisfaction for both me and him, Money came in my mouth.

I swallowed it. The taste was disgusting, but I figured since he was older, that was what grown people did . . . swallowed the nut. I constantly felt like I had to prove to him that I was just as grown as he was.

He hugged me tight and kissed me all over.

"I love you, baby," he said between kisses. I said it back.

I got up and went to brush my teeth. Moments later there was a knock on the door. When he opened it, I knew from the voice that it was Cash.

I couldn't really hear everything he was saying, but I did manage to hear him say something about a Christmas party at Justin's place and that he thought we should all go. I knew that couldn't be the only reason he had come over. At least I hoped it wasn't. I crept down the steps, and Cash was already gone.

"Baby, who was that?" I asked, as if I didn't already know.

"Oh, that was just Cash. He was telling me about a Christmas party that he wants us to go to. Call your girl up. We're about to go," he ordered.

Even though it sounded like fun, something was telling me that there was more to this Christmas party. I had butterflies, and that made me not even want to go. Though I was feeling this way, I did as I was told and called Mari.

"Okay, I'm dressed, so just call me when you get outside," Mari said.

I took this party as an opportunity for her to meet Cash. I did a quick washup and then got dressed. I decided my soft pink Versace dress and my Jimmy Choo shoes would be perfect, while Money wore a cream Versace suit with some cream Mauri gators. We were both hot and out the door. We hopped in his all-white Escalade and made our way to Mari's.

After we picked up Mari, we went over to pick up Cash. In the backseat, Mari and Cash talked each other's ears off. *Great! Less work for me in hooking them up!*

When we arrived at Justin's, we spotted Jasmine and Gip. We immediately approached them. We all exchanged hugs and daps, and then the guys told us that they'd be right back.

"I don't know about this Christmas party," Jasmine said as they walked away.

"Me either! It seems so last minute, and I just don't feel right about it," I stated.

Deep down inside, I knew I couldn't be the only one against it. Mari remained quiet. She didn't care. As long as she was getting out of her cousin's house for a while, she was cool.

We noticed that there were a lot of couples at the party. We also observed the many Italians there.

"You think they trying to join the Mafia?" Mari laughed.

"I am not with that." I chuckled. "Money's going to find himself single!" We all shared a laugh with that comment.

Jasmine wanted to make sure she was still fly, so we went to the bathroom. There was a pretty dark-skinned lady standing in front of the mirror, applying M·A·C mascara, when we walked in.

She looked at us through the mirror. "You ladies must be new here."

We all exchanged looks.

"No, we've been here before," Mari said, an attitude in her tone.

"No, I mean new to the connect party," she said and laughed.

"Connect party?" I repeated.

"Yeah, this is where the Italians connect with the blacks. You know, start selling their product to us black people. Luke said these niggas got the best crack in the nation."

Our facial expressions must have shown that we were upset.

"Y'all look so down. Don't be," she said while placing her hand on my shoulder. "That means more shopping for us!" she said excitedly as she exited the bathroom.

I was pissed. They said this was a Christmas party, not a damn crack party. I had never thought to ask Money how he got his money . . . or did it even matter to me at the time?

I just knew that drug dealers had only two options in this world, and they were death or jail. Either way it went for him, I didn't want to be a part of it. I made plans to check his ass once we got home.

"Girl, just let it ride. Christmas is tomorrow," Jasmine told me.

She was right. This wouldn't be a good day to dog him out. I decided that I would just dismiss all of this from my thoughts until school started back up.

When we finally left the bathroom, we saw Money, Cash, and Gip talking to some Italian man in the most expensive money-green suit I had ever seen. He appeared to be in his forties, had gray hair, and carried a cane in his hand. That man definitely looked like money, and I was certain he smelled like it too.

"That must be the connect," Jasmine whispered in my ear.

Yeah, it had to be, because when I saw him, I saw dollar signs.

The next day I woke up to the smell of breakfast. Before I could get my vision clear, Money was coming in the room with a tray.

"Breakfast in bed for my baby." He seemed very happy.

He set up my tray for me and left the room. I got up to wash my face and brush my teeth, and then I went back to bed to eat.

He came back in with a small box. "This is your first present," he said. I opened it up, and it was a key.

"You got me a car?" I already had a car, so I wasn't excited about receiving another one.

"Yeah, so you can stop driving that nigga's shit around," he replied, as if I should have already known. He had a point, but I never knew that me driving the car that Zae had bought me was a problem. Money had never mentioned it.

"It's a Jag. You're going to love it." He smiled.

After I finished breakfast, I went downstairs to open the rest of the gifts Money had got me . . . a lot of jewelry and clothes. I loved it all. Besides, I had always been an appreciative person, because I grew up with nothing.

Hours passed, and I just wanted to relax and watch some TV with Lovie. One of my favorite shows, *The Game,* was on. Money came downstairs, talking loudly on his cell phone.

"Yeah, I can be on the next flight there. It'll just be me, my brother, and Gip," he said while looking through a pile of papers that was on the dining room table. Ten minutes later he got off the phone and sat next to me on the couch.

"Baby, I know you about to catch an attitude when I tell you what I'm about to tell you, but this is for business," he said while grabbing my hand.

I continued to rub Lovie.

"I have to fly to Miami tomorrow. . . . I'll be back before New Year's," he told me while looking in my eyes for an okay.

There wouldn't be one, because I wasn't fine with his decision at all. How could he just plan a trip without even telling me first? Whether I felt it was okay or not, Money was leaving the next day.

"Whatever, Deneiro." I got up and headed to the stairs.

He followed.

"So you mad, Doll?"

"Money, you know this ain't cool! And another thing . . . the connect party," I said with an attitude and continued to march up the steps.

"Okay, so I lied about the Christmas party. Doll, I sell drugs! What do you expect from me?" He had his hands in the air as if he had given up.

"I expect you to be honest and let me know what's going on." I flopped on the bed. He walked in seconds after.

"Some things are just too much for you to know. Sometimes, it's better that you don't know." He grabbed my face. "Don't let this little shit get in the way, Doll. I'm sorry for lying, but I love you and I'm doing this for us." He kissed me.

I still kept my attitude. I was going to pretend I was okay with it, but deep down inside I was pissed that I would have to spend the majority of my break alone.

Money, Gip, and Cash landed in Miami on the 26th of December. Girls smiled and giggled as they made their way out of the airport in their tan Dickies short set outfits, with their clean white Air Forces on their feet. Their rental was waiting out front with the valet, as planned. They put their bags in the trunk and all got in. Gip was the driver, Money rode shotgun, and Cash sat in the back.

"Do you know how to get there, or do you need me to GPS it?" Cash asked while putting their destination in his phone's GPS.

"I think I know how to get there, but put it in just in case," Gip replied.

Gip played with the radio to find a good station to listen to. Money pulled a Gucci Mane CD out of his back pocket.

"I knew we was going to need this," he said, inserting the disk.

Then they were off. Money sat and thought about Doll the entire way to the Malattos. She was perfect for him. She was young as hell, but she was very mature for her age. He knew she was the one for him, and he planned to start his family with her. He pulled out his phone and sent her a text: Thinking about you.

He knew she was pissed about his last-minute trip, but he had to do what he had to do. The streets were all that he knew. His mom and dad had died when he was a child, so his grandmother had raised him. She later passed away, so he felt that Cash was the only person he had in this world.

He had started selling weed for his mentor, Legend. Legend had taught Money the ropes of the drug business. He told him that he'd let him sell only weed because he was too young and that all he had to do was tell the Feds that he smoked weed if he ever got caught. He would get only a misdemeanor for drug abuse. When Money turned eighteen, Legend introduced him to the white substance called crack. Money had thought weed was bringing in all the money, but he was really balling with crack.

When Money was eighteen, Legend gave him and Cash a condo. Money was pushing a Lexus truck by the time he graduated from high school. Legend was killed in a robbery. Once again, Money felt like somebody he loved had been taken away from him. Losing Legend was like losing a father . . . and his connect. This was what brought him to the Malattos.

Legend had introduced them at a connect party when Money was twenty years old, but Money had lost touch with them after Legend died. He had kept in touch with Mist, Legend's right-hand man, who was always coming up short with money. He realized Mist was his only way to the Malattos, but he too died shortly after. Word on the street was that the Malattos had taken him out of the game.

This left Money with no connect. No connect meant no money. He had had Cash find out through his lady friend, Tonya, when the next connect party was.

"Christmas Eve," she had said.

When Cash came through with the information, Money had had no choice but to go. They came to Atlanta for recruits only once a year, and Christmas Eve was that one time.

His phone vibrated.

Doll had texted him back. Miss you too. That made Money smile.

They pulled up to a mansion with security gates. Gip pressed the call button.

"May I help you?" a female voice asked.

"Yeah! It's Gip for Oatis Malatto."

Seconds later the gate opened. They drove inside and parked in the lot.

"He said the front, right?" Gip asked Money.

"Yeah," Money replied. "Y'all niggas ready?" He looked back at Cash.

"Hell, yeah. Let's get this shit over with." Cash opened his door. He went to retrieve a bag of luggage from the trunk.

Money and Gip stepped out, and they all made their way to the front entrance. A blond-haired woman in a bikini met them at the entrance.

"Follow me," she told them. She led them to the back, where there were many of her kind in the pool. The Malattos sat at a table.

"There," she said and pointed at the Malattos before heading over to dive into the pool.

They walked over to the Malattos and sat down.

"Hello, Money . . . Gip . . . Cash," Oatis Malatto greeted, nodding his head at each one as he said their names.

Oatis Malatto was in his midforties. He was the nicest one out of the Malatto family. He had more patience when it came to fuckups. He had been dealing with Money indirectly for years now, so he wanted to finally get the opportunity to work with him man-to-man. His brother Ruben Malatto sat to the right of him. He had no patience and had a low tolerance for everything. He was in his late thirties. The youngest, Sam Malatto, who was in his midthirties, sat to the left of Oatis. He didn't have any say-so over anything. He just did as he was told. Nothing more. Nothing less.

"So! You guys got what we need . . . and we got what you guys want," Ruben stated.

"Money, you know how we get down, right?" Oatis asked.

"Yeah, I know what it is. We got the money, and we know we'll receive the product a few days from now," Money said, trying to shorten the entire conversation process.

"Correct. Well, then, you should know our policy," Ruben said, hoping they knew the consequences if their money or their product came up short.

"Of course, but we don't have those types of mishaps. We're as legit as they come." Money put his hand on his chest. "If one of my boys fuck up anything, know that I'm going to get out there and fix it."

Money had no intention of being in this game much longer, anyway. His goal was to make a million dollars and bounce out of the game. Unfortunately, he was ten thousand dollars short. After this one exchange he would be set, and he and Cash would be through.

Money didn't live the flashy life. It was apparent he had money, but he didn't spend his money on stupid shit. He treated himself to good things every now and then, but he made sure he put a certain amount in his safe before he spent anything. He was very young but also very wise. Legend had always told him, "Save first and spend later," and that was what his life revolved around.

"Okay, well, it looks like we're all on the same page, then," Oatis said. Money, Gip, and Cash got up, shook hands, and left, heading to their hotel.

They checked in at the Catalina Hotel on Collins and Seventeenth. When they got on the elevator, two girls entered with them. The elevator had a sign that read FOUR PEOPLE ONLY, but they sensed money, so they didn't care. They were attractive, they had nice shapes, and their hair weaves were looking nice. One was mixed, and the other was dark skinned. The mixed one had her eyes on Gip, while the dark-skinned one wanted Money.

"Y'all here with y'all girls?" the mixed one asked, sparking a conversation.

"No, we here on a business trip," Cash replied, keeping the conversation short.

"Oh, really? Well, can we be a part of that business?" the dark-skinned girl asked. The entire time she was staring at Money.

"Business over pleasure," Gip said as the elevator stopped at their floor.

They got off and walked down the dim hall to their separate rooms. Money and Cash had never been the ones to give the girls the time of day. They saw the girls as games and a waste of time. They definitely had their share of girls, but they looked at them all as "good fucks."

On the other hand, Gip loved for females to be all over him. For the most part, he was faithful to Jasmine, but from time to time, he slipped up. The only reason he didn't holler at the girls on the elevator was that he saw Money and Cash pass them up. He didn't want to seem like the only one who was on it . . . or thirsty . . . because he believed he was far from that.

They didn't hit the club or the hoes that filled Miami. Instead, they got together and ordered food up to one of their rooms and let the Xbox occupy their time. There was no reason to go all out into the streets. There wasn't nothing out there but trouble.

"Man, I should have got one of them chicks' number," Gip said, regretting that he hadn't.

"You have to be smarter than that, dawg," said Cash. His eyes never left the TV screen. "Hoes be setting shit up, and at the rate you going, yo' ass is going to get caught slipping." Cash had a point.

"Yeah, you right . . . but a nigga need some!" Even though Gip agreed with Cash, he wasn't really trying to hear what he had to say.

"We'll be home in the morning," Money said and laughed. "Just wait. Jasmine's going to put it on you when you get home. Nigga, you probably got blue balls and shit, with yo' horny ass."

They all laughed.


Money, Gip, and Cash were up by seven' o clock in the morning to catch their flight back home. When they touched down, they all had one thing on their mind: sex. During the car ride home, sex was all they talked about.

"Man, when I say I'm going to fuck the shit out of Jasmine . . ." Gip pictured how it was going to go down.

"Man, you ain't never lied. Dude, I don't even know who to call," Cash said. He had too many options.

"I'm going home to wifey." Money was faithful, and he was pleased with Doll's sex game.

"We know that," Cash said as Gip burst out into laughter.

"Why the hell we acting like we was gone for a week? It's only been two days," Gip said.

"Yeah, but it's been four days for me, 'cause I ain't get none on Christmas or the day after. Doll was mad as hell." Money chuckled.

"Her too? Man, Jasmine thought I was going to meet a bitch up in Miami or something." Gip smiled as he recapped her letting his ass have it. They all laughed again.

This was all they needed. Each other. Their gang had started out with more than the three of them. When push came to shove, they were the last three standing. They had grown up together, had shared the same girls, and had worn each other's clothes from time to time. They fought for one another, gave each other money, and if one needed a shoulder to lean on, they could always depend on each other. Blood couldn't make them any closer, but love did. Even though Cash and Money were blood brothers, you couldn't tell them that Gip wasn't their brother too.

Gip was a dread-wearing, grill-gleaming, rim-riding thug. If there was a fight, he was on it. No ifs, ands, or buts about it. He was malicious and was never afraid to pull a trigger. Respect was what Gip would die for, so if you came incorrect, he came to your doorstep. He was the definition of a *street nigga*.

He had grown up an only child, but when he met Money in junior high, he knew he had met a brother for life. He liked Money because they shared a common interest. The benjamins. Gip also admired the loyalty Money had for his younger brother, Cash. They all vowed to remain tight.

Cash had a study buddy named Jasmine Jones who came over to their house twice a week. Gip practically lived there too, so he got to see her all the time. Cash knew Gip wanted her badly, and Jasmine would constantly tell Cash that she wanted Gip. Eventually, Cash hooked them up, and they'd been together ever since.

Money and Cash had never been big on the whole relationship deal, so oftentimes, they had ended up with different girls. They didn't approach girls. They let the girls approach them. This made the hoes go crazy over them.

"Go make love, nigga!" Cash joked as they pulled up to Money's house first. Cash hopped in the front seat.

Money nodded. It was true. He was in love, and he wasn't afraid to admit that. Doll was something every nigga wanted on their arm. She was street-smart and book smart . . . not to mention, she had his heart.

He unlocked the door and set his bags by the door. Doll was on the couch, asleep. He smiled at the thought of her angelic face. He went over to her, picked her up, and carried her upstairs to bed. He decided he wouldn't wake her, so he kissed her on the lips and watched her sleep. He couldn't help but kiss her again.

"I love you," Money said. She remained asleep. He decided to take a shower and then lie up next to her afterward.

After his shower he pressed up against her warm body. He hadn't slept well in Miami, but lying next to her made him fall asleep right away. She was indeed his soul mate.

# Chapter 14

"We have a test on chapters nine through twelve on Friday, so study, study, study," my professor told our class.

It was the second semester, and I was maintaining a 3.0. Mari, on the other hand, was on academic probation, meaning if she didn't get it together this semester, she would have to sit out. I could tell she was so distracted by Cash that she probably didn't even care about her grades.

After Money and his posse's trip to Miami, Cash started to shower Mari with all types of gifts. This was something she was not used to, so all of a sudden she started missing class. She said that this semester would be better, but who knew, for real?

Money was in the streets heavy. I felt like the streets were his mistress, whom he paid more attention to. Although I wasn't living with him, I spent many nights there. The nights I stayed with him, I wanted him to be there with me.

I was sitting at the table, doing my homework, when he walked through the door.

"Again, Money?" I was reminding him of what he had told me . . . that he would try to be home by midnight.

He looked at me . . . with his fine ass.

"It's three in the morning, Deneiro," I said as I got up from the table.

"I know, Doll." He took everything but his boxers off and sat on the couch. "You like nice shit, don't you?" he asked.

No, the hell he didn't go there.

"That ain't the issue. The issue is me sleeping alone and shit!" I wanted to slap his ass.

"I know. I'll be out the game soon. Just be patient with me. When I reach my goal amount, then I can step out," he explained.

I sat down next to him.

"You know I'm not out there with a bitch or anything. I'm just trying to keep a smile on your face."

I knew he was trying to run that game on me. I wasn't stupid. I didn't think he was cheating, but I was a woman and I did have needs.

Besides the nice shit, I needed quality time. With him being in the streets, I wasn't getting much of that. Being lonely wasn't something I was used to, but practically living with him and him not ever being there made me feel as if I was better off staying in my dorm.

As usual, Mari was at Cash's house. They were playing NBA Live. Whoever lost had to do whatever the winner wanted them to do. Even though she was falling for him, the agenda she had for him wouldn't allow any room for that. If she played her hand the way she was supposed to, she would reap the benefits later.

Cash was beating her by ten points, and he was smashing it in her face.

"Mari! You ass, baby!" He laughed.

"Whatever. This my first time playing this game, so I think I'm doing pretty darn good!"

Hmm. She thought she was good. Her phone started ringing.

"Pause the game," she told Cash as she went to get her phone off the charger. It was her friend Marlen.

"Hey, you," she said.

"What's up? How's it going?" he asked.

"It's going," she said while peeking behind her. She knew she couldn't say too much while Cash was in the room.

"Time is money, and if you keep wasting time, then you won't receive any money. Get on it, Mari," he warned.

"I am. It'll happen sooner than you think," she said before hanging up.

She walked back to the couch and resumed the game. Cash knew something wasn't right about that phone call. He didn't want to show that he cared that much about it, so he didn't question it.

When the game was over, Cash won 105 to 88. He decided to just make her have sex with him. Although they did it on a regular, he couldn't think of anything else he wanted. She was already in her bra and panties, and it took no time to remove them. He pulled his boxers down and put on a condom. She straddled him and bounced up and down quickly. She turned around while keeping his penis inside of her, keeping up the same motion. He was impressed. She kept it at a fast pace. He knew if they stayed in that position any longer, he would come in no time.

He picked her up and got up off of the couch. He placed her on the floor, lifted her ass up in the air and proceeded to hit her from the back. He pumped her fast and hard. She was throwing it back just the way he liked it. He grasped her hair in his hands and lifted one of her legs. As he thrust, she began to run from him. Somehow, someway, he got under her leg, and they ended up in the missionary position.

He pumped her fast as he felt himself coming. When he came, he stayed inside of her. He lay on top of her, breathing heavily. He had put his all into that session. Even if he didn't love Mari, her sex game was something that he loved a lot.

After class, Mari, Jasmine, and I decided to meet up at Chicken and Waffles. I sat in the parking lot, waiting for them to pull up. Trey Songz sang through my speakers. I had the volume up high. I sang along in my own little world until I heard the honk of a horn. I looked to my left to see Mari in a red BMW. I instantly got out of my car.

"Oh my goodness! When the hell did you get this?" I asked, happy to see my girl get some wheels.

I opened the passenger-side door for myself and got in. I rubbed the interior in awe. I was impressed.

"Last night. Cash bought it for me. You like?" she said while looking at the car.

"Do I like?" What kind of question was that? "I *love,*" I said, laughing.

Yeah, I was definitely happy for my girl, but it seemed to me like they were moving way too fast.

We got out of the car and walked into the restaurant and waited for Jasmine to arrive. A few minutes later Jasmine came in, smiling from ear to ear.

"Hey, ladies!" she said before taking a seat.

"What's up with you?" I asked as she sat down. "You got you some dick before you came or what?" I said while giggling.

We all laughed.

"Why is it that every time I'm in a good mood, dick got to be involved?" Jasmine chuckled.

"Probably because your ass ain't ever in a good mood," Mari joked.

"If you must know, I aced my calculus test," she said proudly. That was certainly something to smile about.

The waitress came over to us, and we were all ready to order. After the waitress left our table, a familiar face walked into the restaurant. It was the dark-skinned lady from the connect party. She waved, and then she sat at a booth all alone.

"Should we invite her over here?" Jasmine asked.

"I mean, why not?" I said.

We all decided that I would be the guinea pig, so I went over to her. "Hey! Do you remember me?" I asked her as I slid into her booth. She was fidgeting with her Chanel sunglasses.

Her eyes got big, and she smiled. "Sure do. How are you?" she asked.

"I'm great." Then I got to the punch. "Me and my friends are sitting over there." I pointed at my girls, who played it cool. "Care to join us?"

She paused and looked at me. Then a smile appeared. "Sure," she said. She looked at me the entire time as she gathered her things and followed me to our table.

"I'm uncertain if we shared names," she said while taking a second to look at us.

"Oh, I'm Doll, and this is Mari," I said while pointing at Mari.

"And I'm Jasmine." Jasmine could introduce herself.

"I'm Tonya, ladies." Then her face lit up. "So . . . how did you girls like the party?" she questioned.

We were unsure if we were supposed to like it or not. We didn't even know why we were really there. The looks on our faces must have said it all, because she continued to talk.

"I see I have to school you newbies, 'cause it's obvious that your boyfriends left the three of you in the clouds."

She went on to explain to us that members of the Malatto family, whom our lovers were dealing with, were known to kill anybody and everybody if their money or product came up short. They could be the sweetest people and could seem like a friendly family to you, but once you crossed them, you were officially crossed out. They had an annual "Christmas party" to recruit people to sell their product. After the party, you were sent to Miami to meet the runners who would be delivering the work to Atlanta. You could get robbed, murdered, or caught by the Feds. They didn't care. Your family was responsible for getting the money right, or everyone was as good as dead.

We were all speechless after the rundown she had given us. The information frightened me. I was afraid for Money.

"Well, ladies! I have to go. It was nice chumping it up with you," Tonya said as she got up to leave.

We were still quiet, but we all fixed our lips to smile at her, even though it felt uncomfortable. Tonya put her sunglasses on and smiled again. Then she left. Her heels clicked against the floor as she walked.

It all seemed odd to me, because she wasn't there long and she didn't order anything. I began to think. Maybe she worked for the Malattos . . . but who paid me to think?

Mari's phone went off like an alarm. We all snapped out of it.

"Bitch, you thought you was going to be asleep?" Jasmine asked.

We all giggled.

"No, actually, I have somewhere to be, so, ladies, I'll link up with y'all later," she said as she got up. She then left the restaurant.

***

Mari was to meet up with Marlen at the Sno-Flake at eight o'clock sharp. When she arrived, he was already there and seated. His dreads were pulled back into a ponytail. His caramel skin gleamed in the sunlight.

"You're late," he said as she grabbed a chair and sat with him.

She looked at her phone. "Umm, two minutes late, though," she said sarcastically, not believing that he was tripping over spilled milk.

"The point is you're late! You got two choices . . . to be early or on time next time . . . or there won't be a next time." He didn't give a fuck if she was thirty seconds late. Late was late.

They ordered some ice cream, which neither one of them planned to eat. They were there for business purposes only, and that was the only thing they intended to do.

"How much longer do you need?" Marlen cut to the chase.

"Not long. I can probably get it done while we're on our way home or something. Maybe stall to give y'all some time." That was the best she could come up with.

"Sounds cool. Sneak a text or something. Just . . . try not to be obvious," he told her.

The last thing they needed was to get caught. Then she would be a dead woman.

They sat there and chatted a little while longer, until they noticed a dark-colored Charger with tinted windows creep past.

"You know them?" Mari asked. She kept her eyes on Marlen.

"Hell, naw. Why they riding by slow?" Marlen questioned.

They both thought the other one was up to something. They decided it was best to leave. Mari hopped in her car, and before she could pull off, the Charger stopped alongside her car. The dark color appeared to be navy. She was scared for her life. She was stuck to the seat. Then they pulled off quickly.

"Damn!" she said aloud while locking her doors. She pulled off and headed back to Bankhead.


"Baby! I'm home!" Money had started coming in later and later as the days went by. I was beginning to grow tired of it.

I just stayed in our king-sized bed and watched BET. I didn't bother to acknowledge him. He came in the room with a medium-size box.

"You ain't hear me?" he questioned.

"No. What did you say?" I played dumb.

He only shook his head and set the box down next to me, on a pillow. I looked at him, and I opened it. There was a smaller box inside. I opened that one, and once again there was a smaller box. After about three more of those boxes inside of boxes, I discovered an engagement ring, the five-carat purple diamond I'd been drooling over at Jared.

He got down on one knee.

"Sommer, will you marry me?"

It had been almost eight months since we'd started seeing each other, and Money wanted me to be his wife. I was madly in love with him, so there was no reason why I could say no. It didn't register with me that saying yes would also mean accepting his lifestyle.

"Yes!" I cried out. I jumped up and gave him the biggest hug ever. I couldn't wait to plan the wedding.

He got in the shower after all the excitement had died down, and then he headed back out into the streets like none of that had just happened.

My phone vibrated on the nightstand. It was an unfamiliar number, so I answered it cautiously.

"Hello?" I tried to change my voice.

"So you really making me go through this, Sommer?"

It was Zae. I was instantly annoyed. How in the hell did he get my number?

"Zae, what do you want?"

He knew me well, so I knew that he knew I had an attitude.

"Why are you doing this, Doll?" He paused, and so did I. "I mean, you know I love you and you sitting up here, changing your number on me? You acting like you annoyed with me, Doll." He sounded pathetic.

"Zae, *I am annoyed!*" I yelled. "Quit fucking calling me. Just get over yourself. I don't want you, so move on, because I have. I'm engaged, and I'm pregnant," I lied before slamming the phone shut.

I didn't understand why he was still stuck on me like he was. I was hoping that the things I had said would push him totally away.

I was so lonely at home. It was always just Lovie and me. She wasn't much company, so I still found myself as bored as ever. I decided to call Fall and have her come over. Her phone didn't ring once before she answered.

"What's up, Doll?" she said. Music filled the background. It sounded like she was at a party.

"Fall, where are you?"

"Over at my friend's house," she said after taking a minute to think about it.

"See where he at," someone demanded in the background. Before I could ask who "he" was that they were referring to, she told me she would call me back. Whatever was going on, wherever she was, it all seemed strange. . . . Only time would tell.

I decided to do some homework. I went up to the room that Money had turned into a study for me. I had a five-page research paper due in a few days. It didn't take long before that bored me out.

A chat line pop-up blocker appeared on my computer screen. It was called the Web Site. "A great way to meet people twenty-one and up," was what it read. Everybody talked about this Web site, so I figured it would keep me entertained. I set up a profile. It didn't take long for a few people to invite me to their friends list, and I didn't take any time to add a few people myself.

After an hour, I had a total of twenty-three friends. That was enough for me. My computer made a beeping noise. There was an instant message at the bottom of the screen from someone named Brian Jacobs, my old fling.

I clicked on it.

I'll be in Atlanta for the summer, he wrote.

Okay, well, we can hook up, I told him. I then messaged him my new phone number.

The next instant message I got was from a guy named Marlen. He lived in Atlanta too.

"How are you, gorgeous?" he asked.

I decided to go through his profile. He was caramel, with dreads. He wasn't my type, but he wasn't bad looking, either. I was bored, so I messaged him back.

"I'm doing okay," I wrote back.

He told me to take his number, and then he sent his number to me. He seemed pretty cool, so I took it. On one of my bored days, that number might come in handy. I logged off the site and began doing what I got on the computer to do in the first place, my homework.

\*\*\*

"Money, haven't heard from you in a while," Kita said as she made her way in the store.

Money smacked his lips. Kita knew that what they had had was long gone. She had fucked up when she was in class, running her mouth, knowing that Doll was his girl. If she had played her position correctly, her time would have lasted a little while longer.

For the past few weeks, Money had been posted up on the block with Cash and Gip, trying to make money. Doll didn't quite understand that. He figured she wouldn't, but all the complaints and nagging were starting to tear him down. He loved her dearly; in fact, he had popped the big question earlier that week just to show her that she was his heart.

She reminded him daily that the streets loved no one. Every day and every night, he risked his life and freedom for the love of the dollar bill. He couldn't help it; getting money was an addiction that he couldn't shake. He didn't want to shake it. He loved having a pocket full of cash, buying nice shit, and giving his girl whatever she wanted.

Kita walked out of the store and stopped in front of Money. She was looking good, with her tight black leggings and an even tighter shirt. She tugged at his Pelle blue jeans shorts.

"So we ain't speaking?" she asked.

"What's up?" Money responded.

"I guess you pussy whipped, 'cause lately you been antisocial."

"If that's how you see it," he said, giving her a short answer.

"What is it, Money?"

He was tempted to fuck her, but it wasn't worth losing Doll over, so he erased that thought from his mind. "I'm engaged," he said.

The look on her face let him know she was hurt. He had been messing with Kita since she was eighteen, and now she was twenty-one. In her head, she was coming closer and closer to becoming Mrs. Money, but now that was out the window. Her eyes watered up, and her voice became hoarse.

"You what?" She had to have misunderstood him, because there was no way he was engaged to a bitch who had just got in the game.

"I'm engaged, Kita. I'm engaged to Doll," he repeated.

Kita couldn't hold back the tears or the frustration. She started punching and kicking Money. Cash got her off him. She was crying and screaming as Cash carried her to her car.

"How could you? You fucking liar!" she screamed as she got in her car. She started it up and sped off.

Cash walked back toward the store, laughing.

"Man, that bitch crazy," Money said, shaking his head.

"What you do to her?" Gip laughed.

"I dicked her down real good," Money said and chuckled as he walked to a black Lincoln to make a sale. He did his transaction and was out of the car in no time. They stood on the block a little while longer, and then they headed to their trap.

Their trap was in East Atlanta, a pretty good distance from home. You would never know it was their trap unless they told you. It was fully furnished and decorated. Actually, Kita had decorated it. There was food in the refrigerator and in the cabinets. It was their home away from home.

As soon as they got inside, Money lay down in his room. He was feeling bad about breaking Kita's heart, but it was either hers or Doll's. He wasn't going to stress the situation. He had told her up front that he wasn't looking for a relationship, and she had played as if she felt the same way. He should've known she was too young to control her feelings. Then again, what bitch didn't fall in love with him?

# Chapter 15

It was the week of finals, and I was studying nonstop. Mari, on the other hand, was booed up with Cash. She had told me she didn't need to study, because the exams would be easy. I didn't bother trying to insist that she should, because I really didn't care. I figured she'd flunk and get a reality check. No need for me to help her.

It was a late Monday night, and I was studying for my anatomy exam when Mari called me, crying.

"What's wrong, Mari?" I could barely understand what she was saying.

"He's been shot, Doll! Cash got shot in front of our house. I'm so scared!" she cried.

Was she serious?

"Did you call the police? Is he breathing?" I asked.

I was praying she had called them before she called me. Somehow a dial tone popped up loudly in my ear. I didn't know whether to rush over there or to continue to study.

I tried getting in touch with Money, but he wouldn't answer his phone. I sat up waiting to hear from him, and finally, after two hours, he called me. Atlanta Medical Center popped up on the screen. I knew it had to be about Cash.

"Hello?" I asked as soon as I picked up.

"Baby, Cash got shot, so I probably won't be coming home tonight. You can come up here to the hospital if you want." He sounded angry and sad at the same time.

"Money, you're never here, and you never call me when you don't come . . . so whatever. I have an exam in the morning, so I won't be coming." I hung up.

Once again, I was going to bed alone. This had become a routine that I was growing sick of. Money and I hadn't had sex in a month, and I was going through a dry spell. I know it was kind of selfish to be thinking about sleeping alone when he had just said his brother had been shot, but I was jeopardizing a lot by living with him when I was supposed to be staying at the dorm.

What was a girl to do?

I decided to use my dildo, which I had got at a toy party that one of the girls in my class had thrown a while ago. I turned it on and went straight to work. It didn't make up for a real dick, but it was good enough.

After I finished that, I took a shower. By the time I was done, I noticed that I had twelve missed calls and two text messages. Ten of the calls were from Zae, and two from Money. Zae had sent me one of the texts.

If you keep playing with me, you're going to regret it.

Money had sent the other text, telling me how much he loved me and that he was going to make things better than they currently were.

I was happy to hear that, because loneliness had taken over and the ring was beginning to lose its meaning.

After I took my exam, I decided to head over to AMC to see Cash. Money and Mari were the only visitors he had there.

"Doll, I need to talk to you," Money said as soon as I walked in. He led me into the hallway.

"What's going on?" I asked.

"I just want you to know that I love you and I don't want to lose you. I have lost a lot in my lifetime. I know you have too." He sounded like he was going to cry. "I know I've been busy, but I'm going to slow down and make time for you. My brother's not looking too good, and if I lose him, you'll be all I have left," he said.

I didn't know what to say, so I just gave him a hug.

When we walked back into the room, Mari was at Cash's bedside. I walked over to console her.

"Doll, they don't know if he's going to make it," she told me through tears.

They had been messing around since the night of the party, a good four months. Although it wasn't a long time, they had been rocking hard, so I was sure there were feelings there.

I had to admit, Cash did look as bad as hell.

Two detectives walked in.

"Hello, guys. I'm Detective Harrison, and this is my partner, Detective Johnson," one of them announced.

Detective Harrison was an older, bald black man, and his partner was younger, with a nice clean cut. It was clear that they wanted to talk to Mari and Money.

"Miss, could you please leave so that we can have a word with these two?" Detective Harrison asked me.

A look of confusion came over my face as I looked over at Mari and Money.

"Okay," I said slowly. "Just call me later," I told Money and Mari.

I needed to clear my head. I didn't have another exam until Friday, so I needed a break, anyway. I decided to go to Tiny's Nail Bar to get a balance. Tiny wasn't present, but I didn't go to see her, anyway. My mind was everywhere but on my nails.

As I sat in the chair, I wondered why somebody would want to harm Cash. I prayed it wasn't the Malatto fami-

ly. I also tried to figure out what Money had meant when
he said I would be the only family he had left if he lost
his brother. I was also hoping that the police didn't think
Mari was a suspect. Before I could try to answer my own
questions, my balance was done. I gave them my money
and hopped in my Jag and headed home.

When I got home, Money was there, asleep in our
bed. Instead of waking him or lying down beside him, I
took Lovie for a walk around the block.

We began our little journey, and I saw that there
were more black people than I had thought who lived
in the area. Everyone was friendly, waving and speaking to us. We walked for about twenty minutes before I
decided it was time to return home. It felt good to clear
my mind a bit.

Walking back, I spotted the guy Marlen from the
Web Site getting out of a classic Mustang. I had never
thought I would run into him, so I continued walking,
wondering if he'd recognize me. He definitely looked a
lot better in person. His dreads were pulled back, and
his shirt was off. *Hmm . . . nice body.* He had a few tat-
toos, which I couldn't read from afar. I examined him
up and down.

When I got up to him, I kept walking, and he looked
at me and turned back to his car. Then he looked back.

"Hey!" he yelled.

I stopped.

He began walking up to me. "You remember me
from—"

"The Web site," I interrupted. I looked him up and
down again. I noticed a big tattoo on his chest that read
GB. "Yeah, I do," I admitted. I smiled, while trying to
figure out what "GB" stood for.

"Oh, so why didn't you speak?" he said, then chuckled.

"I didn't think you remembered me," I said.

"Well, you never used the number I gave you, either," he reminded me with a smile on his face.

"Okay, I promise I'll call," I said, flirting. "Well, we have to go," I said, with Lovie in my hands.

"You from this area?" he asked.

"No," I lied. "But I promise . . . I'll call," I said before Lovie and I walked off and went home.

Money was sitting on the couch, watching TV. He didn't look up or acknowledge me. I had played that same role with him before, so I knew he was pondering something.

"Attitude?" I asked as I sat down next to him.

"No, baby, I'm just thinking about a lot of things." He kissed me on my forehead.

"What?" I asked. I was dying to know.

"Baby, I want to get you pregnant. I need something that belongs to me. I'm not saying you don't belong to me, but you know what I mean," he said, hoping I did.

What the hell was he talking about? "Pregnant, though, Money?" I questioned. "Are you serious?"

"Yeah, have my seed. Is that possible?" He was hopeful.

"Anything is possible, but what would make you ask me that?" I was lost when it came to him. One minute he wanted to get married; the next minute he'd be MIA. I just didn't know if having a baby with him would be a good move right now.

"Doll, they don't think Cash is going to make it." A tear fell. "They said if he do, he won't be the same. Those Gib boys robbed my brother, man." He put his face in his hands. "My mom and pops died in a car accident. Our nana raised us. Then she died from cancer, so that just left me and Cash."

He was actually crying now. "I never let these hoes in, just because I can't take another loss. You was different, Doll, so I let you in and there's nothing guaranteed in this world. But my kid will be. I'll raise 'im if you don't want to." He wiped his eyes.

The sight of him crying was sexy. I could've gotten pregnant at that very moment.

"Why wouldn't I want to raise my own child, Deneiro? You never told me what happened to your parents," I told him.

"Why else did you think you didn't meet them? Enough of that." He quickly changed the subject and stood up. "Are you ready?" He grabbed my hand.

This man was really serious.

We went upstairs to create Money's baby. This was far from the other times we had sex. This was passionate. This was what I called making love. After it was all done and over with, Money told me he had to go back to see his brother.

"I'll be back, Doll. Okay?"

"Okay," I sighed.


Mari came knocking at the door maybe an hour later. She was shook up.

"Doll, there's no way I'm staying in that house," she said.

I could totally understand why she wouldn't want to. I led her to the couch.

"Are you cool, Mari?" I questioned.

"Doll, man, they pulled up to the car, and they pointed the gun at his head. I was screaming so loud, and then the other one came and put one to my head and told me to shut the fuck up. The one on Cash's side told him to give him everything." She was in tears. "He wasn't budging, so they shot him."

She started sniffing. "Then he came over to me and opened my door and pulled me out. He told me if I didn't show him where it was, he was going to kill me too. I had no choice." She was balling at this point.

I just sat there looking at her. I felt sorry for my girl, because not only was her man down, but now the Malattos would be at her neck too.

"They're going to kill me, Doll!" she cried out.

I guess she read my mind, because I was thinking the same thing. I just kept telling her everything would be okay, but in the back of my head I questioned what I was saying. She said she needed to go to our dorm to get some clothes because she wasn't getting anything out of Cash's house.

I was in my pajamas and she was in a sweat suit, so, in other words, I was looking tacky and she wasn't. I didn't care, though. I agreed to go with her, as is. We pulled up to our dorm, and there were so many people in front of the building. We walked past them, and that was when I noticed Kita mean mugging me.

I turned around to ask if there was a problem, but she just smacked her lips. I took that as a "There's a problem, but I don't want no problems." When we opened the door to our dorm room and I flicked the lights on, we realized it barely had anything in it, being that we had most of our stuff at Money's and Cash's houses. Mari went through the few things she did have there and grabbed a notebook and two outfits that went with the sandals she had on and stuffed them in a book bag.

"Ready," she said while looking around our vacant dorm room.

"All right. Let's go," I said as I opened the door. When I opened it, there stood Kita and Ona.

"Why the fuck are y'all at our door?" Mari asked with much attitude.

"I mean, damn, if it's a fight, let us know," I snapped. "We don't got time to be prolonging this beef. Kita, if you wanna get it off yo' chest, then do so." This bitch really irritated me, and although I had no problem with her, she was making me want to fight her.

"I just wanna know why my name is in your mouth, Doll," Kita said.

I figured this was her way of starting some other shit so it didn't seem like she was fighting over Money. I just punched her. Hell, that was what she wanted, anyway.

She grabbed my hair and swung me around. The girl was definitely strong. When she let me go, I hit the wall really hard and slid down. As she made her way over to me, Mari kicked her in the back, causing her to fall over. I got up, wrapped my hand around her sew in, and proceeded to punch her in her shit.

Ona hit me in my mouth, causing me to let go of Kita. Mari started whupping her, but being hit that hard from the blind had fucked me up. Next thing I knew, Kita was stomping me. A few boys came and broke it up. They told us to go outside and square up, so that was what we did.

When we got outside under the streetlight, I saw that Kita's face was so fucked up, but I planned to do more damage. I thought of all the shit I had gone through, pretended that she was Imani and took off on her ass. I never stopped swinging or holding on to her collar. I know she was hitting me back, but I couldn't feel it, or was I too pissed to feel it? When I finally let go, she dropped to the ground.

Ona ran over to aid her. I hulked and spit on both of them. Ona stood up, ready to go to war, but Mari hit her so hard, she dropped. Mari grabbed her book bag, and we fled the scene. I knew if it hadn't been for Mari, my ass would have been whupped in that dorm, but ifs and buts didn't count in fights, so therefore, I had the victory.

When we got inside my house, we just lay on the couch. We were worn out. We already knew what tomorrow had in store for us, sore muscles.

"Damn, every trip," Mari said, shaking her head.

"Right. Like why these bitches hating so tough?" I replied.

"Girl, I don't know, but can a bitch live?"

I just shook my head. Mari no longer seemed sad about Cash's situation, but then again, so much had just taken place, I couldn't be too sure. We both were hungry, but neither of us felt like cooking.

We ordered a pizza, talked a little bit more, and eventually she dozed off. I covered her up, and then I retired to my room.

Money and I were eating at an Italian restaurant called La Grotta, talking about our future plans. The waitress brought us our drinks, and then two members of the Malatto family came in and grabbed a seat with us. I was shocked that they were so bold.

One was older, and the other was a little younger. They both wore expensive Armani suits. I was nervous as hell, and Money seemed a little uneasy too. I could tell.

"How do you do, Money?" the older one asked.

"I'm cool. How you?" Money asked and then took a sip of his drink.

"Well, I was doing good until I heard your brother got shot and his girlfriend gave away our shit," he said calmly.

Money just shook his head.

"Now, I personally respect Cash for taking a bullet for our product and our money," the younger-looking one admitted. "But that bitch," he said while shaking his head, "she got to go, Money. That's how the game goes."

Now I was shitting bricks. I prayed they didn't kill my girl.

"By the way, you know that put your brother in fifty thousand dollars' worth of fucking debt," the older one added calmly.

"Now, we know Cash can't get it . . . and you *are* your brother's keeper, right?" The younger one laughed.

"Hell yeah, I am, and I'll get it back. Just don't go fucking with my little brother." Money was serious as hell. "How long y'all need?" he asked them while eyeing the younger one. I guess he intimidated him, because he turned away.

"Because we really love you two, we'll give it two weeks. Can you do that?" the younger one said and looked at Money for an answer.

"Yeah. Now, can y'all excuse me and my fiancée? We're trying to have a romantic dinner," Money said, sounding annoyed.

They got up and left. They didn't push their seats back in.

I thought Money would give me the rundown when they left, but he didn't. We continued to eat in total silence for at least twenty minutes.

Finally, he grabbed my hand while scooting closer to me. "Baby, don't worry. We cool. We're safe, and nothing's going to happen to us. You and my seed are going to be taken care of," he said while rubbing my undeveloped stomach.

"Money, we don't even know if I'm pregnant." I laughed, trying to erase my nervousness.

"If you not today, you will be by tonight." He chuckled before grabbing my face and kissing me.

"I love you, baby," I said and smiled.

"I love you too, Sommer," he said back.

On our way home, I kept thinking about what could
possibly happen to Mari. I figured her best bet was to
flee to Toledo. I also wondered how in the hell Money
was going to come up with fifty thousand dollars in
only two weeks. I decided to put that in the back of my
mind. If my man said he could get it, then hell, he was
going to get it.

Money wanted to go up to the hospital to visit his
brother, so that was what we did. When we got in the
hospital room, Gip, Jasmine, Mari, and Tionna were all
around his bedside. Honestly, Cash was looking even
worse. I had a gut feeling he wouldn't last a week.

"How's he doing?" Money asked. His whole mood
had changed, so I knew he felt the same way I did.

Everyone left his question unanswered. Money
walked up to Cash's bed and stood there staring at
him. Everyone sat in silence, watching Money rub his
brother's waves on his head.

"Cash, man, I know you're fighting for me . . . but if
you're . . . tired, then it's safe to just let go. Just make
sure you watch over me, 'cause this world is wicked."
Tears fell from his eyes. "I don't like seeing you suffer
like this, so if you feel like you want to give up, then
go ahead. Tell Mom and Pops I'll be there sooner or
later. I'm going to hold you down. Forever my brother's
keeper," Money said, then kissed him on the forehead.

He turned to us with lost hope. He shook his head,
and I ran over to console him.

I knew all too well how it felt to lose so much. Money
had lost everything in his bloodline, and I knew that us
having a baby would mean a lot to him. I prayed that

Cash wouldn't leave us, because I didn't think Money would know how to take it.

Gip got up so that Money could sit down. Money sat with his face in his hands.

All of a sudden a loud beep went off, and Cash flatlined. Doctors came rushing in, and they told us to go sit in the waiting room. We all knew this was bad.

Money sat next to me, zoned out. His heart was broken, and I felt so bad for him. We sat there, waiting and waiting. After twenty minutes a male and female doctor came out, and by the look on the their faces, we all knew it was bad news.

"Deneiro Browner . . ." said one of the doctors.

Money looked up and then went over to the doctors. The male doctor had a clipboard in his hand. I followed, of course.

"I'm sorry. We tried everything, but there was nothing more we could do. We tried reviving him, but he didn't give us a response," the female doctor explained.

Money breathed in and out.

"I'm sorry, but Chase Browner didn't make it," the male doctor said. He tried to say other things, but Money broke down right there in the waiting room. He didn't take it well at all. His knees hit the floor as he burst out crying.

"Why, God? Why?" he asked. He was angry.

Mari was crying on Tionna's shoulder. Jasmine shed a few tears too. Gip was in her lap, going through it. I held Money tight and let him let everything out. I desperately needed God to send me an angel.


I got up bright and early the next morning. I wanted to make Money breakfast, but we had nothing to make. I snuck a kiss on Money's cheek before I slid out of bed.

I slipped on a sweat suit and carefully crept downstairs as he slept peacefully. I grabbed my keys off the couch and headed to the grocery store.

I hopped in my Jag, started the ignition, and backed out of the driveway. The nearest grocery store was only ten minutes away. Luckily, I found a close parking spot there. As I grabbed a cart, I started reminding myself of the things that I needed. I went down almost every aisle, grabbing all the things I would need to make my man a hearty breakfast. After I was certain I had everything, I headed to the checkout line. I spotted Tonya as we almost crossed paths.

"Hey, Doll," she said with a box of cereal in her hand.

"Hey, Tonya. How are you?"

"Fine," she said blankly. Then she looked at me. "I heard what happened to Cash." Then she looked away.

I shook my head. I really didn't want to touch that subject.

"I understand you don't want to talk about it." She placed her hand on my shoulder. "Doll, watch your friends," she said as she began to walk away.

I turned around. "What do you mean?" I questioned.

She turned to face me. "Just be careful who you call your friends." She shrugged her shoulders. "You know, choose your friends wisely." Then she walked away. "Have a good breakfast," she yelled back. I figured she had noticed the breakfast items in my cart.

She didn't know enough about me to warn me like she had. I didn't know what to think. Who exactly was she talking about?

I proceeded to the checkout line. While the cashier rang up my items, I looked out the window and noticed Tonya climbing into a navy Charger. She sped off, and I replayed our conversation again and again. Who was she referring to?

She left me lost in my thoughts.

# Chapter 16

Money was cooped up in our bedroom for a whole week straight. He didn't eat, he didn't sleep, and he barely spoke. I washed him up and cooked him meals every day, although he refused to eat. I didn't know what else to do!

I didn't know how he was ever going to get that money in one week. I called my bank to find out what I had in my savings account. I figured I had to have a nice lump sum in there. Debo had wired me 25 percent of Unc's money while I lived in Toledo ,and it had never stopped when I moved here. When I called the bank, the associate told me I had $1.5 million in my account, with a pending deposit of one hundred thousand coming from Toledo, Ohio.

I was amazed! I couldn't believe I had that much money. I had to call back to make sure I had heard correctly. I had never checked to see how much I had in my account in all the years I had had it. It had never mattered, because I had always had a baller to take care of me. This must have been the angel God sent me.

Money fell asleep, and I wasn't going to bother him. He needed to rest. I cleaned up the house, and my sister came to my mind. I decided to call her.

"Hey, Doll darling," she said happily.

"Hey, hon! What you up to?" I asked.

"Nothing. Just doing my homework, ready for school to be out," she answered. "What about you?"

"Nothing. I just miss you . . . haven't talked to you in a little while. Maybe we should hook up soon." I really did miss my sister.

"Okay, cool." She was excited.

I thought about our last conversation, when she abruptly rushed me off the phone. I hadn't forgotten what I heard a man say in the background that day, so I was going to bring up the "See where he at" incident the next time we did get together.

I heard noises upstairs, so I assumed Money was up. I went upstairs to find him in the bathroom, taking a piss. I sat on the bed and watched him.

"What's up?" he asked dryly as he went to lie back down.

"Money, you've been in this room all week long. You have to understand that your brother is in a better place." I wanted Money to live his life and not shut himself up in the bedroom.

"Man, I got to get up and make this money," he said as he got up to search for something to put on.

"I got the money." I grabbed his arm.

He looked at me, puzzled.

"Yeah, I got it, baby. I'll go get it tonight, and you can take it to them in the morning," I assured him.

"How? Where you get the money from? Who?" he questioned.

I smiled at him. "Unc put some money up for me. We can use that."

"Baby, you sure? I don't want to take from—"

"Baby, I swear it's cool," I assured him. I knew that I would still have more than enough money in my account after withdrawing what he needed.

He sat back down, grabbed my face, and kissed me. "Baby, you're always there for me," he said as he stared into my eyes.

Of course, I was going to hold him down, no matter the weather. I was hoping that this money would make them forget about trying to kill Mari. I was still a little nervous when it came to her.

"We gather here today to lay Chase Lamar Browner to rest. He's been with us for twenty long years," the preacher said after we all gathered at the cemetery.

There were a lot of familiar and unfamiliar faces. Money stood there with a blank expression on his face. He didn't utter a word. Mari's face was covered in tears. We tried our best to console her, but our trying to help didn't work.

After the burial, we all headed toward the limo. Two black suburban trucks pulled up. We all stopped to see who it was. We didn't have to wait for long, because four Italians hopped out.

"Money . . . Gip," one of them said as he signaled them over to one of their trucks.

The rest of us continued to the limo. I hurried over to Mari, who was shaking. I wanted to make sure she was all right.

"They're going to kill me," she told me as we got into the limo. She started crying even harder.

I watched Gip and Money's interaction with the Italians through the limo's window. I wanted to know what was going on. A few moments later Gip and Money walked back over to our limo and got in.

"What did they say?" Jasmine immediately asked. Money looked out the window without any words to say.

Gip sighed. "They said Mari got to leave town." He looked down.

"What? Why?" Jasmine wanted all the details.

"Either that or they're going to kill her. They're giving her a week," Gip explained. He had anger in his voice. "Damn, quit asking so many fucking questions." Gip was obviously annoyed.

It was quiet for the rest of the ride. We all either looked down at our laps or out the window.

At least they had spared her life.


"I don't want to leave, guys," Mari told us sadly as we walked around the mall.

"I know. I don't want you to go, either." I put my arm around her.

Her boyfriend had been murdered, and now they were making her leave town. The girl had no time to even heal . . . but it was better than being dead.

Mari was set to head back to Toledo the next day. Though I didn't want her to leave, I didn't want her to die, either. I loved her like a sister, and we had built a bond that couldn't be broken.

"Well, for your last day here, we're going to live it up with you," Tionna said, trying to remain positive. We all knew that "living it up" meant hitting up the club and other fancy places.

After we left the mall, we went to Jasmine's condo. Aunt Sasha had done the décor, so her place was definitely top-notch.

The four of us got to gossiping and laughing like we did in the good ole days.

"I'm pregnant," I blurted out.

"Say what?" Jasmine spit out her drink. "How far are you?"

"About a month." I smiled.

I was finally giving Money the child that he wanted. I couldn't wait to get home to tell my baby the good news. All my girls started congratulating me, and Jasmine started planning the baby shower.

"Yeah, we're going to have the baby shower at Justin's." She had it all figured out.

"Jasmine, she's only a month or so. Calm down," Tionna stated.

We were all happy, except for Mari. I was sure she was happy for me, but she was dwelling on the fact that she wouldn't be in Atlanta to watch the baby grow in my belly.


"Babe, I'm home!" Money yelled out as he walked through the door.

"I'm in the den," I replied.

Finally, I was ready to tell him the big news. I had held the news from him for over two weeks now.

He came in looking good as ever in his Polo fit. Money was just beginning to get his life back to normal.

"What's up, baby?" he asked, licking his lips.

"Sit down." I patted the couch so he could sit next to me. He sat down and turned toward me.

"Guess what," I said excitedly.

"What?" he asked.

"I'm pregnant." I smiled. He grabbed me and hugged me tight.

"Man, that's all I needed to hear. All I need is a hundred thousand more, and I'm out of the game for good," he said while kissing me.

Our doorbell rang, and Money got up to answer it. It was Gip and two other dudes at the door. I could barely make out what they were talking about. I heard only Gip talking. At one point he said, "Yeah, the Gib boys." I heard a few "all rights," and then Gip and the two dudes were out the door.

I knew how the conversation must have gone. They must have figured out where the Gib boys hung out, and they were planning to retaliate.

Money made his way back to the den, where I had remained.

I stepped in front of him. "I hope you're not planning to do anything dumb." I was pissed.

"Man, gone. You just wait 'til I get back," he said, moving me out of the way.

"I don't understand, Money! You're going to be a dad. You don't have time to be doing dumb shit!" I had my fingers in his face by this time.

He snatched me up. "Look, Doll. I owe this to my brother, so understand this and get the fuck out the way." He pushed me a little. I sat down in disbelief.

Money went to our bedroom. I followed him. He put on all black. He went in our safe and got his two Glocks out. He put his bullets in the guns and stuck both of them in his pants. He went downstairs and sat on the couch and waited for his ride.

I stayed upstairs in bed and cried. I kept thinking that something was going to happen to him.

Then I heard a horn beep outside. I ran to the window to see who was picking him up.

"I love you!" Money yelled from downstairs. Through the window, I watched him walk out the door. He got into a black truck.

I went back to cry on the bed. Jasmine called my phone shortly after Money left.

"What's up, Jas?" I said in my "I've been crying" voice.

"Girl, that stupid muthafucka's going to get shot or something." She had been crying too.

"Well, you should come over here so we can wait on them to get back," I told her.

"Okay, I'm on the way," she replied.

I decided to call Mari while I waited for Jasmine's arrival. The phone rang a few times before she answered.

"Hey, hon! How are things down there?" she asked.

"I'm fine. How's the Glass City?" I asked.

"It's cool. Girl, people been saying that Zae's been looking for you . . . or he wants you . . . something like that." She sounded concerned.

"That man is crazy. I'm not worried about him," I said, disregarding the information she had just given me. We chopped it up a little more, and she ended up telling me that Brian's baby was handsome and that he was coming here next month.

"You got to come down here soon," she said.

"Yeah, I will. I have to close that deal on Unc's house," I said while twirling my hair. The doorbell rang, and I knew that it was Jasmine. "Well, sweetie, it's late, so I'll talk to you tomorrow," I said, ending our conversation.

"Okay, and take care of my baby," she said and chuckled.

I opened the door to find Jasmine and Fall.

"Well, I wasn't expecting you, Fall." I laughed.

"Yeah, I know, but you scums always seem to leave me out," she said. We all sat down on the couch.

"So, Fall, what's been up?" I questioned.

"Nothing really, since school's been out. I heard I was about to be an auntie." She smiled.

"Sooner than later," I said while holding my stomach.

"Do my mama know you're out this late?" Jasmine questioned her.

Now that she mentioned it, it was unlike Aunt Sasha to let a sixteen-year-old out this late.

"I'm about to be seventeen, guys. Damn, give me a break," Fall said, annoyed.

"I'm just saying. If Mama don't know you're here, you're going to have to get a break, all right?" Jasmine looked her up and down.

"Her neck's going to get a break," I said, and we all laughed.

I looked at Fall, and I saw me all over. She dressed, acted, and even talked like me. Her mouth was fly, and she was prissy. My aunt Sasha had told me that Fall looked up to me, but it had never been apparent to me until now. I prayed that she would choose a different path than the one I took, because the streets I had been down had a bunch of dead ends and detours.

Her phone rang, and by the way she was talking, I could tell it was a boy.

Jasmine and I shared a glance at each other, and then Fall got up to leave the room. Jasmine waited until Fall was totally out of our sight.

"Girl, your damn sister is hot in the pants. She wants to be you so bad, it's sad," she said while shaking her head.

"What makes you think that?" I asked, as if I couldn't see for myself.

"Bitch, did you not see her? The girl admires you and wants to be Doll Jr. You should really sit and talk to her, because if you don't . . . the rest is history," Jasmine warned.

I sat there in deep thought. Fall had changed a lot since the first day I landed in Atlanta. I knew the time was coming soon when I would have that long talk with her.

Jasmine decided to call her mom to tell her where Fall was. Aunt Sasha was very upset with Fall. She told Jasmine to bring Fall home immediately because she had an ass whupping with her name on it.

"Well, I got to get her home," Jasmine said.

Fall had finished her phone conversation and now stood there with her arms crossed.

"Fall, we'll link up once you get off punishment," I said. I was certain she was going to get on punishment.

After they left, I went upstairs to bed. My phone began to buzz and ring in my head. I grew excited, thinking it was Money, but when I looked at the phone and saw that it was an unfamiliar Ohio number, I just knew who it was. I hesitated to answer it, but I knew that if I didn't, then he would call a million times.

"Yes, Markaylo," I answered. I was annoyed that he was still bothering me.

"Doll, I miss you. Why don't you come home? I know I fucked up, but, baby, everything will be different this time," he pleaded.

"Zae, why don't you get it? It's over. We are done. Can you please leave me the hell alone?"

"Listen, bitch, if I can't have you, then no one will. I told you that you was all I had, and you just say "Fuck me" and think that I'm going to let you live happily ever after with another nigga. I'll kill you before I let that happen," he said.

Chills ran up and down my spine. I kind of figured he was just talking, but being that he was turning into somebody that I didn't know, I wasn't so sure. I hung the phone up and looked around the room. He had me scared straight. I lay down on the bed. I was tired. I looked at the clock, which read 3:00 A.M. . . . and still no word from Money.


Money walked in at eight in the morning.

"Why are you just now walking in the door?" I was furious.

"Baby, I had to handle this business," he said while kissing me on my neck.

He had on a totally different outfit. I knew they must have killed somebody or done something of that nature since he had changed his wardrobe.

He did his usual routine. He kissed me, hopped in the shower, and came back to bed with me. I was annoyed but happy that I could finally sleep and not worry about where he was or what he was doing, because he was right here with me.

He lay there, naked, holding me close. It felt so perfect, and it took no time for me to drift off into dreamland.


"Yes, Aunt Sasha, I know she's been acting up."

I was on the phone with Aunt Sasha, who was fuming with fire. I knew she was ready to wash her hands of Fall. She told me that Fall had been sneaking out and being fast, and that she was on the verge of killing her.

"I'll deal with her," I told my aunt. I decided to meet with Fall to let her know this life was not the life for her.

Fall was young, and she had no idea about all I had been through. I didn't think she truly cared, either. She just saw me living the life, but she had no clue what I had gone through to get where I was. I guess nobody had ever told her that everything that glitters ain't gold. I was far from it. If the truth be told, I was a little rusty.

Fall and I met up at the Waffle House, one of her most favorite places. She had on the tightest pants I had ever seen and a belly shirt. My eyes almost fell out their sockets. She sat down with an attitude.

"Do you think that's appropriate?" I asked in disgust.

"Yeah. Why wouldn't it be?" She laughed. I just shook my head. Couldn't tell this girl nothing. I decided to start from scratch.

"Why are you giving Aunt Sasha such a hard time?" I asked her.

"She be tripping, seriously. I be trying to be cool, but she just don't get it," she said, looking innocent.

"What do you mean by 'She just don't get it'? You're too young, and I can see you're trying to live this life, but, sweetie, there is no future in this," I told her in all honesty.

The more we talked, the more it appeared to me that the things I was telling her weren't sticking. I completely gave up on her. If she didn't know by now, she would soon find out.

She went on to tell me about her boyfriend . . . that they were serious.

"His name is Jamal."

That name sounded so familiar, but I just couldn't put my finger on it.

She kept going. "Yeah, his brother just got shot and killed a few nights ago. My poor baby's down," she said while taking a bite out of her waffle.

It made perfect sense. My sister was sleeping with the enemy. This was too much to swallow.

"So your sister's fucking with one of the Gib boys?" Money was asking me twenty questions. I was tired of answering them and just plain old tired, in general.

"Baby, I'm tired. How about we resume this in the morning?" I was hoping like hell he would agree.

"Okay," he said while kissing me on my forehead.

I was almost two months pregnant, and the sleepiness of pregnancy was taking over earlier than expected.

I tossed and I turned all night long. When I woke up to get a drink of water, Money was nowhere to be found. I headed downstairs and heard an unexpected guest. It was Gip.

*Why in the hell is he here, when he should be home with Jasmine?* I stayed on the steps and listened in on their conversation.

"So both Roscoe and Mickey are done deals?" Gip asked Money while sipping Grey Goose straight from the bottle.

"That's good we took care of that. I think I'm getting out the game for good, man," Money said.

"Word? You should, though. You about to have a seed, and nothing good can come out of these streets." Gip had Money's back no matter what he decided to do. "I'm about to go over Jude house. I'll catch up with you later," Gip said as he got up from the table.

I hurried up the stairs.

That nigga had lost his mind, cheating on my cousin, and he definitely had some nerve. I was going to put an end to that as soon as I opened my eyes the next day. There was nothing that was going to keep me from ratting his black ass out. Jasmine was way too good to him, and if I wasn't mistaken, Jude was a stripper.


I pulled up to Jasmine's house a little after ten. I had already broke the news to her over the phone, but for some odd reason, she wanted me to come over.

When I walked in, Keyshia Cole's "I Remember" was on full blast. Now I knew for a fact that she had shed a few tears over the situation, because everyone knew Keyshia would take you there with her songs.

"Jas!" I hollered. She was nowhere in sight. I decided to check upstairs. When I reached her bedroom, I saw that she was lying in her bed . . . in tears.

"Jasmine, come on, sweetie. Pull it together." I was sad that she was sad.

"Five years, Sommer! And this is how he do me? I want to go to the bitch's job," She gave me that look that told me she was not playing.

Being a lady in love was a hard job, because situations like this caused you to act unladylike. If Jasmine wanted to go to her job, then that was exactly what we were going to do.

I was already dressed for the occasion. I had on a comfortable Rocawear sweat suit. Jasmine put on something similar and pulled her long hair into a ponytail. We hopped in her black Maybach with tinted windows and were on our way to Magic City.

She turned the music up high and put on her game face. I already knew if Jude was there, she was definitely in a whole lot of trouble. I was praying we didn't catch a case.

# Chapter 17

We parked Jasmine's Maybach and made our way inside the club. A lot of the niggas we passed grabbed our arms, but we were on a mission. There was no time to get distracted by guys we could do nothing with. We sat in the front row and waited until Jude hit the stage.

A waitress came over to us. "You ladies drinking anything?" she asked.

"Yeah, I need two shots of Goose and whatever she's drinking," Jasmine said.

"I'm cool." I wasn't in the mood to drink. Somebody had to be sober, and I guessed it had to be me.

The waitress came back with Jasmine's shots, and Jasmine threw them down her throat like it was nothing. I just sat back. I could tell this was tearing a hole in Jasmine's heart. There were a couple of people who came over by us, trying to flirt, but we quickly dismissed them.

The DJ got on the mic. "Y'all make some noise for my girl. She sexy and a little rude. Niggas, get up and tip the infamous Jude!"

U.S.D.A.'s "Throw This Money" came on, and Jude came out. She wasn't what I would call pretty. She was thick, and her weave was definitely on point. Other than that, there wasn't much to say about her. By the response of the crowd, I could tell she was everybody's favorite.

When the light hit her, the niggas were bucking, but they weren't bucking for no reason. They started getting out of their seats and making their way to the stage. We decided to stand up and get close too. When we got all the way to the stage, we spotted Gip.

"Oh, hell no! I'm about to whup his ass," Jasmine yelled as she grabbed my arm. We made our way over to Gip. He spotted us. By then, it was too late to hide.

"What in the fuck are you doing here, Gip? You fucking Jude, so you feel you need to support her trifling ass, you nothing-ass bitch!" Jasmine punched him in his nose.

He grabbed her arm. "Jasmine, calm down." He tried to calm her down.

"Don't tell me to calm down, you sick dick bastard!" She had tears in her eyes.

"Let's go! I don't want everybody in my business," he said as he pulled her in the direction of the door.

"Your business? Did you care about business when you was fucking that one-dollar ho?" Jasmine screamed.

He decided the only way to get Jasmine out of the club was to pick her up, so he did. When we got outside, he told me to drive his car home and he was going to drive hers. I did as I was told.


Money and I sat in the waiting room, waiting for me to get called back to see my ob-gyn. It kind of made me sad, because it seemed like yesterday when I was doing this same routine with Zae.

I sat there daydreaming about how things could have been if Imani hadn't ruined my life. It was crazy how the ones closest to you seemed to hurt you first or worse than the ones who you couldn't stand. Life had lessons, and I felt as though I had learned them all.

Money had turned back into the man I fell in love with. I looked at my engagement ring and then over at him. I couldn't wait to have his child. I wanted to spend the rest of my life with that man, even though we had had our share of ups and downs. I had never caught him cheating, or I'd never heard about it. And even though life had kicked my ass, it was doing me lovely now.

"Sommer Jones, you may come back," the nurse said as she stood in the doorway. Money and I stood up and followed her to my examination room.

"Sit on the table, and Dr. Miller will be with you shortly," she said with a smile.

I sat on the table, and Money sat on a chair. I instantly began to daydream again. I was thinking about what my baby would have looked like if it were Zae's. Our baby would have been almost one year old at this point. It was a hurtful situation.

"What you thinking about, baby?" Money asked me, snapping me out of my thoughts.

"Oh, I was just thinking about a few things, but nothing too big."

I decided not to tell him what I was actually thinking about, because I knew he would accuse me of thinking about Zae.

My doctor came in smiling.

"Hey, Sommer and Deneiro. How are you guys?"

"We're fine," I said, answering for the both of us.

She told me to lie down, and I did. Then she applied a cold gel to my stomach and went to work.

"You're about four months," she said as she looked at the screen.

"Four," Money repeated.

"I thought I was more like two." I was confused.

"No, you're definitely four months. Your due date is Christmas, December twenty-fifth, two thousand and nine," she continued.

I was happy and relieved to know that this pregnancy was going to be over sooner than we had planned.

"Do you want to know what you're having?" she asked.

"Yeah." Money was standing up by this point.

"It's a boy." My doctor smiled.

We had never discussed what we wanted. We just knew we wanted a baby. I figured Money was happy, just because a lot of guys wanted their first child to be a boy, and I was happy I could give him that.

She gave us a little more information and some health tips and told us we were free to leave. I started putting my clothes on.

"Four months," Money repeated once more.

I just couldn't believe it. I really had had no clue I was pregnant for that long.

"Are you happy it's a boy?" I asked him while zipping my pants.

"Yeah, but it really didn't matter to me. We're naming him after me, right?" He already knew the answer to that question.

"You already know how I feel about your ghetto-ass name." I laughed, but at the same time I was serious.


We went to Mr. Chow's to celebrate the news. We ordered our usual, then discussed our future.

"So have you planned the wedding?" Money asked. He bit into his steak.

"No, but I'm unsure if we should get married before or after the baby." I was confused.

"Well, whatever you decide to do, you know where to get the money from," he said, smiling.

This was the life. I had the best man God had created, and we were going to make a family. I would be able to give my son the life I had never had.

"Thanks again for that money, baby. I'm going to give it back to you." He was staring me in the eyes. I knew he was serious.

"No, baby. You don't have to. We're a team." I had my hand on top of his. "This is what we do. We look out for each other." I smiled.

"Man, I swear I love you. I don't know what I'd do without you," he said, kissing me softly.

I couldn't wait to be Mrs. Deneiro Lamont Browner.


I was lounging over at Jasmine's place, listening to Usher's *Confessions* CD while she cleaned her house from top to bottom. She had OCD, because the girl didn't like anything dirty or out of place.

"How about you mop a floor?" She was holding a mop while looking at me. I laughed and got up to mop her kitchen floor.

I started rocking to "Yeah!" as I got her floor to sparkle.

Her doorbell rang loudly, so I went to answer it. It was Tionna, with a bottle of Hennessy and a bottle of Goose. Too bad I couldn't drink. Tionna came in smiling from ear to ear. She was definitely happy about something or someone. Jasmine turned the music down.

"Why the hell you so happy?" Jasmine asked as she sat on the couch.

"Well, if y'all must know . . . I got me a new friend that I think I might like!" She was all smiles.

"Or your ass got you some cutty and you found some dick you might like." Jasmine laughed as she went to go retrieve two glasses for herself and Tionna.

"Whatever! Y'all always thinking nasty. Get yo' minds out of the gutter." She poured the drinks when Jasmine returned with the glasses, and rolled her eyes in the process.

I just sat and laughed. Tionna proceeded to tell us about her new friend, Mike. She claimed she hadn't done anything with him yet, but Jasmine and I knew better. Tionna was just like a nigga. She had to try it out first before she got to know it.

My phone began to ring. It was a 419 area code, so I knew it was somebody from Toledo.

"Turn that down," I told Jasmine, who held the CD player remote. "Hello?" I said in my professional voice.

"Hi, Sommer Jones. This is the Realtor Maggie Voloski. I'm just letting you know that I have an interested buyer for your place on Manchester who is fine with paying the full price. I just wanted to call to let you know that we are very close to sealing the deal, so get your plane ticket ready," she joked.

"Okay. That's good." I was excited.

"Well. I'll be getting in touch with you by the end of this week. Have a great day," she said before we ended our call.

That was definitely a good thing. Unc would definitely be set after this.

My girls and I had decided to get our normal pedicures and manicures at the Glambar. I was soaking my feet in water when I looked over at Jasmine.

"Have you and Gip set aside y'all differences yet?" I asked her.

"Hell no. I just don't think I can trust him anymore. What's a relationship without trust?" She had a point. If you didn't have trust, you always had to worry. There was no happiness in a situation filled with doubt.

"Hey, ladies!" Fall said as she pranced through the door. She was more presentable then she had been the day I met up with her. She sat down next to me.

"You came to get done up?" I asked her.

"No, I just saw y'all cars, and I decided to come speak," she said. She got quiet for a second and looked at her phone and started texting. "Actually, I'm 'bout to leave with my man."

I just screwed my face up in disgust. She was a fool. She was young and naive and thought that she knew it all, but she was as clueless as hell!

"What was that face for, Doll? Are we jealous?" Fall stood up, eyeing me.

No, she didn't.

"Sis, why in the hell would I be jealous of you?" I was offended. "Where you're at . . . I've already been, and like I told you before, the life you're trying to live is a dangerous one." I wanted to slap her so bad, but I had just gotten my nails done. "And to answer your dumb-ass question, no! I'm not jealous of your skinny, anorexic, sickly-looking ass," I yelled.

My friends kind of giggled.

The little girl chose the right one, because unlike Aunt Sasha, I would put my hands on her and would never have to do it again. The beat down I would deliver would be one that haunted her for a lifetime. She was seventeen trying to be twenty-one, and her mentality was still at a fourteen-year-old's level. She'd have to learn the hard way.

Her phone rang. She still had a dumb look on her face as she looked down at her phone.

"I'm on my way out," she told the person on her line. Before she left, she rolled her eyes and slammed the door behind her.

\*\*\*

Fall hopped in the car with her Gib boy, and they made their way to Decatur. They never noticed the car following them, because they were too wrapped up in each other.

"Baby, you missed me?" Jamal Gib asked.

"You know I did," Fall said with the biggest smile ever. "You know my sis is hating on us tough, right? She just jealous, 'cause her and Money don't got what we got," Fall said as she looked out the window.

"Wait, what's her nigga's name?" Jamal Gib had to make sure he had heard right.

"Money?"

Fall gave him her full attention. "His name is Money. Why? Do you know him?" she questioned.

"Yeah, he's one of the niggas that killed my fucking brother Mickey and my cousin Roscoe. I need you to help me set him up." Jamal saw an opportunity.

Fall sat and thought about it. She didn't want any parts of that street war. Money was her sister's love. There was no way she could set him up.

"You going to do it or not? Because there's a lot of bitches who would. I mean, if you the down-ass bitch you claim to be, then you will," he said. He was using reverse psychology, which most older guys used on young girls.

Fall felt offended. She was a down bitch, and she loved Jamal. She would do anything for him. She'd be damned if he had another female do it instead of her. There was no way she was going to let that happen.

"What exactly do you want me to do?" she asked, not really wanting to know.

"Just get back cool with your sister, and then find out when it's just the two of them. We're going to go there then. When you find out, let me know." He had it all figured out. He couldn't wait to tell the Gib boys about his master plan.

"You're not going to kill Doll, are you?" She had to know, because if that was on the agenda, she was not going to go through with it.

"No, baby. Why would I harm your sister?" he said in his sincere voice.

In the back of his vengeful mind, he didn't give a fuck. He would kill her and whoever else was affiliated with Money's crew. They didn't care about killing his brother or his cousin, so why would he care?

He was satisfied.

The sweet revenge.

I sat at my vanity, curling my hair. The ladies and I had decided to have a ladies' night and do some catching up. We all had a taste for some Justin's, so that was where we were going. After putting spirals in my hair, I soaked in the tub. Pregnancy was taking a toll on me, but it was giving me some junk in my trunk.

After soaking for half an hour, I smelled like cucumber and melon. My favorite scent. I dried my body off and then took a glimpse of myself in my body-length mirror. I had no stretch marks yet, and I prayed that I developed none.

I heard Money in the bedroom, on his phone. Moments later he was walking into the bathroom. He grabbed me from behind while kissing on my neck.

"Missed you, baby," he whispered in my ear.

"I missed you too," I said.

"You wanna show me how much?"

"Money," I said as I turned around to face him, "I'm about to go out with the ladies."

"What that mean?" he asked, with a puppy dog look on his face. I smiled. He was so sexy, I couldn't resist.

"Make it quick," I said as I helped him take off his green and white Ralph Lauren polo. He unbuckled his khaki shorts. They dropped to his feet. He stepped out of the shorts and his boxers. Now he was wearing nothing but socks.

"Come on, baby," he said, leading me to the bedroom. When I walked into our room, the lights were off and candles were lit all around our bed. We stopped at the foot of the bed.

"What's the occasion?" I asked. I looked him in his eyes, waiting for an answer.

"I love you, and I like seeing you smile," he said as he pushed me on the bed, "so show me that you love me and make me smile."

He didn't have to ask twice. I sat up to put his dick in my mouth and went to work. I put it all in and eased it out, slow stroking his manhood with my mouth.

He moaned while holding the back of my head. I knew he was into it, but after twenty minutes of that, my neck was getting tired. I stopped. He turned me around, and I tooted it up for him. He went in slow, and then he got in the motion. He sped it up, gripping my hair and smacking my ass.

It felt like we were teenagers getting it on. We normally made slow, passionate love. This was different, but I liked it.

"Let me know when you 'bout to cum," he moaned.

"I'm about to," I said.

He pulled his dick out, flipped me over, and started devouring me. He flicked his tongue across my clit; then he sucked on it. I was on cloud nine. My body started shaking, and I began losing my mind. That was the best nut I had ever had. He came up from my love box and began kissing his way up to my lips. We kissed, and then I hopped up to get freshened up.

***

Money was worn out from the work he had put in with Doll, but there was money to be made. His crew had a meeting to find out where and how they could get rid of more of the Gib boys. His brother couldn't properly rest in peace without more of the Gib boys dying, so this meeting was a must.

After showering, he put on a navy blue Coogi sweat suit with some all-white mid-top Forces and headed out the door. He jumped in his Escalade and headed to the trap. Gip and their other four friends—Louis, Tim, Peppy, and Twan—were already there, waiting for Money's arrival.

When he walked inside, they were all on their knees, shooting dice for hundreds. Money smiled. His niggas didn't care where they were or what the occasion was; they were all about their money.

"Hey, cut that dice game short," he said, bringing the gambling to an end.

They all grabbed their money and got up to head to the dining room table. Everyone got a seat around the glass table, with open ears, ready to hear what Money had to say.

Gip started the conversation. "Well, y'all all know the Gib boys got to go," he said, looking at each one of them. They nodded their heads.

"Yeah, we eliminated two, but I want Marlen and Jamal out," Money said. They all sat and listened, taking mental notes. Money didn't care if it took his last breath; those two were going to die.

The beef between them and the Gib boys had started years ago. Back when Money and Gip were in high school, the Gib boys just never liked them and their crew. They dressed better, had all the cute girls, and were pushing nice whips. The Gib boys, on the other hand, were filthy with nothing.

Jealousy was a deadly disease, and the Gib boys were definitely jealous of Money and his boys. When they were younger, Money and his boys would box with them and play basketball against them to prove which crew was better. As they grew older and their money got longer, the hate that the Gib boys had for them grew stronger.

Money didn't understand how and when they grew the balls to try to rob his little brother, but something told him they had had inside help. No one knew where Cash lived. He had just moved there a few days before Christmas Eve. He wasn't big on company, and most of the hoes he fucked he took to hotel rooms. They were real selective when it came to taking people to their houses and their trap. They would never get caught slipping by being careless.

The meeting was adjourned, and the fellas went back to gambling . . . all but Money and Gip.

"So what you over there thinking 'bout, Big Money?" Gip asked, reading the look on Money's face.

"I think somebody set my brother up," Money said while still staring out into space.

"Word? I do too."

"Hell yeah, but who?"

They both sat there thinking long and hard. They both came up with the same thing, because in their heads the easiest way to a nigga's pocket was through one thing: a bitch.

"Man, I'll kill that ho," Gip said, referring to Mari.

"You think it was her?" Money asked. He couldn't really see Mari doing that. She seemed as if she was head over heels for Cash.

"You can never be too sure. Don't sleep on that bitch. Money talks," Gip said as he stood up to head to the dice game.

Money just sat there thinking. *I guess I got to kill that bitch too.* If that was his only choice, then so be it. Doll would be so hurt, but blood was thicker than water, and he chose his little brother over anybody.

# Chapter 18

Fall had finally come to her senses and had apologized for her embarrassing behavior. I was happy that the little girl was turning into a young lady, no matter how long it took her.

We decided to spend some sisterly time together, so we went to the movies and out to eat. It was fun, and it was well overdue. She asked more than enough questions about Money, and I figured since she wanted to be like me, she also wanted her relationship to resemble mine too. I found it cute.

"So do you and Money go on a lot of dates?" she asked while we headed back to Aunt Sasha's.

"Yeah, for the most part. We've been really busy getting stuff ready for the baby and the wedding," I said, trying to get the conversation off of us. It was like she was taking notes. It was starting to feel weird.

"Does Money leave you at home by yourself a lot?"

This chick was definitely up to something. She was too damn obvious. I just couldn't put my finger on it. We pulled up to her house, and I left her question unanswered.

When I was on my way home, Money called me.

"Yes, baby?" I said, trying to sound sexy.

"What you up to?" I could tell by the wind sound that he was in the car.

"Just left from a date with my sister," I said. I pulled up to the house and decided to sit in the car until we got off the phone.

"I don't want you around her, Doll." He wasn't playing.

"What, Deneiro? That's my only sister, so whatever you and her boyfriend got going on, that has nothing to do with us! How could you? That's my damn blood!" I was irritated and ready to hang up on him.

"I know, but, baby, they might use her to get to me. I just don't want nothing to go bad. I don't want anything to happen to you, either," he said, calming down.

I understood where he was coming from, but I could never choose a nigga over my own flesh and blood. He had to be a fool to even demand that.

We ended our conversation with "I love yous," and I made my way into the house. There was an unfamiliar car sitting across the street, but I figured it was for the neighbors. I went to lie down on the couch because I was drained. I was almost five months pregnant, and it was beginning to take a toll on me. I drifted off to sleep.

I woke up to the ringing of my phone. I had incorporated the ringing into my dream, so I almost missed the call.

"Hello.?" My voice was raspy.

"You were asleep?"

I instantly knew who it was. I tried to clear my throat. "Brian, what's up?" I was happy to hear from him.

"Nothing much. I'm in town." He sounded sexier than ever.

"Really? Well, I can't see you right now . . . but maybe we can hook up later. How long are you here for?" I was hoping a while, because I would have to sneak to see him. Only God knew how long that would take.

"Until mid-August. You got plenty of time to sneak around," he said, giggling.

"Whatever," I said and laughed, because he was right.

"That's cool. Well, let me know," he said before we hung up.

He put an everlasting smile on my face. Although him having a baby with Janeen had affected me, I had put that behind us. I had a love for him that couldn't fade. They say, "Forgive and forget." I forgave.

I had to call Mari. I told her that Brian was officially in town and I really wanted to link up with him, big tummy or not. I didn't have the slightest clue how it was going to occur.

"Don't get killed, Doll. You got a good man, and Brian ain't shit and ain't been shit." She was speaking the real. I felt her.

"I know, Mari, but come on now. It's Brian!" She knew how it was with Brian and me.

"I understand that, Doll, but that stuff ain't worth it. Brian is not worth it! Be smart, sweetie. That's all I'm saying."

She was right. I told her I loved her and that we would get together when I came to close the deal on Unc's house.

It was the Fourth of July. Money and his boys were throwing a party at Club Chaos. I was kind of upset that I couldn't attend. Besides, Money had said too much went down on the Fourth and he was not about to put his wife and son in harm's way. I didn't plan on going, anyway. I was a lady, and being pregnant in a club screamed "hood rat" loud and clear.

Money came in the den to tell me that he was getting ready to go. He wore a Crown Holder outfit with gators. He had on his diamond chain, and he had his grill in his mouth. The Cartier glasses put the icing on the cake.

"Aren't you looking delectable?" I was being honest. He was fine!

"I look that good?" He smiled.

I nodded my head. He reminded me that I was pregnant due to the fact that he always kept himself up. It made me want to jump his bone.

"So what you going to do with it?" He pulled it out on me.

I gasped and got wet.

"It depends on what you have time to do," I said seductively.

"Whatever you want to do, baby. It belongs to you."

I decided to give him a quick blow job so that he could make it to his party at a decent time. If I put "this" on him, he probably wouldn't make it there at all. I looked at the cable box, which read 11:55 P.M. Yeah, I definitely had to make it quick.

I gave him the head he loved, and it took all of five minutes for him to come and conquer. He went to the bathroom to freshen up. He left his phone behind, and when it rang, I looked at the caller ID.

It was Gip, so I answered it.

"What's up, Gip?"

"Tell Money to stay at home. The party just got shut down. Niggas was shooting up in this bitch," he said, out of breath. I figured it was from running to safety.

"Money!" I yelled.

Money hurried out and got on the phone. After they ended their conversation, he looked up at me.

"I think it was them punk-ass Gib boys!" he said angrily.

I didn't doubt it. We got in bed and cuddled. I was happy I didn't have to stay at home alone.

"I think I want us to move out of town. What you think?" Money saw no opportunities in Atlanta.

"Whatever you want. I don't really want our son growing up here, anyway." I felt like my chapter here in Atlanta was done.

I finally got the opportunity I was waiting for . . . to see Brian. Money was at the gym with Gip, and I knew that it always took him hours to work out. I decided to meet up with Brian at Justin's.

When he walked in, he was looking better than ever and was licking his lips like he always did. I was so happy to see him. I couldn't hide the expression on my face.

"You cheesing." He smiled.

"Boy, hush. You're always talking." I laughed. He had me on cloud nine.

All the memories ran through my thoughts as we sat there laughing.

"I missed you, man."

He must have read my mind.

"I missed you too. We shared good times, B." I was ready to close this chapter of my life as well. I wanted to see him one last time, and here I was, doing exactly that.

"So I heard you were pregnant." He sounded kind of disappointed.

My baby bump definitely couldn't hide itself.

"Yeah, and I heard your son was a cutie," I said, striking back. "Why didn't you tell me you got her pregnant?" I decided to throw that in the air.

"Well, Doll, I just didn't want to hurt you," he said.

"Well, you managed to do that, anyway," I said, as if he should have known.

"Sorry." He was cute when he apologized.

"No problem. The past is what we don't dwell on." Even though I didn't have a problem discussing the situation, I was over it.

He explained to me that his relationship with Janeen was completely over and that her crazy ass wouldn't let him see his son when he wanted. I blamed him. He should have done his research first.

As we packed up to leave, a face that I hadn't seen in a long time and a face I should have never seen with hers came into the restaurant.

It was Auny and Clyde.

She had me fucked all the way up! "Hold this." I gave Brian my purse and keys, then made my way over to their table. Auny saw me, and her face dropped. I pulled up a chair and sat at the table with them.

"Leslie, what are you doing here with Clyde?" I quizzed, looking at him in a disgusted way. "Isn't this the man who *you* said set Unc up? How trifling and gold digging can you be?"

I waited for her to answer, but I knew she didn't have anything to say.

I got up and punched her so hard in the face, she flipped out of the chair. Before I made my way to the door, I spit on her.

I don't know how slick the bitch thought she was, but to play my uncle, she had to be insane! She had hers coming. . . . That was just a sample. I grabbed my things from Brian and proceeded out of the restaurant. I jumped in my Jag and made my way home. I needed to sleep on this.


"Yes! The nasty bitch was with Clyde! Can you believe it?" I explained to Mari and Jasmine on a three-way. I couldn't tell Unc about it, because I didn't think his heart could take that type of pain without wanting to snap her neck.

"So she thought she was safe in Atlanta?" Mari asked.

I didn't know what Auny thought, but whatever it was, she was sadly mistaken.

Jasmine switched the subject. "Girl, has your sister been trying to be buddy-buddy with you lately?" she asked, sounding like she sensed Fall was up to no good.

"Yeah, girl. She called me, apologizing and stuff. We went on a little date not too long ago." I was happy things were turning around.

"No, something just ain't right, Doll," Jasmine said. She was sticking to her no-good feeling about Fall.

"What you mean?" I was thinking the same thing, but I wanted to make sure we were on the same page.

"I'm just saying. She came over here, asking me a million questions. It just was . . . unlike her." Jasmine already knew there was something to all of Fall's questions.

"What has she been doing?" Mari asked, butting in.

"Well, Fall is messing with one of the Gib boys, and at first she was acting like a rebel. Now she's sweet as pie, but something just ain't right. You feel me?" Jasmine was not playing.

I just shook my head. I had a feeling Jasmine was telling the truth, but I couldn't believe that my sister would try something slick.

I told them that I would call them back, because I needed a moment to ponder the situation. I went up to bed, where Money was. He could probably tell something was on my mind, because I didn't say too much. He sat at the foot of the bed and started massaging my feet.

"What's wrong, baby?" he asked, sensing I was upset.

"Jasmine thinks that Fall is up to something." I felt bad having to say it.

He gave me that "I told you so" look. "Stay away from her," he demanded.

I rolled my eyes. I didn't feel like arguing. It was too much for me.

"At least until I figure this out. Yeah, I understand that's your sister, but that's my baby." He pointed at my stomach. He was definitely right, so for the time being, I would grant him his wish.

He crawled over next to me. He rubbed my stomach. "Somebody's birthday is coming up," he said excitedly.

I had forgotten all about it. "Yeah, it's only the first of August. We got plenty of time." I didn't have a clue how I was going to celebrate my birthday. I thought I'd just have the baby shower, since there wasn't anything else to do.

"Baby, I'm about to go to the gym with the crew. Dinner's going to be done when I get back." He laughed as he kissed my lips.

"If dinner's made, you're going to know something," I joked.

Money put on his Nike workout clothes and was out the door in no time. Although our house was clean, I decided to do some cleaning, anyway, to stay busy. It could use a sweep or a mop, and that was what I intended to give it. I started my mop water, turned on my Monica's *The Makings of Me* CD, and began my cleaning duties.

Once the house glistened, I started lighting incense. A house was never completely clean without the scent of Pine-Sol and other lovely things. Well, at least that was what Auny had taught me when I was younger.

I was taking a nice, long, and peaceful bubble bath when my phone started vibrating on the sink. It almost vibrated to the floor. I got out of the tub to answer it.

It was the Realtor.

"Hello," I said, sounding professional.

"Hey, Sommer! It's official! They want the house, and like I said the other day, they want to pay full price." She was excited about the deal.

"Really? I'm excited." I was smiling from ear to ear.

"So when will you be in town?" she asked.

"I don't know. I'm going to call my travel agent to see when I can get a flight. I'll be in touch, though," I said, knowing that Unc would be so proud of me.

We hung up, and I got back in the tub. I was planning to move Unc wherever Money and I decided to move to. I already knew I wasn't walking down any aisle unless Unc was there to give me away. Besides, he was the only one who could do the job any justice. I was sure Money would understand. A wedding was a major part of a girl's life, and Unc was the only father figure I had.

My phone began to ring again. I had it lying on the toilet, and it was moving all around from the vibration. I dried my hand off with my towel and looked to see who it was. Private caller. I answered.

"Hello."

"Baby, I miss you." It was Zae. He hadn't called me in a few weeks. Just when I thought he had gotten the picture, it became apparent he hadn't.

"Zae, what do you want?" I said calmly.

"You. Just hear me out, Doll," he said, hoping I would stay on the phone to hear what he had to say. "I love you. Baby, there's not a day that goes by that I don't think about you. Come home." I shook my head. He really needed to give it up.

"Zae, you fucked my friend. Not to mention, you left me when I needed you the most. How could you have possibly loved me?" I questioned.

Amour

"Only once," he said, like that made a difference. I caught a feeling at the fact that they had had sex. Although I suspected it, I didn't know for sure. I was over him, but I still cared about that for some odd reason. I got mad instantly.

"Fuck you, Zae. Die slow," I said, then hung up. He called multiple times after that, but I didn't answer. I thought to get my number changed, but I knew it would be pointless, because he *always* got my numbers. I just couldn't win for losing with him.

# Chapter 19

I touched down in Detroit, Michigan. Mari was waiting for me in the parking lot. It took me a while to spot her red BMW, since there were a million red cars out there. Mari got out of the car and waved her arms so that I could see her. I made my way over to her car, and we hugged.

"Missed you, sweetie!" she said, grabbing my bag and putting it in the backseat.

"I missed you too!" I opened the passenger-side door and got in.

It took us a little shy of an hour to get to Toledo from Detroit. There wasn't anything in Unc's house, and I refused to sleep on the floor, so we decided I would stay at her house. That was our first stop. I put my things in her guest room, and then we went downstairs to watch TV.

"So how's the pregnancy?" she said, trying to spark up a conversation.

"It's cool. I sleep more than usual. How are you liking it here at home?" I asked, regretting that I did.

"Girl, I hate it here. I wish I didn't have to come back, but hey! It beats a coffin," she said in a nonchalant way.

"Girl, it's cool. We're all planning to leave Atlanta soon. Then you can come wherever we are." I got excited thinking about it.

"How am I going to afford to do all that, Doll?" she asked. Cash was her source for money, and now that he was gone, she didn't have it made like she used to.

I was sure that Money would help my girl out, but I had to clear it with him before I made any offers.

We turned in early. I had to be up bright and early, and I needed to be prompt. Being back in Toledo let me know I would never return for good. This city offered no opportunities. Plus, there were way too many haters and people who hated to see the next person shine. . . . They were always talking down or envying one another. Some people were afraid of change, and so they bonded in Toledo forever.

Not I, though. I had made sure to go beyond Toledo. I would rise. I'd be that nurse I had always dreamed I'd be. Money and I would give our son the life that neither one of us had had. I just couldn't wait to see my dreams come true.


Mari dropped me off at Unc's house. My appointment with the Realtor was set for five o'clock that evening. I arrived a little earlier. I went in and dusted off a couple of things. The house was beautiful, and it looked much bigger than it did when we brought life to it. I took time to look back on all the memories that the house held . . . both good and bad. They said you had to close one door in order for another to open.

I was slamming this one shut.

The doorbell rang, so I fixed myself up and walked to the door.

"Wish me luck," I said as I opened it. My mouth hit the floor. It was Zae.

I tried my hardest to close the door, but Zae was so much stronger than me. As he pushed the door open, I fell onto the floor.

"Bitch, you trying to shut me out? Didn't I tell you I was going to find you?" he asked as he approached me. He bent over and grabbed me by my hair.

"Zae, stop please!" I was scared for my life, as well as my baby's.

"Zae, stop please!" he mocked me. "Sommer, you're not cute when you beg." He stood me up and dragged me up the stairs.

He saw my ring and instantly got mad.

"What the fuck is this? Bitch, so you are engaged? Oh! So you went down to Atlanta to start a new life, huh? Didn't I tell you we were forever? The only way out of this"—he pointed at both of us—"is death! Since you ain't being loyal to that, you must die." He spit in my face. His breath smelled like alcohol.

I was dead meat. Him plus drunk, plus a broken heart . . . equaled me in the danger zone. I prayed to God that I would leave this situation alive.

Zae threw me to the floor. I hit my head so hard, it started spinning. I worried about my growing baby.

"So . . . Sommer, tell me. Are you carrying this man's baby?"

I didn't know whether I should lie or keep it real. If he knew the truth, lying would result only in an even worse ass whupping.

"Yes," I cried. My head was spinning out of control.

He kicked me in the stomach. The pain was excruciating. I was now in the fetal position. He got on the floor with me and started punching my face. I could hardly cry because I felt swollen and sore. He started to choke what was left in me, wrapping his hands around my neck, lifting my head from the floor while the rest of my body struggled.

Death flashed before my eyes. I knew I was about to die. He had his thumb pressed against my throat. I was changing colors and gasping for air.

After I turned blue, purple, and black, Zae let me go. I crawled to the window and opened it with all my might. I begged for oxygen.

"Get the fuck out that window!" he yelled.

Helpless, I did as I was told. I looked at my first love and saw another man. He was a fucking monster. He didn't give a fuck about me. At least I still had some type of love for him left in me.

He started unbuckling his pants.

"What are you doing?" I questioned between breaths.

"You like to fuck niggas while you're pregnant, don't you?"

I knew better than to say no. I started crying loudly. This man was a psychopath. He dragged me by the legs and flipped me over onto my stomach. I didn't know how this would be, either too rough or just plain old disgusting. He put on a condom and put it in. I was as dry as a desert, so it hurt like hell.

I cried the entire time. I kept having flashbacks of when his dad tried to rape me. I felt like this was almost the same thing, except in a different form. Although I didn't say "No" or "Stop," he knew I didn't want any parts of this.

After he was done having his way with me, he lay down right there with me and fell asleep. I lay there too, waiting until I heard a snore so that I could get up and search for my phone.

I damn near crawled down the steps. I was in so much pain, but thank God, I was able to get my phone out of my purse. I had a few missed calls from the Realtor. She had texted, asking if it would be okay to close the deal at a later date because there was an emergency that had come up for the couple to tend to.

Thank God again. I needed the extra time.

My phone read 9:12 P.M. I just couldn't believe this was happening to me all over again. How could the man who I had once thought was so right be so wrong? I had to call Mari. She probably wasn't even awake, being that she went to bed so early, but I decided to try my luck and call her, anyway. The phone rang about five times before she answered dryly.

"Hello."

"Mari, please get up. I need to come over there," I breathed heavily into the phone.

"What happened, Sommer?" I could tell she was sitting up now, worried about what was going on with me.

"Zae beat me up," I cried. My life had been nothing but letdowns. My mom had been on drugs, Unc was gone, and now my first love was holding me captive in Toledo. What had the world come to?

We ended the phone call once Mari told me that she would meet me on the corner of Bancroft and Secor. I hung up the phone and proceeded to sneak out. I was barefoot, but I didn't give a damn how I was getting the hell up out of there. I crept through the window because I knew opening the door would make too much noise while Zae's drunk ass slept. That man had really turned into a monster, and I hated him with a passion. Our meeting spot was a block or two from Unc's house, so I jogged my way on over there. At this moment, I was very paranoid, so I kept looking over my shoulder, making sure no one was behind me.

As we planned, her red BMW was at the corner, waiting on me. I jumped in. I knew she would question the whole situation, and I didn't feel like discussing it . . . but hell, as long as she saved me, I owed her any explanation she asked for.

She looked over at me, and from the expression on her face, she was telling me that my face was a mess.

"What the hell happened, Doll?" she asked while touching my face.

"Girl, he's crazy. I came to finalize the offer on Unc's house, and when I got there, Zae pulled up. He pushed himself into the house and asked me if I was pregnant by Money. I told him yeah, and he started choking me. It escalated from there," I said, crying my heart out.

I felt as though I had bad luck. Why did my life have to be so bad? It felt like I was cursed.

"We're going to the hospital," Mari stated.

"No, Mari. What if he comes up there?" I asked. I knew that I needed to see about my son, but Zae had me so shook that I didn't want to go.

"Doll, you need to see if your baby is okay," she said while staring at me.

I sat back in my seat, and tears began to fall. I was scared for my life and wished that Money was here to console me.

"Look, I'll stay with you, but you need to go for sure."

"They gon' ask me a million questions, and I'm not tryin'a start a case here. After Unc house is sold, I have no plans on returning," I said while sobbing.

"That's fine and dandy, but you could just tell them that you got jumped by some girls you don't know."

She was right. I needed to see about my child, and I would just have to feed them a lie so that I wouldn't have to deal with the police trying to make me press charges.

We pulled up to Mari's house, and I was frightened to get out of the car. I didn't know if he was lurking around or not. I just didn't feel safe in Toledo anymore. I knew that when I woke up, I would be on the next thing smoking to Atlanta.

I was happy to know that my son was okay. The doctor had put me on bed rest for two weeks, and the way my body was feeling, I was sure that I wouldn't be moving much, anyway.

We walked upstairs to her bedroom to lie down. We talked until she dozed off. I had the worst time trying to go to sleep. I kept thinking that Zae was going to come out of nowhere and kill me.

I woke up, scared, to the vibration of my phone. I was afraid to answer it. It was only my younger sister, Fall.

"Hey, Fall," I managed to say with my sore jaw.

"Doll, when are you coming back? I miss you," she said happily.

Fall was seventeen and living her life up. I thought back to those careless days of mine, and those were the same days I wanted back so badly. My younger sister wanted to be so much like me, but little did she know, I was a hard act to follow. If she knew better, she would decide that I was an act that she *would not* want to follow. I couldn't bump my head for her. I could only warn her. I was hoping she would listen to me, because my life was not one to live. I was a prisoner in my own little world.

When I got off the phone with Fall, Mari's phone began to ring. I knew it wasn't for me, so I just let it go off. The caller called twice before I decided to go put her phone on vibrate so that it would no longer bother me. When I picked the phone up, it read TWO MISSED CALLS FROM MARK. I wondered who he was, because Mari had never told me about a Mark. I pressed IGNORE on the phone, and then her text message conversation with him popped up. I looked over at Mari to make sure she was still asleep; then I started reading the messages.

There were no incoming messages from him. There were only messages from her to him. As I read, I realized a few of the messages were talking about me, and I didn't understand why. One message read: She'll be in town to sell the house. That will be the perfect time, if you ask me.

*The perfect time to do what?* I thought. I heard Mari moving in the bed, so I quickly laid her phone back down and got back in the bed with her. I kept replaying that message in my head. It didn't make any sense to me.


The next morning Mari drove me to Detroit Metro Airport, where I paid an arm and a leg for my emergency flight to Atlanta. The entire car ride I wanted to ask her about that message, but I didn't want her to know that I was in her phone. It took everything in me not to question her.

At the airport all eyes were on me. I wanted to curse everyone out, but I didn't need that extra attention. When they called my flight to board, I made sure I was the first person in line. As I sat in my seat, I prayed the plane took off into the sky as soon as possible. They did their announcements, even mentioning that the use of cell phones was prohibited, before we took off to Atlanta. My phone continued to vibrate. It was a text message from Zae.

You can run, but you can't hide.

I closed my phone and started praying aloud. I didn't care who heard me, as long as God could. "God, please don't let this man find me."


I snuck into the house, praying Money wasn't there. He was sleeping in the den, so I headed directly up the stairs. I went to our bathroom and locked the door. I damn near scared myself when I looked in the mirror. I was a mess indeed. My jaw was swollen, and my eye was black. I was disgusted. I touched my face softly, but even that hurt.

My lip was busted. It too was swollen. I began to cry. I couldn't believe I looked this bad. There was no way I was going to be able to hide this ugliness from Money. I didn't want him to harm Zae . . . not because I cared about Zae, but because I knew there was a chance that things could get deadly.

I heard Money twist and turn the doorknob.

*Damn, what am I going to do?*

I decided to open the door. I had to face him sooner or later.

I kept my head down. Money picked my face up. He gasped.

"What happened to you, Doll?"

*Should I lie or tell the truth?*

"Imani and her girls jumped me, but they went to jail, so I'm cool," I said with a smile that hurt like hell to form.

"Are you sure that's what happened?" It was obvious that he knew I was lying. He just couldn't prove it.

"Yeah, I'm sure. I just need to get some rest," I responded. My entire body ached.

"Well, is my son all right? You definitely don't look like you are," he stated.

"He's fine, Money. They didn't hit me in the stomach." I prayed he would end the questions there.

"You want to go to the spa to get a massage or something?" He helped me to the bed. I lay down, and he started massaging my feet the way I liked. That hurt too.

"No, I don't want anybody seeing me like this," I told him.

There was no way in hell I would be seen walking around, looking like the ugly duckling. He told me to rest up and that he was going to get me some cocoa butter for my face.

"I'm going to get a massage therapist to come to the house," he promised. My man always went out of his way to please me.

I just nodded my head. He left the room, and I lay there, replaying the ass whupping Zae had given me, remembering the hate and hurt he had had in his eyes. I had thought he would always love me, but it was clear that love had turned into resentment.

The smell of his breath, how roughly he handled me, the words he said to me, the tone he used with me, and the love he lost for me caused me to shed tears. I didn't know why I still had a place for him in my heart, but I did.

I started to reflect on the day we first met and how I just knew he would be mine in due time. I recalled the day he saved me from his drunken father. Those sandpaper hands that had held my neck so tight were the same hands Zae had used on me. I held my stomach. Reminding myself of that situation always made me sick to my stomach.

How did Zae even know I would be at Unc's house? I didn't talk to anybody in Toledo but Mari. I couldn't imagine her telling him. She wasn't that grimy. I started to get tired, and I yawned. My body felt a little better lying between our Gucci satin sheets. Sleep was what I needed, so sleep was what I got, but would life be better if I never woke up. . . .


Mari had been calling my phone nonstop, but I didn't answer. I didn't know if she had something to do with Zae knowing my whereabouts or not. I just had a strong feeling that she did. Or was I overreacting? I paced back and forth in the kitchen while I talked to Jasmine on the phone.

"I mean, if no one else knew you was going to be there, then there you have it," Jasmine said.

"But she did come pick me up," I reminded her.

"What the hell that mean? She ain't have no choice, 'cause if she didn't, you would have been suspicious."

"I don't know. She is blowing my phone up, though."

"Making sure her cover ain't blown."

"You don't trust her, huh?"

"I don't trust me, so hell no, I don't. I mean, she never cross me as a fake bitch, but then again, none of them do before you realize they fake as fuck. Then again, we could be jumping to conclusions, so just play things normal, but the next fake shit she do . . . you know the rest," Jasmine preached before we ended our call. She made perfect sense, so I decided to answer Mari's next call, which came shortly after I hung up with Jasmine.

"What's up?" I answered.

"Girl, what the hell were you doing?" she questioned.

"Can a bitch get some sleep?" I giggled.

"My bad, Sleeping Beauty, but I whupped that bitch ass for you." She sounded proud.

"What? Wait. What bitch?"

"Justine."

Now, I had made a mental note years ago that Justine had to be got. She was a fake-ass bitch that I should have detected from the jump. I had been just so vulnerable at the time that I had let her pass the fake-bitch inspection. She'd been playing around like a true friend, when all along she'd been working for Imani. She had come just to let me know that Zae and Imani were creeping. I had really trusted her tacky ass, and I was glad to hear she got her ass whupped. She deserved to be dead.

"Really! What happened?" I was eager to know.

She began to tell me that she saw Justine at the Eclipse, a new club in Toledo. She was with Imani and a couple of other hood rats, and she asked Imani if it was true that she had sent Justine to me, and Imani said yeah. Mari waited till Justine was on the dance floor, dropping it, and she dropped her. I couldn't help but laugh as I visualized how the fight went. Justine wasn't a fighter, but she was definitely a shit talker.

There was no way my girl had set that Zae thing up. She was too loyal to me. Always had been and always would be. I was upset with myself for even thinking that of her. She was my only *real* friend, and I cherished our friendship. Real bitches did real things, and she had always been legit.

# Chapter 20

Fall and her love, Jamal, were on their way to Cascade. The Gib boys were throwing a party there, which they had to attend. She was sitting on the passenger side of his old-school Regal, with her window down. She had to let all his hoes see who was worthy of riding shotgun in his whip.

They were waiting at a red light when he decided to check Fall's progress on the assignment he had given her.

"So what's up? It's been a minute since I asked that favor out of you," he said. He was growing impatient with her.

He had never wanted to be her boyfriend. She had just turned seventeen, and he was already twenty-one. They didn't have a damn thing in common. She was young and easy to convince. She was just too naive to be his woman.

"Doll's out of town, so I haven't really talked to her," she replied, hoping he would understand.

"Fall, you need to pick up the pace. My brother can't rest in peace until this is done." He was annoyed. "He tossing in his muthafucking grave, man," he almost yelled.

"Okay. I'll call her."

"Hello?" I was in so much pain. It was Fall, and I knew I shouldn't have answered it, but I did.

"Where you at, sis?" she asked anxiously. I decided to play as if I was still in Toledo.

"Oh, I'm at Unc's house. Where're you?" I said, not really caring.

"In the car, on the way to Cascade. There's a traffic jam going toward the rink," she sighed.

"Yeah, I heard there's been a lot of traffic. Who you with?" I was hoping she would say her boyfriend.

There was a pause.

"Jamal," she finally said.

"Well, enjoy yourself. I'm going to call you after I nap. Love you, babe," I said before hanging up.

I hated to have to do this, but it was either us or them. I called Money and told him where he could find Jamal.

"Do not hurt Fall," I told him, making it as clear as day. I didn't care about Jamal, and I figured he was better dead than alive. That way I wouldn't have to worry about having my sister grow up fast.

I asked God for forgiveness. "God, please forgive me for the sin I just committed. I hope you can understand my reasons for this. If not, I'll still continue to praise and worship you. No weapon formed against me shall prosper. . . . Amen." With that, I fell back asleep.


Traffic was out of control. There were, like, a million cars on the road, and it seemed as though each car was moving only a mile a minute.

"This shit is ridiculous," Jamal complained.

He rolled his window all the way down. He never paid any attention to the black Magnum that pulled over next to him. Two guys dressed in all black jumped out and made their way to the Regal. Jamal continued to complain, while Fall sat and listened.

Before they knew it, their car was getting shot up. Fall tried to get out of the car, but she got hit before she made a complete exit. She hit the ground. She was in so much pain that she didn't know what to do. She held her arm tight. Blood leaked everywhere.

The two guys fled the scene.

Jamal had been hit five times. The sight of him made Fall throw up. He was definitely gone. Fall had been shot in the arm, which was nothing fatal. An ambulance rushed them to AMC. Jamal died upon arrival. The doctors did the painful procedure of removing the bullet from Fall's arm.

There was a lesson to be learned in this situation, I realized. *When you're a kid, be that. You have all the time in the world to grow up. The same years you skip trying to be older than you are become the years that you'll never get back.* Fall got the message, all right! She sat in the hospital bed, crying her eyes out.

My face was healing, and I was feeling a lot better. There was nothing that the gift of M·A·C couldn't cover. When I got the news that Fall had been shot in the arm while her boyfriend was gunned down, I immediately went to Money and dogged his ass. I had specifically demanded that my sister not be touched. He explained to me that it was an accident and that he wasn't present when it happened. That didn't stop me from being pissed.

Aunt Sasha was irritated about Fall crying over her no-good, dead boyfriend.

"Fall, shut the hell up!" she yelled. She was tired of the fast lane Fall was trying to go down.

"Aunt Sasha, you don't understand! That was my boyfriend," Fall explained, blowing her nose.

"Whatever! You are only seventeen. What the hell are you going to do with some twenty-one year-old gangbanger?"

Fall couldn't come up with an answer.

"Fall, you're falling victim to a lifestyle that your ass don't know anything about!" Aunt Sasha sat in the chair, waiting for Jasmine and me to arrive.

Jasmine and I arrived at the hospital at the same time.

"Gip told me what went down," she whispered.

"Yeah, I know." I didn't really want to talk about it.

"They should have shot her mouth out, 'cause the little bitch talk too much," she said with an attitude.

"Cut it out," I told Jasmine, letting her know I wasn't playing around.

We walked into Fall's room. She was crying and getting dogged by Aunt Sasha. We instantly started laughing. Aunt Sasha never cursed, and to hear her cursing like a sailor was hilarious. It was obvious that she was tired of Fall.

"Okay, Aunt Sasha, I understand," Fall cried.

Aunt Sasha got up. "Talk some sense into her. I have to go meet with a client," she said, then kissed us on the cheek and left the room.

"I don't want to hear none of y'all mouths. I know what I need to do," Fall said, letting us know in advance.

"Do you really? From the looks of it, it appears you don't." I was annoyed that Fall was still carrying an attitude.

"You're just dumb as hell." Jasmine was done trying too. She sat down in the chair.

The same detectives that had questioned Mari came to question Fall.

"Autumn Jones, can you tell us what happened?" Detective Harrison asked. They were sick of all the gang violence going on and wanted to get to the bottom of it all.

"I got shot," Fall said.

"Do you know who did this?" Detective Johnson asked with his pen and pad in his hand.

"I have no idea. I just know his family's been beefing with guys named Money and Gip," she said, as if Jasmine and I weren't sitting there.

*Bitch!*

"Oh, we know who they are. Well, we'll pick them up and question them," Detective Johnson said before leaving.

Jasmine jumped out of her chair as soon as the detectives walked out of the room. "Bitch, have you lost your fucking mind? Gip and Money ain't have shit to do with that!" she yelled.

Fall just sat there smiling. I got up and walked out. Jasmine followed. If I had said anything, I probably would have strangled her.

I wanted to save her in every way that I could, and here she was, trying to blame my man for a murder! I didn't get it. Why was the world made like this? You gave someone all your love and loyalty, and all they gave you back was their ass to kiss.

I didn't want to call Money to tell him what had happened. I had seen plenty of *Law & Order* episodes and knew that phone records were always used to get closer to a case. I had to wait until Money and I were face-to-face.

When I got to our street, all I saw were flashing red and blue lights. It was too late. I drove down the street slowly. I saw Money sitting in the backseat of a police car as it rolled past me, almost in slow motion. He looked me in the eyes and mouthed "I love you." I said it back, but the police car had already driven by.

At that moment, I started wishing that they had killed Fall's ass when they had the chance. She didn't give a fuck about me, so there was no point in sparing her. I went to Jasmine's house. I wanted to wait until the police cleared out before I went home. Everything felt unreal. It was like a scene from a movie. If it was one, I was praying the director would soon say, "Cut!"

When I got to Jasmine's, she was sitting in her car, crying. I opened her car door and helped her into her house. The inside of her house had been torn apart.

"Look at my damn house!" she cried loudly. I could only imagine how my house was looking. I flipped the couch over and told her to sit. I was hurt too, but I figured I had to be strong for both of us.

I called Tionna.

"Get here, like, right now," I said as soon as she answered.

A half an hour passed before Tionna came through the door.

"Oh my goodness! What the hell?" she asked as she looked around. Before she arrived, I had tried to clean up the majority of the stuff. I ended up throwing away a lot of stuff that had been ripped apart.

"Long story," Jasmine said and sat up. Her eyes were bloodshot.

"Okay, um, I have time," Tionna said as she sat on the floor.

We told her everything, from the beginning to the end.

"What you got to drink? 'Cause I think I need some alcohol for this," Tionna said while heading toward the kitchen.

Jasmine's house phone rang. She answered it in a raspy voice. "Hello?"

"You have a collect call from . . . Gip. Do you accept the charges?" the operator asked.

"Yes," she replied and put the phone on speaker.

"Baby, you cool?" Gip asked. He was worried about her.

"Yeah, I'm cool. What's up? What are they saying, and where is Money?" She could barely get it out.

"They said we're both suspects in some murder that happened a week ago." Gip sounded innocent. "They took us in for questioning."

"Why did they suspect y'all, out of all people?" she asked, playing dumb.

"I guess one of the victims told the police that we had a beef with the dude that got killed. Baby, I don't know what the fuck is going on, but my lawyer said they're not going to hold us, 'cause they ain't got enough proof. You stay strong, baby. I love you." He grew silent.

"Love you too," she said and started crying again. He put Money on the phone, and she handed me the phone.

"Doll?" Money asked.

"I'm here, baby." I kept replaying what Fall had said. I wanted to turn back the hands of time and whup her ass.

"You heard what Gip said, right?" he asked, making sure I knew what was going on.

"Yeah, I did. Do you know when they're going to release y'all?" I was hurt. I couldn't imagine a day without him.

"No, but it'll be soon. Daddy will be there sooner than you think," he assured me.

He didn't know how long he was going to be in there, and that was the part about it that killed me. My nineteenth birthday was two weeks away, and I was seven months pregnant. There was too much going on for me to be all alone.

"I know you're thinking about your birthday and the baby, but I'll be there for all of that." The sound of his voice let me know that he was worried that he wouldn't.

"Okay, love you," I told him.

"Love you more. Have faith, Doll. Nothing is impossible," he said before we hung up.

He must have read my mind, because I didn't see how he was going to pull this one off. I wiped my eyes and straightened myself up. We finished cleaning up Jasmine's house, and then we went to see what mine was looking like.

We walked in with caution. Nothing in the house was out of place at all.

"Oh, so because y'all are living in the rich neighborhood, they won't tear y'all shit up." Jasmine was pissed.

It wasn't my fault. We decided that it would be better to stay at my house. Fall took turns blowing both of our phones up. We wondered what she wanted, but we didn't answer.

"The bitch is crazy to think that I'm going to fuck with her," Jasmine said as she watched her phone ring uncontrollably. I felt the same way. I was cutting Fall off completely. There was no way that I would affiliate with her anymore. I couldn't believe she had done what she did to us. Maybe we had been a little too nice.

"I can't believe Fall," Tionna said from the kitchen. She was making us tacos.

"You? Hell, I practically grew up with her." Jasmine was sipping her Moscato.

I didn't know what Jamal was telling her. Whatever it was, he told it well, because she had turned her back on her blood. We continued talking about Fall, and that was when I decided to go and write Unc.

*Dear Unc,*

*Hey. I know you'll be a free man before we know it. I can't wait. It's been so long since you've been directing me down the right path to take. Now I have to figure it all out by myself. I have so much I want to tell you, but it's too much to write. I don't think I told you, but I'm pregnant! I know, I know . . . not a smart move, but it's by a great guy and we were engaged before we found out. I know he's the one for me, Unc.*

*Well, anyway, I also wanted to tell you that I feel like the world is against me at this time in my life. It seems like you are the only person who truly cares about me. You've always wanted what was best for me. I kind of wished you could have called me or asked me to come visit you. You're such a mystery to me, and I hate it. I pray for you every night. I pray that God lets you come be with me soon. Well, I didn't want much.*

*Love you.*
*xoxox, Doll*

I had so much that I wanted to say, but I thought my words could possibly be used as evidence against Unc. I couldn't wait until Unc got out of jail. I really needed someone to tell all these problems to. I needed someone who could tell me to do this or not do that. I needed that parent type of love. I fell asleep with my thoughts. Life was so much better in my dreams.

# Chapter 21

I had been holding on to Unc's letter for about a week. I woke up early in the morning so that I could send it out to him. That entire week, Jasmine had stayed at my house with me. We needed each other's company.

I was tired and drained. My body was still in pain from the beat down that Zae had given me. I decided to take a relaxing bath. Fall continued to blow my phone up. What could she want? I pinned my hair up and got in the tub. My body needed this.

Once again, Fall was calling.

"What, Autumn?" I said with an attitude to let her know that we weren't cool at all.

"Doll, I just wanted to tell you that I was sorry." She tried to convince me, but I didn't care how she felt.

"Okay . . . anything else you'd like to add before I end this call?" I wasn't in the mood for her.

"Yeah." She paused. "I'm pregnant again—"

"You need to tell Aunt Sasha or something!" I interrupted. "I'm pretty sure your grown ass will think of a strategy." I hung up my phone.

We might not beef for the rest of our lives, but she was dead to me for now.

I continued to relax in the tub until Jasmine burst through the door.

"How rude," I said, covering my breasts.

"Girl, please! I seen all of that." She waved me off and sat down on the toilet.

"Guess who just called me, talking about they're sorry *and* pregnant."

I already knew Jasmine would know.

"That damn sister of yours! She sad as I don't know what." Jasmine rolled her eyes. "Anyway, we need to get out of this house." That sounded like a plan to me.

"And go where, Jas?" I asked.

There wasn't any place to go. I began filling my washcloth with Dial body wash.

"I don't know. The mall, the movies, a spa? Just anywhere but here," Jasmine suggested.

We decided to go to the spa. A full body massage was exactly what I needed.


"How did he know that you were in town?" Jasmine asked as we sat and ate at Mr. Chow's.

"I have no idea. I opened the door, thinking it was the Realtor, and it was him. I thought I was going to die, y'all," I said. I almost felt a tear fall down.

"That's crazy. It's like he's obsessed with you. Has he been calling?" Tionna questioned. She took a sip of her lemonade and waited on my answer.

"No, but on my flight back to Atlanta, he texted me, talking about I can run but I can't hide." I got chills thinking about it.

"Wow," Jasmine said.

"Wow" didn't fully describe the situation at all.

I was finally free of bruises and had started my weekly doctor visits. It was depressing because Money wasn't there to join me.

***

It was the morning of my nineteenth birthday, and Jasmine, Tionna, and Mari, to my surprise, were jumping on my bed, forcing me to wake up.

"Y'all are tripping! It's nine in the damn morning." I was pissed. Every lady needed her beauty sleep, so why cut mine short?

It was a special day, because it was also the day of my baby shower, so we all had to go get dolled up. We all got in Money's Escalade and turned Beyoncé's "Video Phone" on full blast.

Once the song was over, I looked over at Mari. We all knew it was dangerous for her to step either foot of hers out of Toledo.

"Do the Malattos know you're in town?" I asked her. I was concerned.

She explained that they had allowed her to come visit, but she wasn't allowed to live here. That was cool with me, because sooner or later, we wouldn't be here, either. We went to the Glambar, as usual, and got done up. Then we went home to get dressed.


My baby shower was at an Atlanta club called Velvet Room. Jasmine and Mari were the hosts, and they definitely did a lovely job. I had gifts on top of gifts, and I was sure that my son had everything he needed and more.

I sat at my table, wishing Money was there to take in both of these moments. I was now nineteen, and here we were, celebrating the arrival of our firstborn. There were a lot of familiar and unfamiliar faces, but I was just happy that I was enjoying myself for the most part.

The food was catered, and the cake was enormous. It was much bigger than the one I had had for my eighteenth birthday. The guests played all the games and won gifts. Then we all ate.

Mari walked up to the microphone. "I have a surprise for the birthday girl," she told the guests. She turned to me. "I got something for you," Mari mouthed.

"I thought *you* were the surprise." I smiled. Everyone laughed.

Everyone looked at the door, and in walked the love of my life. He was holding two big bags, and so was Gip. I jumped up and ran to show him some love. He picked me up and spun me around.

"I told you I'd be here," he whispered.

I just kissed him. I didn't care about the gifts. Being in his presence was a present. The crowd aahed. We looked at them while we held one another and smiled.

I was definitely happy, no doubt about it. After I opened my gifts, I had only a few words to say.

"I just want to thank my gals. They did an amazing job!" I winked at them. "They really made my day with this shower and with surprising me with my man. I couldn't have done it better. . . . Thanks, ladies!" I handed the mic over to Money, who had made it clear he wanted it.

"I just want to say that I love you more than words can describe," he said while holding my hand. "Real talk, I don't know where I'd be if I hadn't met you, Doll. You made the pain of losing my brother bearable. Being locked up made me realize how much I can't stand being away from you. I'm glad that I met you. You make my life worth living," he said before kissing me.

The crowd clapped, and then we cut the cake.

The door flew open, and to everyone's surprise, it was Fall, with a gift in her hand. Money gave me that "Get her" look, so I walked up to her.

"Fall, what's the deal?"

"Sommer, I'm only human," she said, looking like a lost puppy.

"I understand all of that, but you've hurt a lot of people by just being human," I said sarcastically.

It hurt me to be so mean to her, but truth be told, she didn't give a fuck about me. I couldn't trust her. I took the gift.

"I'll call you later," I said. I stood there until she got the point that she wasn't invited.

She left, sad.


When we got home, we got down to business.

"I miss this," he said while peeling my clothes off. I grabbed his dick.

"No, I miss this," I said while smiling.

He whipped it out. "Show me how much," he said.

By the time he was lying on his back, I was already devouring him. I had totally missed my man, and I'd been beyond lonely during his two-week absence.

He turned me around, and we did the sixty-nine. That quickly turned into me riding him. I was a better lover from all the things he had taught me, and our sex was something to die for. After we climaxed, we lay in each other's arms. As we breathed heavily, he broke the silence.

"Did you figure out when you want to be Mrs. Deneiro Browner?" he asked as he rubbed my stomach.

"I don't know. I'm ready now, but I want my uncle to walk me down the aisle."

I was ready, but it was only right to wait for Unc. We ended up falling asleep naked. *In love* weren't the words to use. I was way past that. I was more like dangerously in love.


The next morning there was a letter from Unc sitting on the nightstand. I was excited. I wondered what he had to say. I got up to look for Money. He and Gip were in the nursery, painting.

"Aww, look at Daddy and Goddaddy getting ready," I said and laughed.

"Yeah, young Money will be here before you know it. When you get dressed, you and Jasmine can take my black card and get shit to decorate." Money looked around the room. "My little nigga," he said.

I went back to our bedroom to open Unc's letter. I unfolded it and held it close to me. I missed my uncle more than ever.

> *Dear Sommer,*
>
> *I miss you too. You should already know that. I haven't wrote you or called, because I wanted you to enjoy your life and not worry about me. I'll be out before you know it. As a matter of fact, I'll be out September 26th. Debo will be in touch with you shortly. I'll make up for the lost time. You're the child I never had. Well, both you and Debo are. Y'all have shown me loyalty like my right-hand man had. I really appreciate it.*
>
> *I'm glad to hear you're getting married. That's the best way to go. Tell Zae I said hi.*
>
> *Love you much.*
> *Unc*
>
> *P.S. Happy Nineteenth Birthday.*

I put the letter back in the envelope and placed it in the drawer. I knew it wasn't going to be a long letter, because Unc never was the type to express himself.

Unc was definitely lost, because Zae was history in my life. It was already the 19th of September, so that meant Unc would be getting out in a week. I was sure Debo had something special planned for him. I just didn't know if his taste was up to par, like Unc's and mine.

I jumped in the shower and got dressed. I was ready to do this shopping for my child. I picked Jasmine up, and we were on our way to the Gucci Baby Depot.

"So what color are we doing this room?" Jasmine asked while we parked my Jag.

"I don't know . . . something nice. You know how we do."

Once we got in the store, we decided to do his room in green and red. They had a lot of cute stuff in that color scheme. We went over to the clothing department and admired the baby outfits.

"You come up with any names yet?" she asked me while throwing the cutest comforter set into the cart.

"I was thinking about naming him after Cash. I don't like Money's name too much." I was being brutally honest.

"Hmm, Deneiro or Chase? That's a tough one. I'm sure either way it goes, Money's going to be satisfied." Jas had a point.

We purchased our items and loaded them into the car and headed over to the mall to do a little bit more shopping.

We ran into Tionna at Underground Station.

"This is like the only store you hoes come to," she said and laughed. She had some dude on her arm.

"Where you about to go? Turn a trick?" I asked, and we all shared a laugh.

"Fuck the both of you," she joked as she and her new little friend walked out.

We bought a few items and made our way to the food court. We found Fall sitting at a table filled with boys. It seemed like everybody was up in the mall today.

I caught a bad feeling, and from the look of Jasmine's face, she did too.

"Should we?" Jasmine was on the same thing that I was on. I wanted to go and snatch her ass up, but at the same time, Fall was known to embarrass us.

We agreed to eat Chinese food, and even though I wanted to go holler at Fall, I decided to let it go and order something to eat. After we ordered our food, we sat two tables away from Fall's. I could hear the boys calling her all types of hoes as she sat there in silence. Surprisingly, she didn't defend herself.

"Yeah, Fall suck us for a buck," one of them teased.

"Let us run a train on you, bitch!" another shouted.

I couldn't take it. I had had enough. Jasmine and I looked at each other and got up. We walked over to where they were.

"If you don't get your little toddler dick ass away from my sister, I'm going to snatch it off and shove your damn balls down your throat!" I was all in his rude-ass face.

"Talking about getting your dick sucked! Do you even have one? 'Cause it looks like you wearing a fucking size three," Jasmine joked as she looked down at his feet.

"Well, you know what they say."

All his boys started laughing. Then they all got up and walked away.

One came back. He was actually cute, and he looked mixed.

"I'm sorry about that, Fall, but call me sometime." He gave her a small piece of paper.

He was rocking Hollister, so we could tell that he was far from a thug. She needed his type in her life, because thugs were just too much for her. She was a rookie who had just gotten pushed off the bench. She took the paper and smiled. We went back to our table, and she got up and followed us.

"Hey, y'all! Thank you," she said, trailing behind us. We sat down, and she embraced both of us, trying to wrap her arms around us at the same time. "Love you guys," she told us.

"We love you too, Fall," Jasmine said.

We were back to normal.

# Chapter 22

It was the 24th of September, and our flight back to Toledo would be the following morning. I was anxious as hell and excited that Money and Gip would be joining us. I knew Unc would love Money. He really didn't have a choice, since Money was my fiancé *and* the father of my son.

I packed only a few bags for both Money and me because we were going to stay for only a weekend.

"Baby, you need to get some sleep. We have to get up early," Money said while peeking his head in the bedroom.

"Then why aren't you asleep?" I questioned.

"You know the game's on. I can't miss it," he said, looking like a little kid.

"Okay, but only one game, Money. Then bring your ass back up here," I demanded.

"Okay. Love you, Doll," he said, then shot back down the stairs.

I zipped our suitcases and got in bed. When I talked to Debo, he told me that he had hired some party planners to take care of Unc's homecoming. Debo was old-fashioned, so the weight had definitely lifted from my shoulders. He was so far stuck in the nineties, it was ridiculous.

I said my prayers, and then I got some rest.

\*\*\*

The next morning was hectic. We all rushed to the airport. We sat in the lobby, cracking jokes and laughing, while we waited to board our flight.

"Now boarding Flight two-eleven to Toledo, Ohio. I repeat, now boarding Flight two-eleven to Toledo, Ohio," the lady said on the intercom.

We all got up and boarded the plane. Money and I sat together. So did Jasmine and Gip, and Aunt Sasha and Fall.

"You nervous?" I asked Money.

"No. What should I be nervous for?" he questioned.

"I don't know." I really didn't know why I had asked.

"Well, you know since I have some family in Toledo, I'm going to get up with them. I want you to spend some time with your family," he told me.

I just wanted to see Mari. That was it, and that was all.

The flight was long and boring.

"You ever did it on a plane?" Money asked me.

I smiled. "No, Deneiro, and I don't think I'm going to, either. My aunt is on here!" He should have known I was not going to be down with that.

It seemed like days later when we landed in Toledo. A chill ran across my body when I got off the plane. It wasn't because it was chilly outside. It was because I knew that there was a lot waiting for me.

We arrived at the Holiday Inn Splash Bay, and we all felt like kids. Well, everybody except for Aunt Sasha, who wasn't messing her wrap up for nothing. I couldn't enjoy myself like I wanted to, because I was pregnant. It was cool, though. Jasmine and Fall were getting thrown left and right into the pool, while I wiggled my toes in the water. I couldn't wait until the day I dropped this load, so that I could bounce back. I had three months to go until I could finally meet the man I had been waiting for.

Mari came strolling in with Kola. I stood up.

"Oh, hell no, Mari! What you on?" I didn't know what she was thinking. I looked Kola up and down, and then I pulled Mari to the side.

"Doll, she's cool. She's been our ace for years, and that shit was foul, but really what did she do? She said they were only playing to make you mad." Mari was trying to squash the beef.

Honestly, I didn't care. It had been about two years since we were friends. I didn't need any new friends, nor did I want her as my friend.

"Mari, I don't know." I really didn't.

"I know," she shot back. "We're supposed to be better than that."

I looked at her, and then I looked over at Kola.

"Y'all don't have to be tight like y'all used to be, but let's be grown," Mari said, hoping I would agree.

"No, that's your friend. Me and her could never be close!" I said angrily.

I went back to my spot by the pool. They came over and sat next to me.

I sighed. "So you're still rocking with Imani?" I decided to ask Kola, looking her dead in the face.

"No. Girl, we never rocked to begin with. I told y'all, Malcolm and I pulled up, and the two of them were in Zae's car. I didn't know shit about that," she explained. She was sticking to her story.

Mari gave me the "I told you so" look. I turned my head.

"So, I see life's treating you good. . . ," Kola said as she admired my Christian Dior bikini. My baby pudge was poking out, but I was still looking good.

"Mmm-hmm, I can't complain," I began splashing my feet in the water.

The entire time we were at the pool, Kola threw her two cents into every conversation I started. I knew she was really trying to be my friend. We were Thelma and Louise back in the day.

The truth was, she used to be Mari back then. I did miss her, but once you crossed me, it was hard for me to forgive and forget.

The guys all went with Money to visit his Toledo family, while all the girls ended up having dinner at Applebee's since it was the only restaurant open after ten o'clock. Aunt Sasha went to visit a few of her old friends. We suspected that at least one of her "old friends" was an old booty call, but we knew she wouldn't tell.

We all sat down and ordered drinks and the boneless wings appetizer. The food came out in no time.

"Is this shit old? How in the hell they bring this out that quick?" Mari complained. We all laughed. After all this time, she was still crazy.

"Mari, calm down," Fall said.

"I'm just saying," Mari said, looking at each and every last one of us. "Don't y'all want fresh shit?" She had a point.

"So this is Fall?" Kola smiled.

"Yes, I'm Fall. You probably heard some horrible things about me," Fall said.

I had never told Fall or Jasmine why I wanted to move to Atlanta in the first place, and I had no intention to.

"Um, no. Actually, Doll spoke nothing but good things about you," Kola assured her.

Moments later Ashley, BJ, and Jerrica walked through the door. They came over to our table once they spotted us.

"Long time no see, Doll," Jerrica said as they pulled up chairs.

It was like a Rogers High reunion when we were all together. It was the best feeling ever.

"Y'all are going to make me cry," I said as I wiped my tears of joy away.

"Are you pregnant?" BJ asked.

"Yes, honey. I'm seven months. By the way, this here is my younger sister, Fall." I pointed. "And that's my cousin Jasmine." I introduced the ladies to my family. "This is BJ, Ashley, and Jerrica." I introduced my family to the ladies.

When the clock struck twelve, we all decided it was time to go. My friends promised that they would be present at Unc's surprise party, and then we all hugged and laughed and departed.

When we got to our hotel, the guys still hadn't made it back. We all went up to Fall's room to relax before bed.

"Why you and Kola fall out?" nosy-ass Fall had to know.

*Always asking questions.*

"I just felt as though she disrespected me, so I got my space . . . nothing too big." I made it sweet and simple.

After Aunt Sasha and Fall dozed off, Jasmine followed me to my and Money's room.

"Do you think old boy is still looking for you?" Jasmine asked me as we watched *Why Did I Get Married?*

"Girl, you never know with Zae. I don't even know him for real, but I hope he don't show up." I was scared, to be honest.

"Are you scared?" She never stopped with the questions.

I nodded my head no, but in reality I was scared to death.

Money walked in.

"Jasmine, go tend to your man," he joked.

She laughed. She said, "Good night, you two," and went to her room.

Money took everything but his beater and boxers off and climbed in bed. "What you watching?" he asked as he got comfortable.

*"Why Did I Get Married?"* I said while I scooted closer to him. "But since you're here, I can go to sleep now," I added, kissing him all over his face. I turned off the TV.

"It's like that with you too?" He chuckled.

"I swear, I only sleep good when I'm next to you," I replied.

He kissed me back.

"That's how you know it's real," I said as I drifted off to sleep.

# Chapter 23

The next morning was nothing but pandemonium. We went from getting our hair done to having our nails and eyebrows done. Then we went to the mall. It felt like time was flying, because the hours passed us by. Everybody wanted to get Unc a gift, but we had no clue what to get him. Aunt Sasha's idea was to buy him clothes so that he could look nice on his first day home. We ended up buying him a maroon Armani suit, matching Mauri gators, a Rolex, and a two-carat diamond earring. We knew Unc would love what we got him because it wasn't flashy, but it still screamed money, loud and clear.

We gave the gifts to Debo so that he could give them to Unc when he picked him up. We picked up his cake and made sure the caterers had the menus correct. We didn't want any mistakes. We wanted things to be perfect for Unc, so we didn't have any room for errors.

I called to see how much money Unc was sitting on, just to make sure he was all the way taken care of.

"The remaining balance is five hundred million, nine hundred fifty thousand, seven hundred thirty-five dollars. In your savings account, you have a remaining balance of one million dollars," the bank associate said.

Unc was a multimillionaire, and the money still wasn't done being collected.

The party was scheduled to begin at seven o'clock. Around five, we rushed back to the hotel to get dressed. It was a proper attire affair.

Unc was a fly cat when it came to being dressed. We had to bring him home in his flavor. The party had to represent Unc well.

I wore a Versace dress, and Money wore a matching suit.

"I'm so nervous," I said as Money zipped my dress up.

"You're going to bust up out of this," he noted and laughed.

"Ha-ha, not funny." I smirked. He chuckled.

"Why are you nervous, though?" he asked as we sat on the bed.

Money didn't understand that it had been a long time since I had seen Unc.

"It's just been so long since I've seen him. There's so much that he doesn't know. I'm not nervous. . . . I'm more like afraid," I said, clearing it up.

I was ready. I missed Unc so much, and this was the day I had been waiting for ever since I learned that he had got arrested.

Aunt Sasha called my phone and told me that it was time for us to head to the party. The party was at the Omni. It was a big, elegant club. It was perfect for the event. "I need you guys to be hostesses, like helping people out," Aunt Sasha told us when we arrived.

We all frowned. That was not what we had planned to do. We wanted to party like everybody else.

"I know y'all are not frowning up at my orders," Aunt Sasha said with authority.

Grown or not, we knew not to talk back to Aunt Sasha. "No," we said in unison.

Guests began to arrive at 6:45 P.M. There were so many pimp-like, older-looking men with young women on their arms. We couldn't help but laugh. We knew they were definitely Unc's old friends, because he liked his women to be legally young.

When my girlfriends walked into the party, Aunt Sasha gave them their party duties too, which were the same as ours. They didn't have a problem with that, so they started walking up to people, asking if they needed anything. Jasmine, Fall, and I stood around.

There were a lot of familiar faces who came up to me and hugged me. Folks constantly asked me when was I due and how was I doing. I smiled, answered the questions, and kept it moving.

Eventually, I sat down with Money. My feet were starting to hurt in my heels. I was holding up a lot of weight.

"Baby, are you cool?" Money asked. He rubbed my stomach.

"Yeah, I'm fine. My feet are just bothering me," I said.

"You want me to rub 'em, baby?" he asked next. I smiled.

"No, Money. Thanks, though."

Money didn't care where we were. If I needed anything, he made sure to accommodate me.

More people started to pour into the party. The Omni was jam-packed by the time 7:30 hit. We all were waiting on Unc to arrive.

I watched Kola walk over to me.

"You nervous, Doll?" Kola asked.

"Girl, nervous ain't the word. I can't wait," I said as I got up. I went to stand by the door.

I wanted to be the first person he saw. Everybody smiled and moved out of my way. They must have known what I was aiming to do.


Unc sat on the couch at Debo's house, waiting on him to arrive with his clothes. The door opened, and in came Debo with a maroon suit and a shoe box. Unc stood up.

"This for you," Debo said, handing Unc his gifts. Unc grabbed them and looked them over.

"My style," he said as he admired the Armani suit. He laughed and placed the suit and the shoe box on the couch. He opened the shoe box, and there were the Mauri gators, which he loved.

"They got yo' man together." He smiled, knowing that it had to be Sommer who had picked out his clothes.

He gathered his things and then headed up the stairs to take a shower. He ran his water, and then he took all his clothes off and jumped in.

Unc was nervous. This was the day he had been waiting for ever since the police had handcuffed him and taken him away. He couldn't wait to get his hands on Clyde. He also wanted to cross paths with Auny. The bitch had disappeared on him when he needed her the most.

He scrubbed his body clean. He hadn't had a shower like this one in years. When he stepped out, he was smelling just like Old Spice. He dried his body off and wrapped himself up in his towel. Then he went into Debo's guest room to get dressed.

When he was all done, he took a good look at himself in the mirror. He struck a few poses, knowing he was looking and smelling like a million bucks. He went downstairs, finding Debo waiting patiently on the couch, in a navy suit with matching gators.

Debo stood up. He had to admit Unc looked good. That was the Unc he knew. He handed him the Rolex, which Unc quickly slid over his hand and locked shut. Then he gave Unc the diamond earring. Unc didn't waste any time putting it through his ear.

"You ready, Unc?" Debo asked him.

"Yeah. This is the moment I've been waiting for," Unc replied.

Debo grabbed the keys, and they were on their way to Unc's party. Unc sat quietly on the way there. He looked at the streets he hadn't been down for a long time.

When they pulled in, the parking lot was full of cars. Unc grew excited. He was happy to see that a lot of people had come out to show they loved him and couldn't wait to see him again. He couldn't wait to see who was inside.

Unc took a deep breath as they walked toward the entrance. He paused. Debo extended his arm to open the door for him.

The door flew open, and in came Unc and Debo. They both were looking like a million bucks. I hurried and ran into Unc's arms. His warm embrace brought tears to my eyes. The pregnancy also had my emotions going.

Unc stepped back and took a look at me, glancing down at my stomach. He pulled me back in and hugged me tighter than before. We definitely had an audience. Everybody stood there, watching us. It had been way too long, and now my fairy tale was finally becoming a reality.

After our reunion, I went to sit back down. Unc had to mingle and entertain his guests, of course. I planned to steal him away at some point, because we had a lot of catching up to do.

"Are you happy now?" Money smiled.

"Yes. I'm very happy. I have to introduce you two." I got up to get Unc again. I grabbed him and walked him over to our table.

I turned to Unc.

"Unc, this is Money, my fiancé and the father of my son," I said. "And, Money, this is my father slash uncle, Unc." I gave them a formal introduction.

"Not to be rude, but what happened to Zae?" Unc asked.

I could tell Money got offended by his facial expression.

"Well, Zae did me so wrong, Unc. I'll explain it all to you at a later time," I told him. "Right now I'm celebrating you, Unc," I said, trying to make things sound better.

"I'm sorry if I offended you, young buck. Zae's the last guy I knew Sommer was with before I went away. I was just curious. I'm glad you're making her happy," Unc said while extending his hand.

Money stood up and gave him a handshake. Unc pulled him in.

"You're a part of the family, and family don't shake hands. . . . They show love," Unc said as he gave Money a manly hug.

My two favorite men were getting along just fine, and that was all I needed. Unc's right-hand man and marketing partner, Mitch, came in with a mink on. He had bought Unc a new chinchilla as a "welcome home" gift.

All the ballers and pimps, and even the sluts, gave Unc some top-notch gifts. Unc had a smile on his face the entire night.

"He's so happy," Aunt Sasha said to me, rubbing my shoulders as we watched him open his gifts.

"I know. I'm glad we made this a special night for him." This was definitely a night to remember.

Aunt Sasha and I went over to the DJ booth, and the DJ handed her a microphone.

"Okay, ladies and gents! I got some announcements for y'all!" Aunt Sasha said loudly.

Everybody took a seat somewhere so that they could hear what she had to say.

"Sommer's going to go first," she said, then handed me the mic.

I wasn't expecting to start it off, but I went along with the flow. "I really don't know where to start," I said, straightening the hanging cord. I sighed and looked up at everybody. "This man has been more than an uncle to me. He took me in when my mom couldn't do a thing for me. He made my life worth living." I paused and thought back. I could feel tears filling my eyes. "There were so many lonely nights when I wanted to take my own life . . . and he showed me a love that made me happy enough to choose not to terminate my life."

Tears fell one by one.I went on. "He showed me the definition of *love*. He took me in as his very own, he gave me the finer things in life, *and* he always pushed me to do better. I'm glad to say that Unc made me the woman I am today." I looked at Unc. "Yes, I may be pregnant, but I'm a sophomore in college. I'm living the life my mother could have never given me. I owe it all to you, Unc." I smiled and handed the mic back to Aunt Sasha.

Unc got up and gave me a hug. "I love you," he told me.

Life was changing for the better.

Aunt Sasha and a few friends made their announcements, and then they told the DJ to cut the music back on. We danced and partied. This was the good life.

At some point during the evening I noticed my phone was ringing. It was the Realtor. *Why is she calling me this late?* I figured I should go outside to answer it. Money looked at me.

"Baby, I'll be right back," I told him as I headed outside.

I noticed how crowded the parking lot was. I smiled at the tremendous turnout. I realized that I had missed the Realtor's call, so I called her back. The phone rang and rang. Suddenly, out of nowhere, a hand covered my mouth, and then someone dragged me into the backseat of a car and pushed me down onto the floor. The car pulled off, and I struggled, screaming as much as I could.

When I managed to get up off the floor of the car, I saw the face I had been avoiding. It was Zae. I started crying as we got farther and farther away from the club.

"You thought I wouldn't find you, huh, Sommer?"

I didn't say anything. I was only thinking of a way to get out of the car. He was driving so fast that if I jumped out, I would die and kill my baby. I looked down on the floor of the car and saw my cell phone. I had forgotten that it was in my hand when he grabbed me. I pushed the volume all the way down to vibrate.

We drove so far that we were now on the highway. I didn't know where we were going. I texted Mari.

Zae kidnapped me. Tell Unc and Money I love them. I don't think I'm going to make it.

After sending that message, I dialed 911. I knew I couldn't make a plea for help, so when the 911 operator answered, I started to ask Zae questions.

"Markaylo, why are you doing this?" I cried, giving the operator his first name.

"I told you I was going to catch up with you. This time, there won't be no running. I hope you kissed your fucking baby daddy good-bye." He laughed in an evil way.

"Someone please help me!" I cried out loudly.

"Shut up!" he yelled.

I hung up on the police, and all I could do was hope that they recorded everything and tracked down the call. Money started calling my cell phone nonstop. I couldn't answer. That broke my heart even more. I was as good as dead.

Money texted me.

> Baby, just listen to what he says. I'm going to come get you. Believe that. I love you so much. I'll never let you die.

I read it over and over, and it made me cry even more. There was no saving me. How would anyone know where I was? Zae noticed I had my phone in my hands, so he grabbed it and threw it out on the highway.

I began to weep.

His phone rang.

"Don't do no dumb shit, Doll!" he yelled. "That pisses me off!" he said, then answered his phone. "Yeah, Mari?"

Then it hit me, Mark was short for Markaylo. Mari had set me up. My eyes welled up to the point where I could barely see. I was hurt to the core. I tried to stop crying, but I couldn't help it. I started to cry even more. I saw a sign that reassured me that I was as good as dead.

It read: LEAVING TOLEDO.

# Notes